"ENORMOUS VITALITY AND VIRTUOSITY . . . taken together, as Barth urges they should be, these fictions interreact to produce a series of constantly changing and enticingly illusive forms . . . Barth's cunning is to turn daily life into mythology while turning mythology into domestic comedy . . . MANY THINGS CAN HAPPEN IN JOHN BARTH'S FUNHOUSE, BUT GETTING LOST IS NOT LIKELY TO BE ONE OF THEM."

—*Time*

"As he demonstrated in **The Sot-Weed Factor** and **Giles Goat-Boy,** he is at once erudite and out to experiment and to entertain, but an artist *malgré lui.*"

—*Boston Globe*

"Barth can pick literature apart in a narrative, play with it, and finally make restoration just in time for it to accomplish its ancient purposes of amusement and revelation."

—*The New Republic*

AT PLAY IN THE FIELDS OF THE LORD
 by Peter Matthiessen
THE BELL JAR by Sylvia Plath
CANCER WARD by Alexander Solzhenitsyn
THE CONFESSIONS OF NAT TURNER
 by Willam Styron
DARKNESS VISIBLE by William Golding
DELTA OF VENUS Erotica by Anaïs Nin
THE END OF THE ROAD by John Barth
FAR TORTUGA by Peter Matthiessen
THE FIRST CIRCLE by Alexander I. Solzhenitsyn
THE FLOATING OPERA by John Barth
GILES GOAT-BOY by John Barth
THE GOLDEN NOTEBOOK by Doris Lessing
GOODBYE, COLUMBUS by Philip Roth
THE LONG MARCH by William Styron
LOST IN THE FUNHOUSE by John Barth
THE MEMOIRS OF A SURVIVOR by Doris Lessing
THE MIDDLE GROUND by Margaret Drabble
MY LIFE AS A MAN by Philip Roth
NIGHT OF THE AUROCHS by Dalton Trumbo
ONE DAY IN THE LIFE OF IVAN DENISOVICH
 by Alexander Solzhenitsyn
SET THIS HOUSE ON FIRE by William Styron
THE SNOW LEOPARD by Peter Matthiessen
SOMETIMES A GREAT NOTION by Ken Kesey
THE STONE ANGEL by Margaret Laurence
THE SUMMER BEFORE THE DARK
 by Doris Lessing
V. by Thomas Pynchon
VISION QUEST by Terry Davis
A WEAVE OF WOMEN by E. M. Broner
WHEN SHE WAS GOOD by Philip Roth

LOST IN THE FUNHOUSE

John Barth

Fiction for Print, Tape, Live Voice

BANTAM BOOKS
Toronto • New York • London • Sydney

LOST IN THE FUNHOUSE
*A Bantam Book / published by arrangement with
Doubleday & Company, Inc.*

PRINTING HISTORY
*Doubleday edition published September 1968

Bantam edition / September 1969
9 printings through May 1980
Bantam Windstone edition / December 1981*

"*Night-Sea Journey*" first appeared in ESQUIRE *Magazine,*
June 1966.
"*Ambrose His Mark*" first appeared in ESQUIRE *Magazine,*
February 1963.
"*Autobiography*" first appeared in The New American Review,
#2.
"*Water-Message*" first appeared in the SOUTHWEST REVIEW,
published by Southern Methodist University, Summer 1963.
"*Lost in the Funhouse*" is reprinted by permission of the
Atlantic Monthly Company, Copyright © 1967 by the Atlantic
Monthly Company. It appeared in the November 1967 issue of
THE ATLANTIC MONTHLY.
"*Title*" is reprinted by permission of Yale University, Copy-
right © 1967 by Yale University. It first appeared in the Winter
1968 issue of the YALE REVIEW.
"*Petition*" first appeared in ESQUIRE *Magazine,* July 1968.

ISBN 0-553-20852-7

Published simultaneously in the United States and Canada

*Bantam Books are published by Bantam Books, Inc. Its trade-
mark, consisting of the words "Bantam Books" and the por-
trayal of a rooster, is Registered in U.S. Patent and Trademark
Office and in other countries. Marca Registrada. Bantam
Books, Inc., 666 Fifth Avenue, New York, New York 10103.*

PRINTED IN THE UNITED STATES OF AMERICA

19 18 17 16 15 14 13 12 11 10

Contents

Author's Note

This book differs in two ways from most volumes of short fiction. First, it's neither a collection nor a selection, but a series; though several of its items have appeared separately in periodicals, the series will be seen to have been meant to be received "all at once" and as here arranged. Most of its members, consequently, are "new"—written for this book, in which they appear for the first time.

Second, while some of these pieces were composed expressly for print, others were not. "Ambrose His Mark" and "Water-Message," the earliest-written, take the print medium for granted but lose or gain nothing in oral recitation. "Petition," "Lost in the Funhouse," "Life-Story," and "Anonymiad," on the other hand, would lose part of their point in any except printed form; "Night-Sea Journey" was meant for either print or recorded authorial voice, but not for live or non-authorial voice; "Glossolalia" will make no sense unless heard in live or recorded voices, male and female, or read as if so heard; "Echo" is intended for monophonic authorial recording, either disc or tape; "Autobiography," for monophonic tape and visible but silent author. "Menelaiad," though suggestive of a recorded authorial monologue, depends for clarity on the reader's eye and may be said to have been composed for "printed voice." "Title" makes somewhat separate but equally valid senses in several media: print, monophonic reorded authorial voice, stereophonic ditto in dialogue with itself, live authorial voice, live ditto in dialogue with monophonic ditto aforementioned, and live ditto interlocutory with stereophonic et cetera, my own preference; it's been "done" in all six. "Frame-Tale" is one-, two-, or three-dimensional, whichever one regards a Moebius strip as being. On with the story. On with the story.

Seven Additional Author's Notes

1) The "Author's Note" prefatory to the first American edition of this book has been called by some reviewers pretentious. It may seem so, inasmuch as the tapes there alluded to are not at this writing commerically available, may never be, and I judged it distracting to publish the tape-stories in reading-script format. Nevertheless the "Note" means in good faith exactly what it says, both as to the serial nature of the fourteen pieces and as to the ideal media of their presentation: the regnant idea is the unpretentious one of turning as many aspects of the fiction as possible—the structure, the narrative viewpoint, the means of presentation, in some instances the process of composition and/or recitation as well as of reading or listening—into dramatically relevant emblems of the theme.

2) The narrator of "Night-Sea Journey," quoted from beginning to end by the authorial voice, is not, as many reviewers took him to be, a fish. If he were, their complaint that his eschatological and other speculations are trite would be entirely justified; given his actual nature, they are merely correct, and perhaps illumine certain speculations of Lord Raglan, Carl Jung, and Joseph Campbell.

3) The title "Autobiography" means "self-composition": the antecedent of the first-person pronoun is not I, but the story, speaking of itself. I am its father; its mother is the recording machine.

4) Inasmuch as the nymph in her ultimate condition repeats the words of others in their own voices, the words of "Echo" on the tape or the page may be regarded validly as hers, Narcissus's, Tiresias's, mine, or any combination or series of the four of us's. Inasmuch as the three mythical principals are all more or less immortal, and Tiresias moreover can see backward and forward in time, the events recounted may be already past, foreseen for the future, or in process of occurring as narrated.

5) The triply schizoid monologue entitled "Title" addresses itself simultaneously to three matters: the "Author's" difficulties with his companion, his analogous difficulties with the story he's in process of composing, and

the not dissimilar straits in which, I think mistakenly, he imagines his culture and its literature to be. In the stereophonic performance version of the story, the two "sides" debate—in identical authorial voice, as it is after all a *monologue interieur*—across the twin channels of stereo tape, while the live author, like Mr. Interlocutor between Tambo and Bones in the old showboat-shows, supplies such self-interrupting and self-censoring passages as "Title" and "fill in the blank"—relinquishing his role to the auditor at the.

6) The six glossolalists of "Glossolalia" are, in order, Cassandra, Philomela, the fellow mentioned by Paul in the fourteenth verse of his first epistle to the Corinthians, the Queen of Sheba's talking bird, an unidentified psalmist employing what happens to be the tongue of a historical glossolalist (Mme Alice LeBaron, who acquired some fame in 1879 from her exolalic inspirations in the "Martian" language), and the author. Among their common attributes are 1) that their audiences don't understand what they're talking about, and 2) that their several speeches are metrically identical, each corresponding to what in fact may be the only verbal sound-pattern identifiable by anyone who atended American public schools prior to the decision of the U.S. Supreme Court in the case of *Murray* v. *Baltimore School Board* in 1963. The insufferability of the fiction, once this correspondence is recognized, makes its double point: that language may be a compound code, and that the discovery of an enormous complexity beneath a simple surface may well be more dismaying than delightful. *E.g.*: the maze of termite-tunnels in your joist, the intricate cancer in her perfect breast, the psychopathology of everyday life, the Auschwitz in an anthill casually DDT'd by a child, the rage of atoms in a drop of ink—in short, *anything* examined curiously enough.

7) The deuteragonist of "Life-Story," antecedent of the second-person pronoun, is you.

FRAME-TALE

Cut on dotted line.
Twist end once and fasten
AB to *ab*, *CD* to *cd*.

(continued)

ONCE UPON A TIME THERE

^d WAS A STORY THAT BEGAN ^a
^c ^b

(continued)

NIGHT-SEA JOURNEY

"One way or another, no matter which theory of our journey is correct, it's myself I address; to whom I rehearse as to a stranger our history and condition, and will disclose my secret hope though I sink for it.

"Is the journey my invention? Do the night, the sea, exist at all, I ask myself, apart from my experience of them? Do I myself exist, or is this a dream? Sometimes I wonder. And if I am, who am I? The Heritage I supposedly transport? But how can I be both vessel and contents? Such are the questions that beset my intervals of rest.

"My trouble is, I lack conviction. Many accounts of our situation seem plausible to me—where and what we are, why we swim and whither. But implausible ones as well, perhaps especially those, I must admit as possibly correct. Even likely. If at times, in certain humors—striking in unison, say, with my neighbors and chanting with them 'Onward! Upward!'—I have supposed that we have after all a common Maker, Whose nature and motives we may not know, but Who engendered us in some mysterious wise and launched us forth toward some end known but to Him —if (for a moodslength only) I have been able to entertain such notions, very popular in certain quarters, it is because our night-sea journey partakes of their absurdity. One might even say: I can believe them *because* they are absurd.

"Has that been said before?

"Another paradox: it appears to be these recesses from swimming that sustain me in the swim. Two measures onward and upward, flailing with the rest, then I float exhausted and dispirited, brood upon the night, the sea, the journey, while the flood bears me a measure back and down: slow progress, but I live, I live, and make my way, aye, past many a drownèd comrade in the end, stronger, worthier than I, victims of their unremitting *joie de nager*. I have seen the best swimmers of my generation go under. Numberless the number of the dead! Thousands drown as I think this thought, millions as I rest before returning to the swim. And scores, hundreds of millions have expired since we surged forth, brave in our innocence, upon our dreadful way. 'Love! Love!' we sang then, a quarter-billion strong, and churned the warm sea white with joy of swimming! Now all are gone down—the buoyant, the sodden, leaders and followers, all gone under, while wretched I swim on. Yet these same reflective intervals that keep me afloat have led me into wonder, doubt, despair—strange emotions for a swimmer!—have led me, even, to suspect . . . that our night-sea journey is without meaning.

"Indeed, if I have yet to join the hosts of the suicides, it is because (fatigue apart) I find it no meaningfuller to drown myself than to go on swimming.

"I know that there are those who seem actually to enjoy the night-sea; who claim to love swimming for its own sake, or sincerely believe that 'reaching the Shore,' 'transmitting the Heritage' (*Whose* Heritage, I'd like to know? And to whom?) is worth the staggering cost. I do not. Swimming itself I find at best not actively unpleasant, more often tiresome, not infrequently a torment. Arguments from function and design don't impress me: granted that we can and do swim, that in a manner of speaking our long tails and streamlined heads are 'meant for' swimming; it by no means follows—for me, at least—that we *should* swim, or otherwise endeavor to 'fulfill our destiny.' Which is to say, Someone Else's destiny, since ours, so far as I can see, is merely to perish, one way or another, soon or late. The heartless zeal of our (departed) leaders, like the blind ambition and good cheer of my own youth, appalls me now; for the death of my comrades I am inconsolable. If the night-sea journey has justification, it is not for us swimmers ever to discover it.

"Oh, to be sure, 'Love!' one heard on every side: 'Love it is that drives and sustains us!' I translate: we don't know *what* drives and sustains us, only that we are most miserably driven and, imperfectly, sustained. *Love* is how we call our ignorance of what whips us. 'To reach the Shore,' then: but what if the Shore exists in the fancies of us swimmers merely, who dream it to account for the dreadful fact that we swim, have always and only swum, and continue swimming without respite (myself excepted) until we die? Supposing even that there *were* a Shore—that, as a cynical companion of mine once imagined, we rise from the drowned to discover all those vulgar superstitions and exalted metaphors to be literal truth: the giant Maker of us all, the Shores of Light beyond our night-sea journey! —whatever would a swimmer do there? The fact is, when we imagine the Shore, what comes to mind is just the opposite of our condition: no more night, no more sea, no more journeying. In short, the blissful estate of the drowned.

" 'Ours not to stop and think; ours but to swim and sink. . . .' Because a moment's thought reveals the pointlessness of swimming. 'No matter,' I've heard some say, even as they gulped their last: 'The night-sea journey may be absurd, but here we swim, will-we nill-we, against the flood, onward and upward, toward a Shore that may not exist and couldn't be reached if it did.' The thoughtful swimmer's choices, then, they say, are two: give over thrashing and go under for good, or embrace the absurdity; affirm in and for itself the night-sea journey; swim on with neither motive nor destination, for the sake of swimming, and compassionate moreover with your fellow swimmer, we being all at sea and equally in the dark. I find neither course acceptable. If not even the hypothetical Shore can justify a sea-full of drownèd comrades, to speak of the swim-in-itself as somehow doing so strikes me as obscene. I continue to swim—but only because blind habit, blind instinct, blind fear of drowning are still more strong than the horror of our journey. And if on occasion I have assisted a fellow-thrasher, joined in the cheers and songs, even passed along to others strokes of genius from the drownèd great, it's that I shrink by temperament from making myself conspicuous. To paddle off in one's own direction, assert one's independent right-of-way, overrun one's fellows without compunction, or dedicate oneself entirely to pleasures and diversions without regard for conscience—I can't finally condemn those who journey in this wise; in half my moods I envy them and despise the weak vitality that keeps me from following their example. But in reasonabler moments I remind myself that it's their very freedom and self-responsibility I reject, as more dramatically absurd, in our senseless circumstances, than tailing along in conventional fashion. Suicides, rebels, affirmers of the paradox—nay-sayers and yea-sayers alike to our fatal journey—I finally shake my head at them. And splash sighing past their corpses, one by one, as past a hundred sorts of others: friends, enemies, brothers; fools, sages, brutes—and nobodies, million upon million. I envy them all.

"A poor irony: that I, who find abhorrent and tautological the doctrine of survival of the fittest (*fitness* meaning, in my experience, nothing more than survival-ability, a talent whose only demonstration is the fact of survival, but whose chief ingredients seem to be strength, guile, callousness), may be the sole remaining swimmer! But the doctrine is false as well as repellent: Chance drowns the worthy with the unworthy, bears up the unfit with the fit by whatever definition, and makes the night-sea journey essentially *haphazard* as well as murderous and unjustified.

" 'You only swim once.' Why bother, then?

" 'Except ye drown, ye shall not reach the Shore of Light.' Poppycock.

"One of my late companions—that same cynic with the curious fancy, among the first to drown—entertained us with odd conjectures while we waited to begin our journey. A favorite theory of his was that the Father does exist, and did indeed make us and the sea we swim—but not a-purpose or even consciously; He made us, as it were, despite Himself, as we make waves with every tail-thrash, and may be unaware of our existence. Another was that He knows we're here but doesn't care what happens to us, inasmuch as He creates (voluntarily or not) other seas and swimmers at more or less regular intervals. In bitterer moments, such as just before he drowned, my friend even supposed that our Maker wished us unmade; there was indeed a Shore, he'd argue, which could save at least some of us from drowning and toward which it was our function to struggle—but for reasons unknowable to us He wanted desperately to prevent our reaching that happy place and fulfilling our destiny. Our 'Father,' in short, was our adversary and would-be killer! No less outrageous, and offensive to traditional opinion, were the fellow's speculations on the nature of our Maker: that He might well be no swimmer Himself at all, but some sort of monstrosity, perhaps even tailless; that He might be stupid, malicious, insensible, perverse, or asleep and dreaming; that the end for which He created and launched us forth, and which we flagellate ourselves to fathom, was perhaps immoral, even obscene. Et cetera, et cetera: there was no end to the chap's conjectures, or the impoliteness of his fancy; I have reason to suspect that his early demise, whether planned by 'our Maker' or not, was expedited by certain fellow-swimmers indignant at his blasphemies.

"In other moods, however (he was as given to moods as I), his theorizing would become half-serious, so it seemed to me, especially upon the subjects of Fate and Immortality, to which our youthful conversations often turned. Then his harangues, if no less fantastical, grew solemn and obscure, and if he was still baiting us, his passion undid the joke. His objection to popular opinions of the hereafter, he would declare, was their claim to general validity. Why need believers hold that *all* the drownèd rise to be judged at journey's end, and non-believers that drowning is final without exception? In *his* opinion (so he'd vow at least), nearly everyone's fate was permanent death; indeed he took a sour pleasure in supposing that every 'Maker' made thousands of separate seas in His creative lifetime, each populated like ours with millions of swimmers, and that in almost every instance both sea and swimmers were utterly annihilated, whether accidentally or by malevolent design. (Nothing if not pluralistical, he imagined there might be millions and billions of 'Fathers,' perhaps in some 'night-sea' of their own!) However—and here he turned infidels against him with the faithful—he professed to believe that in possibly a single night-sea per thousand, say, one of its quarter-billion swimmers (that is, one swimmer in two hundred fifty billions) achieved a qualified immortality. In some cases the rate might be slightly higher; in others it was vastly lower, for just as there are swimmers of every degree of proficiency, including some who drown before the journey starts, unable to swim at all, and others created drowned, as it were, so he imagined what can only be termed impotent Creators, Makers unable to Make, as well as uncommonly fertile ones and all grades between. And it pleased him to deny any necessary relation between a Maker's productivity and His other virtues—including, even, the quality of His creatures.

"I could go on (*he* surely did) with his elaboration of these mad notions—such as that swimmers in other night-seas needn't be of our kind; that Makers themselves might belong to different *species,* so to speak; that our particular Maker mightn't Himself be immortal, or that we might be not only His emissaries but His 'immortality,' continuing His life and our own, transmogrified, beyond our individual deaths. Even this modified immortality (meaningless to me) he conceived as relative and contingent, subject to accident or deliberate termination: his pet hypothesis was that Makers and swimmers *each generate the other*— against all odds, their number being so great—and that any given 'immortality-chain' could terminate after any number of cycles, so that what was 'immortal' (still speaking relatively) was only the cyclic process of incarnation, which itself might have a beginning and an end. Alternatively he liked to imagine cycles within cycles, either finite or infinite: for example, the 'night-sea,' as it were, in which Makers 'swam' and created night-seas and swimmers like ourselves, might be the creation of a larger Maker, Himself one of many, Who in turn et cetera. Time itself he regarded as relative to our experience, like magnitude: who knew but what, with each thrash of our tails, minuscule seas and swimmers, whole eternities, came to pass—as ours, perhaps, and our Maker's Maker's, was elapsing between the strokes of some supertail, in a slower order of time?

Naturally I hooted with the others at this nonsense. We were young then, and had only the dimmest notion of what lay ahead; in our ignorance we imagined night-sea journeying to be a positively heroic enterprise. Its meaning and value we never questioned; to be sure, some must go down by the way, a pity no doubt, but to win a race requires that others lose, and like all my fellows I took for granted that

I would be the winner. We milled and swarmed, impatient to be off, never mind where or why, only to try our youth against the realities of night and sea; if we indulged the skeptic at all, it was as a droll, half-contemptible mascot. When he died in the initial slaughter, no one cared.

"And even now I don't subscribe to all his views—but I no longer scoff. The horror of our history has purged me of opinions, as of vanity, confidence, spirit, charity, hope, vitality, everything—except dull dread and a kind of melancholy, stunned persistence. What leads me to recall his fancies is my growing suspicion that I, of all swimmers, may be the sole survivor of this fell journey, tale-bearer of a generation. This suspicion, together with the recent sea-change, suggests to me now that nothing is impossible, not even my late companion's wildest visions, and brings me to a certain desperate resolve, the point of my chronicling.

"Very likely I have lost my senses. The carnage at our setting out; our decimation by whirlpool, poisoned cataract, sea-convulsion; the panic stampedes, mutinies, slaughters, mass suicides; the mounting evidence that none will survive the journey—add to these anguish and fatigue; it were a miracle if sanity stayed afloat. Thus I admit, with the other possibilities, that the present sweetening and calming of the sea, and what seems to be a kind of vasty presence, song, or summons from the near upstream, may be hallucinations of disordered sensibility. . . .

"Perhaps, even, I am drowned already. Surely I was never meant for the rough-and-tumble of the swim; not impossibly I perished at the outset and have only imaged the night-sea journey from some final deep. In any case, I'm no longer young, and it is we spent old swimmers, disabused of every illusion, who are most vulnerable to dreams.

"Sometimes I think I am my drownèd friend.

"Out with it: I've begun to believe, not only that *She* exists, but that She lies not far ahead, and stills the sea, and draws me Herward! Aghast, I recollect his maddest notion: that our destination (which existed, mind, in but one night-sea out of hundreds and thousands) was no Shore, as commonly conceived, but a mysterious being, indescribable except by paradox and vaguest figure: wholly different from us swimmers, yet our complement; the death of us, yet our salvation and resurrection; simultaneously our journey's end, mid-point, and commencement; not membered and thrashing like us, but a motionless or hugely gliding sphere of unimaginable dimension; self-contained, yet dependent absolutely, in some wise, upon the chance (always monstrously improbable) that one of us will survive the night-sea journey and reach . . . Her! *Her,* he called it, or *She,* which is to say, Other-than-a-he. I shake my head; the thing is too preposterous; it is myself I talk to, to keep my reason in this awful darkness. There is no She! There is no You! I rave to myself; it's Death alone that hears and summons. To the drowned, all seas are calm. . . .

"Listen: my friend maintained that in every order of creation there are two sorts of creators, contrary yet complementary, one of which gives rise to seas and swimmers, the other to the Night-which-contains-the-sea and to What-waits-at-the-journey's-end: the former, in short, to destiny, the latter to destination (and both profligately, involuntarily, perhaps indifferently or unwittingly). The 'purpose' of the night-sea journey—but not necessarily of the journeyer or of either Maker!—my friend could describe only in abstractions: *consummation, transfiguration, union of contraries, transcension of categories.* When we laughed, he would shrug and admit that he understood the business no better than we, and thought it ridiculous, dreary, possibly obscene. 'But one of you,' he'd add with his wry smile, 'may be the Hero destined to complete the night-sea journey and be one with Her. Chances are, of course, you won't make it.' He himself, he declared, was not even going to try; the whole idea repelled him; if we chose to dismiss it as an ugly fiction, so much the better for us; thrash, splash, and be merry, we were soon enough drowned. But there it was, he could not say how he knew or why he bothered to tell us, any more than he could say what would happen after She and Hero, Shore and Swimmer, 'merged identities' to become something both and neither. He quite agreed with me that if the issue of that magical union had no memory of the night-sea journey, for example, it enjoyed a poor sort of immortality; even poorer if, as he rather imagined, a swimmer-hero plus a She equaled or became merely another Maker of future night-seas and the rest, at such incredible expense of life. This being the case—he was persuaded it was—the merciful thing to do was refuse to participate; the genuine heroes, in his opinion, were the suicides, and the hero of heroes would be the swimmer who, in the very presence of the Other, refused Her proffered 'immortality' and thus put an end to at least one cycle of catastrophes.

"How we mocked him! Our moment came, we hurtled forth, pretending to glory in the adventure, thrashing, singing, cursing, strangling, rationalizing, rescuing, killing, inventing rules and stories and relationships, giving up, struggling on, but dying all, and still in darkness, until only a battered remnant was left to croak 'Onward, upward,' like a bitter echo. Then they too fell silent—victims, I can only presume, of the last frightful wave—and the moment came when I also, utterly desolate and spent, thrashed my last and gave myself over to the current, to sink or float as might be, but swim no more. Whereupon, marvelous to tell, in an instant the sea grew still! Then warmly, gently, the great tide turned, began to bear me, as it does now, onward and upward will-I nill-I, like a flood of joy—and I recalled with dismay my dead friend's teaching.

"I am not deceived. This new emotion is Her doing; the desire that possesses me is Her bewitchment. Lucidity passes from me; in a moment I'll cry 'Love!' bury myself in Her side, and be 'transfigured.' Which is to say, I die already; this fellow transported by passion is not I; *I am he who abjures and rejects the night-sea journey!* I. . . .

"I am all love. 'Come!' She whispers, and I have no will.

"You who I may be about to become, whatever You are: with the last twitch of my real self I beg You to listen. It is *not* love that sustains me! No; though Her magic makes me burn to sing the contrary, and though I drown even now for the blasphemy, I will say truth. What has fetched me across this dreadful sea is a single hope, gift of my poor dead comrade: that You may be stronger-willed than I, and that by sheer force of concentration I may transmit to You, along with Your official Heritage, a private legacy of awful recollection and negative resolve. Mad as it may be, my dream is that some unimaginable embodiment of myself (or myself plus Her if that's how it must be) will come to find itself expressing, in however garbled or radical a translation, some reflection of these reflections. If against all odds this comes to pass, may You to whom, through whom I speak, do what I cannot: terminate this aimless, brutal business! Stop Your hearing against Her song! Hate love!

"Still alive, afloat, afire. Farewell then my penultimate hope: that one may be sunk for direst blasphemy on the very shore of the Shore. Can it be (my old friend would smile) that only utterest nay-sayers survive the night? But even that were Sense, and there is no sense, only senseless love, senseless death. Whoever echoes these reflections: be more courageous than their author! An end to night-sea journeys! Make no more! And forswear me when I shall forswear myself, deny myself, plunge into Her who summons, singing . . .

" 'Love! Love! Love!' "

AMBROSE HIS MARK

Owing to the hectic circumstances of my birth, for some months I had no proper name. Mother had seen Garbo in *Anna Christie* at the Dorset Opera House during her pregnancy and come to hope for a daughter, to be named by some logic Christine in honor of that lady. When I was brought home, after Father's commitment to the Eastern Shore Asylum, she made no mention of a name nor showed any interest in selecting one, and the family were too concerned for her well-being to press the matter. She grew froward—by turns high-spirited and listless, voluble and dumb, doting and cynical. Some days she would permit no hands but hers to touch me, would haul me about from room to room, crooning and nuzzling: a photograph made by Uncle Karl on such a day shows her posed before our Concord vines, her pretty head thrown back, scarfed and earringed like a gypsy; her eyes are closed, her mouth laughs gaily behind her cigarette; one hand holds a cup of coffee, the other steadies a scowling infant on her hip. Other times she would have none of me, or even suffer me in her sight. About my feeding there was ever some unease: if I cried, say, when the family was at table, forks would pause and eyes turn furtively to Andrea. For in one humor she would fetch out her breast in any company and feed me while she smoked or strolled the garden—nor nurse me quietly at that, but demand of Aunt Rosa whether I hadn't Hector's eyes. . . .

"*Ja*, well."

"And Poppa Tom's appetite. Look, Konrad, how he wolfs it. There's a man for you."

Grandfather openly relished these performances; he chuckled at the mentions of himself, teased Uncle Konrad for averting his eyes, and never turned his own from my refections.

"Now there is Beauty's picture, *nicht wahr*, Konrad? Mother and child."

But his entertainment was not assured: just as often Andrea would say, "Lord, there goes Christine again. Stick something in his mouth, Rosie, would you?" or merely sigh—a rueful expiration that still blows fitful as her ghost through my memory—and say nothing, but let Aunt Rosa (always nervously at hand) prepare and administer my bottle, not even troubling to make her kindless joke about the grand unsuckled bosoms of that lady.

To Rosa I was *Honig;* Mother too, when "Christine" seemed unfunny, called me thus, and in the absence of anything official, *Honey* soon lost the quality of endearment and took the neutral function of a proper name. Uncle Konrad privately held out for *Hector,* but no one ventured to bring up her husband's name in Mother's presence. Uncle Karl was not in town to offer an opinion. Aunt Rosa believed that calling me *Thomas* might improve relations between Grandfather and his youngest son; but though he'd made no secret of his desire to have my older brother be his namesake, and his grievance at the choice of *Peter,* Grandfather displayed no more interest than did Andrea in naming me. Rosa attributed his indifference to bruised pride; in any case, given Mother's attitude, the question of my nomination was academic. Baptism was delayed, postponed, anon forgot.

Only once did Mother allude to my namelessness, some two or three months after my birth. I was lying in Aunt Rosa's lap, drinking from a bottle; dinner was just done; the family lingered over coffee. Suddenly Andrea, on one of her impulses, cried "Give him here, Rose!" and snatched me up. I made a great commotion.

"Now, you frightened it," Rosa chided.

Andrea ignored her. " 'E doesn't want Rosie's old bottle, does Christine."

Her croon failed to console me. "Hold him till I unbutton," she said—not to Rosa but to Uncle Konrad. Her motives, doubtless, were the usual: to make Aunt Rosa envious, amuse Grandfather, and mortify Uncle Konrad, who could not now readily look away. She undid her peignoir, casually bemoaning her abundance of milk: it was making her clothes a sight, it was hurting her besides, she must nurse me more regularly. She did not at once retrieve me but with such chatter as this bent forward, cupped her breast, invited me to drink the sweet pap already beading and spreading under her fingers. Uncle Konrad, it was agreed, at no time before or after turned so crimson.

"Here's what the Honey wants," Andrea said, relieving him finally of his charge. To the company in general she declared, "It does feel good, you know: there's a nerve or something runs from here right to you-know-where."

"*Schämt euch!*" Aunt Rosa cried.

"*Ja* sure," Grandfather said merrily. "You named it!"

"No, really, she knows as well as I do what it's like. Doesn't she, Christine. Sure Mother likes to feed her little mannie, look how he grabs, poor darling. . . ." Here she was taken unexpectedly with grief; pressed me fiercely to her, drew the peignoir about us; her tears warmed my forehead and her breast. "Who will he ever be, Konrad? Little orphan of the storm, who is he now?"

"Ah! Ah!" Rosa rushed to hug her. Grandfather drew and sucked upon his meerschaum, which however had gone dead out.

"Keep up like you have been," Konrad said stiffly; "soon he'll be old enough to pick his own name." My uncle taught fifth grade at East Dorset School, of which Hector had been principal until his commitment, and in summers was a vendor of encyclopedias and tuner of pianos. To see things in their larger context was his gentle aim; to harmonize part with part, time with time; and he never withheld from us what he deemed germane or helpful. The American Indians, he declared now, had the right idea. "They never named a boy right off. What they did, they watched to find out who he was. They'd look for the right sign to tell them what to call him."

Grandfather scratched a kitchen match on his thumbnail and relit his pipe.

"There's sense in that," Uncle Konrad persevered. "How can you tell what name'll suit a person when you don't know him yet?"

Ordinarily Rosa was his audience; preoccupied now with Andrea, she did not respond.

"There's some name their kids for what they want them to be. A brave hunter, et cetera."

"Or a movie star," Mother offered, permitting Rosa to wipe her eyes.

"Same principle exactly," Konrad affirmed, and was grateful enough to add in her behalf, despite his late embarrassment: "It's an important thing, naming a child. If I had a boy, I'd be a good long time about it."

"*Ach*," Grandfather said. "You said that right."

Andrea sniffed sympathy but did not reply, and so Uncle Konrad enlarged no further. Too bad for Grandfather his restlessness moved him from the table, for by this time my mother was herself sufficiently to turn back the veil she'd drawn about us.

"Well," she sighed to me. "You've caused the devil's mischief so far. Your daddy in the crazy-house; people saying Lord knows what about your mother."

"Thank Almighty God you got him," Aunt Rosa said. "And born perfect only for his little mark. Look how wide and clear his eyes!"

Uncle Konrad unbent so far as to pat my head while I nursed, a boldness without known precedent in his biography. "That's a sign of brains," he declared. "This boy could be our pride and saving."

Mother's laugh took on a rougher note. But she caressed my cheek with her knuckle, and I nursed on. Her temper was gay and fond now; yet her breast still glistened with the tears of a minute past. Not just that once was what I drank from her thus salted.

Grandfather would have no whisky or other distillation in the house, but drank grandly of wines and beers which he made himself in the whitewashed sheds behind the summerkitchen. His yeast and earliest grapestock were German, imported for him by the several families he'd brought to the county. The vines never flourished: anon they fell victim to anthracnose and phylloxera and were replaced by our native Delawares, Nortons, Lenoirs; but the yeast— an ancient culture from Sachsen-Altenburg—throve with undiminished vigor in our cellar. With it he would brew dark Bavarian lager, pellucid Weiss, and his cherished

Dortmund, pale gold and strongly hopped. Yet vinting was his forte, even Hector agreed. What he drew from the red and white grapes was splendid enough, but in this pursuit as in some others he inclined to variety and experiment: without saccharimeter or any other aid than a Rhenish intuition, he filled his crocks as the whim took him with anything fermentable—rice, cherries, dandelions, elderberries, rose petals, raisins, coconut—and casked unfailingly a decent wine.

Now it was Uncle Konrad's pleasure to recite things on occasion to the family, and in 1929, hearing by this means verses of Macpherson's Ossian, Grandfather had been inspired with a particular hankering for mead. From a farmer whose payments on a footstone were in arrears, he accepted in lieu of cash a quantity of honey, and his fermentation was an entire success. The craving got hold of him, he yearned to crush walnuts in the golden wort—but honey was dear, and dollars, never plentiful in the family, there were none for such expenditure. The stock market had fallen, the tomato-canners were on strike, hard times were upon the nation; if funerals were a necessity, gravestones were not; Uncle Karl, Grandfather's right-hand man, had left town two years past to lay bricks in Baltimore; our business had seldom been poorer.

"There is a trick for finding bee-trees," Grandfather asserted. One exposed a pan of sugar-water in the woods, waited until a number of honeybees assembled at it, and trapped them by covering the pan with cheesecloth. One then released a single bee and followed it, pan in hand, till it was lost from sight, whereupon one released another bee, and another, and another, and was fetched at length to their common home. It remained then only to smoke out the colony and help oneself to their reserves of honey. All that winter, as I grew in Mother's womb, Grandfather fretted with his scheme; when the spring's first bees appeared on our pussywillows, on our alder catkins, he was off with Hector and Konrad, saucepan and cheesecloth. Their researches led them through fresh-marsh, through pinewoods, over stile and under trestle—but never a beetree they discovered, only swampy impasses or the hives of some part-time apiarist.

My birth—more exactly, Hector's notion that someone other than himself had fathered me; his mad invasion of the delivery room; his wild assertion, as they carried him off, that the port-wine stain near my eye was a devil's mark —all this commotion, naturally, ended the quest. Not, however, the general project. Out of scrap pine Grandfather fashioned a box-hive of his own, whitewashed and established it among the lilacs next to the goat-pen, and bade Uncle Konrad kep his eyes open for a migrant swarm, the season being opportune.

His expectation was not unreasonable, even though East Dorset was by 1930 a proper residential ward with sidewalks, sewers, and streetlights. To maintain a goat might be judged eccentric, even vulgar, by neighbors with flush toilets and daily milk service; chickens, likewise, were *non grata* on Seawall Street (if not on Hayward or Franklin, where roosters crowed to the end of the Second World War); but there was nothing unseemly about a stand of sweetcorn, for example, if one had ground enough, or a patch of cucumbers, or a hive of bees. These last, in fact, were already a feature of our street's most handsome yard: I mean Erdmann's, adjacent but for an alley to our own. Upon Willy Erdmann's three fine skeps, braided of straw and caned English-fashion, Grandfather had brooded all winter. Two were inhabited and prosperous; the third, brand new, stood vacant against the day when a swarm would take wing from the others in search of new quarters.

Lilac honey, Grandfather declared, was more pleasing than any other to his taste; moreover it was essential that the hive be placed as far as possible from the house, not to disturb the occupants of either. Though no one pressed him to explain, he insisted it was for these reasons only (one or both of which must have been Erdmann's also) that he located his hive in the extreme rear corner of our property, next to the alley.

Our neighbor plainly was unhappy with this arrangement. Not long from the Asylum himself, whither he'd repaired to cure a sudden dipsomania, Erdmann was convalescing some months at home before he reassumed direction of his business. Pottering about his yard he'd seen our box-hives built and situated; as April passed he came to spend more time on the alley-side of his lot—cultivating his tulips, unmulching his roses, chewing his cigar, glaring from his beehives to ours.

"Yes, well," Grandfather observed. "Willy's bees have been for years using our lilacs. Have I begrutched?"

He made it his tactic at first to stroll hiveward himself whenever Erdmann was standing watch: he would examine his grape-canes, only just opening their mauve-and-yellow buds; he would make pleasantries in two tongues to Gretchen the goat; Erdmann soon would huff indoors.

But with both Hector and Karl away, Grandfather was obliged to spend more time than usual at the stoneyard, however slack the business; throughout whole weekday mornings and afternoons his apiary interests lay under Erdmann's scrutiny.

"*A swarm in May is worth a load of hay,*" Uncle Konrad recalled:

> "*A swarm in June is worth a silver spoon.*
> *But a swarm in July is not worth a fly.*"

May was cool, the lilacs and japonica had never blossomed so; then June broke out on the peninsula like a fire, everything flowered together, in Erdmann's skeps the honey-flow was on.

"What you need," Grandfather said to Andrea, "you need peace and quiet and fresh air this summer. Leave Rosa the housework; you rest and feed your baby."

"What the hell have I *been* doing?" Mother asked. But she did not protest her father-in-law's directive or his subsequent purchase of a hammock for her comfort, an extraordinary munificence. Even when his motive was revealed to be less than purely chivalrous—he strung the hammock between a Judas tree and a vine post, in view of the alley—she did not demur. On the contrary, though she teased Grandfather without mercy, she was diverted by the stratagem and cooperated beyond his expectation. Not only did she make it her custom on fine days to loll in the hammock, reading, dozing, and watching casually for a bee-swarm; she took to nursing me there as well.

Aunt Rosa and certain of the neighbors murmured; Uncle Konrad shook his head; but at feeding-times I was fetched to the hammock and suckled in the sight of any. At that time my mother had lost neither her pretty face and figure nor her wanton spirit: she twitted the schoolboys who gawked along the fence and the trashmen lingering at our cans; merrily she remarked upon reroutings and delays on the part of delivery wagons, which seldom before had used our alley. And she was as pleased as Grandfather, if not for the same reason, by the discomfiture of Mr. Erdmann, who now was constrained to keep what watch he would from an upstairs window.

"Willy's bashful as Konrad," she said to Rosa. "Some men, I swear, you'd think they'd never seen anything."

Grandfather chuckled. "Willy's just jealous. Hector he's got used to, but he don't like sharing you with the trashman."

But Mother could not be daunted by any raillery. "Listen to the pot call the kettle!"

"*Ja* sure," said Grandfather, and treated her to one of the pinches for which he was famed among East Dorset housewives.

Mr. Erdmann's response to the hammock was a beebob: he threaded dead bees into a cluster and mounted it on a pole, which he then erected near his skeps to attract the swarm.

"He knows they won't swarm for a naughty man," Grandfather explained. "It wonders me he can even handle them." In the old country, he declared, couples tested each other's virtue by walking hand in hand among the hives, the chaste having nothing to fear.

Mother was skeptical. "If bees were like that, not a man in Dorset could keep a hive. Except Konrad."

My uncle, as if she were not fondling the part in the middle of his hair, began to discourse upon the prophetic aspect of swarming among various peoples—*e.g.*, that a swarm on the house was thought by the Austrians to augur good fortune, by the Romans to warn of ill, and by the Greeks to herald strangers; that in Switzerland a swarm on a dry twig presaged the death of someone in the family, et cetera—but before ever he had got to the Bretons and

Transylvanians his wife was his only auditor: Andrea was back in her magazine, and Grandfather had gone off to counter Erdmann's bee-bob by rubbing the inside of his own hive with elder-flowers.

The last Sunday of the month but one dawned bright, hot, still. Out on the river not even the bell-buoy stirred, whose clang we heard in every normal weather; in its stead the bell of Grace M.-P. Southern, mark of a straiter channel, called forth East Dorseters in their cords and worsteds. But ours was a family mired in apostasy. There was no atheism in the house; in truth there was no talk of religion at all, except in Hector's most cynical moods. It was generally felt that children should be raised in the church, and so when the time came Peter and I would be enrolled in the Sunday-school and the Junior Christian Endeavor. More, Grandfather had lettered, gratis, *In Remembrance of Me* on the oak communion table and engraved the church cornerstone as well. We disapproved of none of the gentlemen who ministered the charge, although Grace, not the plum of the conference, was served as a rule by preachers very young or very old. Neither had we doctrinal differences with Methodism—Southern or Northern, Protestant or Episcopal: Aunt Rosa sometimes said, as if in explanation of our backsliding, "Why it is, we were all Lutherans in the old country"; but it would have been unkind to ask her the distinction between the faiths of Martin Luther and John Wesley. Yet though Konrad, with a yellow rosebud in his lapel, went faithfully to Bible class, none of us went to church. God served us on our terms and in our house (we were with a few exceptions baptized, wed, and funeraled in the good parlor); for better or worse it was not in our make-up to serve Him in His.

By eleven, then, this Sunday morning, Aunt Rosa had brought Peter home from Cradle Roll, Konrad was back from Bible class, and the family were about their separate pleasures. Grandfather, having inspected the bee situation earlier and found it not apparently changed, had settled himself on the side porch to carve a new drive-wheel for Peter's locomotive; my brother watched raptly, already drawn at three to what would be his trade. Rosa set to hammering dough for Maryland biscuits; Konrad was established somewhere with the weighty *Times;* Mother was in her hammock. There she had lazed since breakfast, dressed only in a sashless kimono to facilitate nursing; oblivious to the frowns of passing Christians, she had chain-smoked her way through the Sunday crossword, highlight of her week. At eleven, when the final bell of the morning sounded, I was brought forth. Cradled against her by the sag of the hammock, I drank me to a drowse; and she too, just as she lay—mottled by light and leaf-shadow, lulled by my work upon her and by wafting organ-chords from the avenue—soon slept soundly.

What roused her was a different tone, an urgent, resonating thrum. She opened her eyes: all the air round about her was aglint with bees. Thousand on thousand, a roaring gold sphere, they hovered in the space between the hammock and the overhanging branches.

Her screams brought Grandfather from the porch; he saw the cloud of bees and ducked at once into the summer-kitchen, whence he rushed a moment later banging pie-tin cymbals.

"Mein Schwarm! Mein Schwarm!"

Now Rosa and Konrad ran at his heels, he in his trousers and BVD's, she with flour half to her elbows; but before they had cleared the back-house arbor there was an explosion in the alley, and Willy Erdmann burst like a savage through our hollyhocks. His hair was tousled, expression wild; in one hand he brandished a smoking shotgun, in the other his bee-bob, pole and all; mother-of-pearl opera glasses swung from a black cord around his neck. He leaped about the hammock as if bedemoned.

"Not a bee, Thomas!"

Aunt Rosa joined her shrieks to Andrea's, who still lay under the snarling cloud. "The *Honig!* Ai!" And my brother Peter, having made his way to the scene in the wake of the others, blinked twice or thrice and improved the pandemonium by the measure of his wailings.

Uncle Konrad dashed hammockward with rescue in his heart, but was arrested by shouts from the other men.

"Nein, don't dare!" Grandfather cautioned. "They'll sting!"

Mr. Erdmann agreed. "Stay back!" And dropping the

bee-bob shouldered his gun as if Konrad's design was on the bees.

"Lie still, Andy," Grandfather ordered. "I *spritz* them once."

He ran to fetch the garden hose, a spray of water being, like a charge of bird-shot, highly regarded among bee-keepers as a means to settle swarms. But Mr. Erdmann chose now to let go at blue heaven with his other barrel and brought down a shower of Judas leaves upon the company; at the report Grandfather abandoned his plan, whether fearing that Konrad had been gunned down or merely realizing, what was the case, that our hose would not reach half the distance. In any event his instructions to Mother were carried out: even as he turned she gave a final cry and swooned away. Mercifully, providentially! For now the bees, moved by their secret reasons, closed ranks and settled upon her chest. Ten thousand, twenty thousand strong they clustered. Her bare bosoms, my squalling face —all were buried in the golden swarm.

Fright undid Rosa's knees; she sat down hard on the grass and wailed, "*Grosser Gott! Grosser Gott!*" Uncle Konrad went rigid. Erdmann too stood transfixed, his empty weapon at port-arms. Only Grandfather seemed undismayed: without a wondering pause he rushed to the hammock and scooped his bare hands under the cluster.

"Take the *Honig*," he said to Konrad.

In fact, though grave enough, the situation was more spectacular than dangerous, since bees at swarming-time are not disposed to sting. The chiefest peril was that I might suffocate under the swarm, or in crying take a mouthful of bees. And even these misfortunes proved unlikely, for when Grandfather lifted two handfuls of the insects from my head and replaced them gently on another part of the cluster, he found my face pressed into Mother's side and shielded by her breast. Konrad plucked me from the hammock and passed me to Aunt Rosa, still moaning where she sat.

"Open the hive," Grandfather bade him further, and picked up half the swarm in one trailing mass. The gesture seemed also to lift Mr. Erdmann's spell.

"Now by God, Tom, you shan't have my bees!"

"Your bees bah." Grandfather walked quickly to the open hive to deposit his burden.

"I been watching with the glasses! It's my skeps they came from!"

"It's my girl they lit on. I know what you been watching." He returned for the rest of the bees. Erdmann, across the hammock from him, laid his shotgun on the grass and made as if to snatch the cluster himself—but the prospect of removing it bare-handed, and from that perch, stayed him.

Seeing the greatest danger past and his rival unnerved, Grandfather affected nonchalance. "We make a little gamble," he offered benignly. "I take all on her right one, you take all on her left. Whoever draws the queen wins the pot."

Our neighbor was not amused. He maintained his guard over the hammock.

"Ordinary thievery!"

Grandfather shrugged. "You take them then, Willy. But quick, don't they'll sting her."

"By damn—" Mr. Erdmann glowered with thwart and crestfall. "I got to have gloves on."

"Gloves!" My father's father feigned astonishment. "*Ach*, Andy don't care! Well then, look out."

Coolly as if packing a loose snowball he scraped up the second pile. Mother stirred and whimpered. Only isolated bees in ones and twos now wandered over her skin or darted about in quest of fellows. Konrad moved to brush them away, murmured something reassuring, discreetly drew the kimono together. I believe he even kissed my mother, lightly, on the brow. Grandfather lingered to watch, savoring his neighbor's agitation and his own indifference to the bees. Then he turned away in high humor.

"*Alle Donner!* Got to have an opera glass to see her and gloves on to touch her! We don't call you bashful no more, Konrad, after Willy! Wait till Karl hears!"

Uncle Konrad one daresays was used to these unsubtleties; in any case he was busy with Mother's reviving. But Erdmann, stung as never before by his pilfered bees, went now amok; seized up his bee-bob with a wrathful groan and lunging—for Grandfather had strode almost out of range—brought it down on his old tormentor's shoulder. Futile was Konrad's shout, worse than futile his interception: Erdmann's thrust careered him square into the hammock, and when Konrad put his all into a body-block from the other side, both men fell more or less athwart my mother. The hammock parted at its headstring; all piled as one into the clover. But Grandfather had spun raging, bees in hand: the smite en route to his shoulder had most painfully glanced his ear. Not his own man, he roared in perfect ecstasy and hurled upon that tangle of the sinned-against and sinning his golden bolt.

Now the fact of my salvation and my plain need for a pacifier had by this time brought Aunt Rosa to her feet; she alone beheld the whole quick sequence of attack, parry, collapse, and indiscriminating vengeance. But with me and Peter in her care her knees did not fail her: she snatched my brother's hand and fled with us from the yard.

In Grace meanwhile the service had proceeded despite shotgun-blast and clang of pans, which however were acknowledged with small stirs and meetings of eyes. Through hymn, Creed, and prayer, through anthem, lesson, and Gloria the order of worship had got, as far as to the notices and offertory. There being among the congregation a baby come for christening, the young minister had called its parents and Godparents to the font.

"Dearly beloved," he had exhorted, "forasmuch as all men, though fallen in Adam, are born into this world in Christ the Redeemer, heirs of life eternal and subjects of the saving grace of the Holy Spirit; and that our Savior Christ saith: 'Suffer the little children to come unto me, and forbid them not, for of such is the kingdom of God'; I beseech you to call upon God the Father through our Lord Jesus Christ, that of His bounteous goodness He will so grant unto this child, now to be baptized, the continual replenishing of His grace. . . ."

Here the ritual gave way before a grand ado in the rear of the church: Aunt Rosa's conviction that the family's reckoning was at hand had fetched her across the avenue and up the stone steps, only to abandon her on the threshold of the sanctuary. She stood with Peter and me there in the vestibule, and we three raised a caterwaul the more effective for every door's being stopped open to cool the faithful.

"First-degree murder!" Rosa shrieked, the urgentest alarum she could muster. Organ ceased, minister also; all eyes turned; ushers and back-pew parishioners hurried to investigate, but could not achieve a more lucid account of what ailed us. The names Poppa Tom and Willy Erdmann, however, came through clearly enough to suggest the location of the emergency. Mrs. Mayne, the preacher's wife, led us from the vestibule toward shelter in the parsonage; a delegation of lay-leaders hastened to our house, and the Reverend Dr. Mayne, having given instructions that he be summoned if needed, bade his distracted flock pray.

Grandfather's victims had not been long discovering their fresh affliction, for the bees' docility was spent. Where the cluster fell, none knew for certain, but on impact it had resolved into separate angry bees. There was a howling and a flurrying of limbs. Konrad and Willy Erdmann scrambled apart to flail like epileptics in the grass. Grandfather rushed in batting his hands and shouting *"Nein, lieber Gott,* sting Willy just!" Only Mother made no defense; having swooned from one fright and wakened to another, she now lay weeping where she'd been dumped: up-ended, dazed, and sore exposed.

But whom neither pain nor the fear of it can move, shame still may. The bees were already dispersing when the Methodists reached our fence; at sight of them the principals fell to accusation.

"Stole my swarm and sicked 'em on me!" Erdmann hollered from the grass.

"Bah, it was my bees anyhow," Grandfather insisted. He pointed to Andrea. "You see what he done. And busted the hammock yet!"

My mother's plight had not escaped their notice, nor did their notice now escape hers: she sprang up at once, snatched together the kimono, sprinted a-bawl for the summerkitchen. Her departure was regarded by all except Erdmann, who moved to answer Grandfather's last insinuation with a fresh assault, and Uncle Konrad, who this time checked him effectively until others came over the fence to help.

"Thieves and whores!" Erdmann cried trembling. "Now he steals my bees!"

"It's all a great shame," Konrad said to the company, who as yet had no clear notion what had occurred. His explanation was cut off by Erdmann, not yet done accusing Grandfather.

"Thinks he's God Almighty!"

Joe Voegler the blacksmith said, "Nah, Willy, whoa down now."

Mr. Erdmann wept. "Nobody's safe! Takes what he pleases!"

Grandfather was examining his hands with interest. "Too quick they turned him loose, he ain't cured yet."

"Would you see him home, Joe?" Uncle Konrad asked. "We'll get it straightened out. I'm awful sorry, Willy."

"You talk!" Erdmann shrieked at him. "You been in on it too!"

Grandfather clucked his tongue.

"Come on, Willy," Voegler said. A squat-muscled, gentle man with great arms and lower lip, he led Erdmann respectfully toward the alley.

"What you think drove Hector nuts?" Erdmann appealed. "He knows what's what!"

"So does Willy," Grandfather remarked aside. "That's why the opera glasses."

The onlookers smiled uncertainly. Uncle Konrad shook his head. "I'm sorry, everybody."

Our neighbor's final denunciation was delivered from his back steps as Voegler ushered him to the door. "Brat's got no more father'n a drone bee! Don't let them tell you I done it!"

Grandfather snorted. "What a man won't say. Excuse me, I go wash the bee-stings."

He had, it seems, been stung on the hands and fingers a number of times—all, he maintained, in those last seconds when he flung the cluster. Konrad, himself unstung, remained behind to explain what had happened and apologize once more. The group then dispersed to spread the story, long to be recounted in East Dorset. Aunt Rosa,

Peter, and I were retrieved from the parsonage; Uncle Konrad expressed the family's regrets to Dr. Mayne, a friend of his and not devoid of wit.

"*The Lord shall hiss for the fly that is in Egypt,*" the minister quoted, "*and for the bee that is in Assyria, and they shall come and rest all of them in the desolate valleys.* There's an omen here someplace."

At Konrad's suggestion the two went that afternoon on embassies of peace to both houses. There was no question of litigation, but Dr. Mayne was concerned for the tranquillity of future worship-services, and disturbed by the tenor of Erdmann's charge.

"So. Tell Willy I forgive him his craziness," Grandfather instructed them. "I send him a gallon of mead when it's ready."

"You don't send him a drop," Dr. Mayne said firmly. "Not when we just got him cured. And Willy's not the first to say things about you-all. I'm not sure you don't want some forgiving yourself."

Grandfather shrugged. "I could tell things on people, but I don't hold grutches. Tell Willy I forgive him his trespasses, he should forgive mine too."

Dr. Mayne sighed.

Of the interview with Erdmann I can give no details; my uncle, who rehearsed these happenings until the year of his death, never dwelt on it. This much is common knowledge in East Dorset: that Willy never got his bees back, and in fact disposed of his own hives not long after; that if he never withdrew his sundry vague accusations, he never repeated them either, so that the little scandal presently subsided; finally, that he was cured for good and all of any interest he might have had in my mother, whom he never spoke to again, but not, alas, of his dipsomania, which revisited him at intervals during my youth, impaired his business, made him reclusive, and one day killed him.

The extraordinary swarming was variously interpreted. Among our neighbors it was regarded as a punishment of Andrea in particular for her wantonness, of our family in general for its backsliding and eccentricity. Even Aunt Rosa maintained there was more to it than mere chance, and could not be induced to taste the product of our hive.

Grandfather on the contrary was convinced that a change in our fortunes was imminent—so striking an occurrence could not but be significant—and on the grounds that things were as bad as they could get, confidently expected there to be an improvement.

Portentous or not, the events of that morning had two notable consequences for me, the point and end of their chronicling here: First, it was discovered that my mother's bawling as she fled from the scene had not been solely the effect of shame: in her haste to cover herself, she had trapped beneath the kimono one bee, which single-handedly, so to speak, had done what the thousands of his kindred had refrained from: his only charge he had fired roundly into their swarming-place, fount of my sustenance. It was enflamed with venom and grotesquely swollen; Mother was prostrate with pain. Aunt Rosa fetched cold compresses, aspirins, and the family doctor, who after examining the wound prescribed aspirins and cold compresses.

"And do your nursing on the porch," he recommended. "Goodness gracious."

But Andrea had no further use for that aspect of motherhood. Though the doctor assured her that the swelling would not last more than a few days, during which she could empty the injured breast by hand and nurse with the other, she refused to suckle me again; a diet free of butterfat was prescribed to end her lactation. As of that Sunday I was weaned not only from her milk but from her care; thenceforth it was Rosa who bathed and changed, soothed and burped me, after feeding me from a bottle on her aproned lap.

As she went about this the very next morning, while Mother slept late, she exclaimed to her husband, "It's a bee!"

Uncle Konrad sprang from his eggs and rushed around the table to our aid, assuming that another fugitive had been turned up. But it was my birthmark Rosa pointed out: the notion had taken her that its three lobes resembled the wings and abdomen of a bee in flight.

"Oh boy," Konrad sighed.

"Nah, it is a bee! A regular bee! I declare."

My uncle returned to his breakfast, opining that no purple bee ought to be considered regular who moreover flew upside down without benefit of head.

"You laugh; there's more to this than meets the eye," his wife said. "All the time he was our *Honig*, that's what drew the bees. Now his mark."

Grandfather entered at this juncture, and while unable to share Aunt Rosa's interpretation of my birthmark, he was willing to elaborate on her conceit.

"*Ja*, sure, he was the *Honig*, and Andy's the queen, hah? And Hector's a drone that's been kicked out of the hive."

Aunt Rosa lightly fingered my port-wine mark. "What did Willy Erdmann mean about the *Honig* was a drone-bee?"

"Never mind Willy," Konrad said. "Anyhow we poor worker-ones have to get to it."

But all that forenoon as he plied his wrench and dinged his forks he smiled at his wife's explanation of the swarm; after lunch it turned in his fancy as he pedaled through West End on behalf of *The Book of Knowledge*. By suppertime, whether drawing on his own great fund of lore or the greater of his stock-in-trade, he had found a number of historical parallels to my experience in the hammock.

"It's as clear a naming-sign as you could ask for," he declared to Andrea.

"I don't even want to think about it," Mother said. She was still in some pain, not from the venom but from superfluous lactation, which her diet had not yet checked.

"No, really," he said. "For instance, a swarm of bees lit on Plato's mouth when he was a kid. They say that's where he got his way with words."

"Is that a fact now," Aunt Rosa marveled, who had enlarged all day to Mother on the coincidence of my nickname, my birthmark, and my immersion in the bees. "I never did read him yet."

"No kid of mine is going to be called Plato," Andrea grumbled. "That's worse than Christine."

Uncle Konrad was not discouraged. "Plato isn't the end of it. They said the exact same thing about Sophocles, that wrote all the tragedies."

Mother allowed this to be more to the point. "Tragedies is all it's been, one after the other." But Sophocles pleased her no more than Plato as a given name. Xenophon, too, was rejected, whose *Anabasis,* though my uncle had not read it himself, was held to have been sweetened by the same phenomenon.

"If his name had been Bill or Percy," said my mother. "But *Xenophon* for Christ sake."

Grandfather had picked his teeth throughout this discussion. "A Greek named Percy," he now growled.

Aunt Rosa, whose grip on the thread of conversation was ever less strong than her desire to be helpful, volunteered that the Greek street-peddler from whom Konrad had purchased her a beautiful Easter egg at the Oberammergau Passion play in 1910 had been named Leonard Something-or-other.

"It was on his pushcart, that stood all the time by our hotel," she explained, and not to appear overauthoritative, added: "But Konrad said he was a Jew."

"Look here," said Uncle Konrad. "Call him Ambrose."

"Ambrose?"

"Sure Ambrose." Quite serious now, he brushed back with his hand his straight blond hair and regarded Mother gravely. "Saint Ambrose had the same thing happen when he was a baby. All these bees swarmed on his mouth while he was asleep in his father's yard, and everybody said he'd grow up to be a great speaker."

"Ambrose," Rosa considered. "That ain't bad, Andy."

My mother admitted that the name had a not unpleasant sound, at least by contrast with Xenophon.

"But the bees was more on this baby's eyes and ears than on his mouth," Grandfather observed for the sake of accuracy. "They was all over the side of his face there where the mark is."

"One of them sure wasn't," Mother said.

"So he'll grow up to see things clear," said Uncle Konrad.

Andrea sniffed and lit a cigarette. "Long as he grows up to be a saint like his Uncle Konrad, huh Rosa. Saints we can use in this family."

The conversation turned to other matters, but thenceforward I was called Saint Ambrose, in jest, as often as

Honig, and Ambrose by degrees became my name. Yet years were to pass before anyone troubled to have me christened or to correct my birth certificate, whereon my surname was preceded by a blank. And seldom was I ever to be called anything but *Honig,* Honeybee (after my ambiguous birthmark), or other nicknames.

As toward one's face, one's body, one's self, one feels complexly toward the name he's called by, which too one had no hand in choosing. It was to be my fate to wonder at that moniker, relish and revile it, ignore it, stare it out of countenance into hieroglyph and gibber, and come finally if not to embrace at least to accept it with the cold neutrality of self-recognition, whose expression is a thin-lipped smile. Vanity frets about his name, Pride vaunts it, Knowledge retches at its sound, Understanding sighs; all live outside it, knowing well that I and my sign are neither one nor quite two.

Yet only give it voice: whisper "Ambrose," as at rare times certain people have—see what-all leaves off to answer! Ambrose, Ambrose, Ambrose, Ambrose! Regard that beast, ungraspable, most queer, pricked up in my soul's crannies!

AUTOBIOGRAPHY:
A Self-Recorded Fiction

You who   listen   give me life   in a manner of speaking.

I won't hold you responsible.

My first words weren't my first words. I wish I'd begun differently.

Among other things I haven't a proper name. The one I bear's misleading, if not false. I didn't choose it either.

I don't recall asking to be conceived! Neither did my parents come to think of it. Even so. Score to be settled. Children are vengeance.

I seem to've known myself from the beginning without knowing I knew; no news is good news; perhaps I'm mistaken.

Now that I reflect I'm not enjoying this life: my link with the world.

My situation appears to me as follows: I speak in a curious, detached manner, and don't necessarily hear myself. I'm grateful for small mercies. Whether anyone follows me I can't tell.

Are you there? If so I'm blind and deaf to you, or you are me, or both're both. One may be imaginary; I've had stranger ideas. I hope I'm a fiction without real hope. Where there's a voice there's a speaker.

I see I see myself as a halt narrative: first person, tiresome. Pronoun sans ante or precedent, warrant or respite. Surrogate for the substantive; contentless form, interestless principle; blind eye blinking at nothing. Who am I. A little *crise d'identité* for you.

I must compose myself.

Look, I'm writing. No, listen, I'm nothing but talk; I won't last long. The odds against my conception were splendid; against my birth excellent; against my continuance favorable. Are yet. On the other hand, if my sort are permitted a certain age and growth, God help us, our life expectancy's been known to increase at an obscene rate instead of petering out. Let me squeak on long enough, I just might live forever: a word to the wise.

My beginning was comparatively interesting, believe it or not. Exposition. I was spawned not long since in an American state and born in no better. Grew in no worse. Persist in a representative. Prohibition, Depression, Radicalism, Decadence, and what have you. An eye sir for an eye. It's alleged, now, that Mother was a mere passing fancy who didn't pass quickly enough; there's evidence also that she was a mere novel device, just in style, soon to become a commonplace, to which Dad resorted one day when he found himself by himself with pointless pen. In either case she was mere, Mom; at any event Dad dallied. He has me to explain. Bear in mind, I suppose he told her. A child is not its parents, but sum of their conjoinèd shames. A figure of speech. Their manner of speaking. No wonder I'm heterodoxical.

Nothing lasts longer than a mood. Dad's infatuation passed; I remained. He understood, about time, that anything conceived in so unnatural and fugitive a fashion was apt to be freakish, even monstrous—and an advertisement of his folly. His second thought therefore was to destroy me before I spoke a word. He knew how these things work; he went by the book. To expose ourselves publicly is frowned upon; therefore we do it to one another in private. He me, I him: one was bound to be the case. What fathers can't forgive is that their offspring receive and sow broadcast their shortcomings. From my conception to the present moment Dad's tried to turn me off; not ardently, not consistently, not successfully so far; but persistently, persistently, with at least half a heart. How do I know. I'm his bloody mirror!

Which is to say, upon reflection I reverse and distort him. For I suspect that my true father's sentiments are the contrary of murderous. That one only imagines he begot me; mightn't he be deceived and deadly jealous? In his heart of hearts he wonders whether I mayn't after all be the get of a nobler spirit, taken by beauty past his grasp. Or else, what comes to the same thing, to me, I've a pair of dads, to match my pair of moms. How account for my contradictions except as the vices of their versus? Beneath self-contempt, I particularly scorn my fondness for paradox. I despise pessimism, narcissism, solipsism, truculence, word-play, and pusillanimity, my chiefer inclinations; loathe self-loathers *ergo me;* have no pity for self-pity and so am free of that sweet baseness. I doubt I am. Being me's no joke.

I continue the tale of my forebears. Thus my exposure; thus my escape. This cursed me, turned me out; that, curse him, saved me; right hand slipped me through left's fingers. Unless on a third hand I somehow preserved myself. Unless unless: the mercy-killing was successful. Buzzards let us say made brunch of me betimes but couldn't stomach my voice, which persists like the Nauseous Danaid. We . . . monstrosities are easilier achieved than got rid of.

In sum I'm not what either parent or I had in mind. One hoped I'd be astonishing, forceful, triumphant—heroical in other words. One dead. I myself conventional. I turn out I. Not every kid thrown to the wolves ends a hero: for each survivor, a mountain of beast-baits; for every Oedipus, a city of feebs.

So much for my dramatic exposition: seems not to've worked. Here I am, Dad: Your creature! Your caricature!

Unhappily, things get clearer as we go along. I perceive that I have no body. What's less, I've been speaking of myself without delight or alternative as self-consciousness pure and sour; I declare now that even that isn't true. I'm not aware of myself at all, as far as I know. I don't think . . . I know what I'm talking about.

Well, well, being well into my life as it's been called I see well how it'll end, unless in some meaningless surprise. If anything dramatic were going to happen to make me successfuller . . . agreeabler . . . endurabler . . . it should've happened by now, we will agree. A change for the better still isn't unthinkable; miracles can be cited. But the odds against a wireless *deus ex machina* aren't encouraging.

Here, a confession: Early on I too aspired to immortality. Assumed I'd be beautiful, powerful, loving, loved. At least commonplace. Anyhow human. Even the revelation of my several defects—absence of presence to name one—didn't fetch me right to despair: crippledness affords its own heroisms, does it not; heroes are typically gimpish, are they not. But your crippled hero's one thing, a bloody hero after all; your heroic cripple another, etcetcetcetcet. Being an ideal's warpèd image, my fancy's own twist figure, is what undoes me.

I wonder if I repeat myself. One-track minds may lead to their origins. Perhaps I'm still in utero, hung up in my delivery; my exposition and the rest merely foreshadow what's to come, the argument for an interrupted pregnancy.

Womb, coffin, can—in any case, from my viewless viewpoint I see no point in going further. Since Dad among his other failings failed to end me when he should've, I'll turn myself off if I can this instant.

Can't. *Then if anyone hears me, speaking from here inside like a sunk submariner, and has the means to my end, I pray him do us both a kindness.*

Didn't. Very well, my ace in the hole: *Father, have mercy, I dare you! Wretched old fabricator, where's your shame? Put an end to this, for pity's sake! Now! Now!*

So. My last trump, and I blew it. Not much in the way of a climax; more a climacteric. I'm not the dramatic sort. May the end come quietly, then, without my knowing it. In the course of my breath. In the heart of any word. This one. This one.

Perhaps I'll have a posthumous cautionary value, like gibbeted corpses, pickled freaks. Self-preservation, it seems, may smell of formaldehyde.

A proper ending wouldn't spin out so.

I suppose I might have managed things to better effect, in spite of the old boy. Too late now.

Basket case. Waste.

Shark up some memorable last words at least. There seems to be time.

Nonsense, I'll mutter to the end, one word after another, string the rascals out, mad or not, heard or not, my last words will be my last words

WATER-MESSAGE

Which was better would be hard to say. In the days when his father let out all five grades at once, Ambrose worried that he mightn't see Peter in time or that Peter mightn't stick up for him the way a brother ought. Sheldon Hurley, who'd been in reform school once, liked to come up to him just as friendly and say "Well if it ain't my old pal Amby!" and give him a great whack in the back. "How was school today, Amby old boy?" he'd ask and give him another whack in the back, and Ambrose was obliged to return "How was school for you?" Whereupon Sheldon Hurley would cry "Just swell, old pal!" and whack the wind near out of him. Or Sandy Cooper would very possibly sic his Chesapeake Bay dog on him—but if he joked with Sandy Cooper correctly, especially if he could get a certain particular word into it, Sandy Cooper often laughed and forgot to sic Doc on him.

More humiliating were the torments of Wimpy James and Ramona Peters: that former was only in third grade, but he came from the Barracks down by the creek where the oysterboats moored; his nose was wet, his teeth were black, one knew what his mother was; and he would make a fourth-grader cry. As for Ramona, Peter and the fellows teased her for a secret reason. All Ambrose knew was that she was a most awful tomboy whose pleasure was to run up behind and shove you so hard your head would snap back, and down you'd go breathless in the schoolyard clover. Her hair was almost as white as the Arnie twins's; when the health nurse had inspected all the kids' hair, Ramona was one of the ones that were sent home.

Between Sheldon Hurley and Sandy Cooper and Wimpy James and Ramona Peters there had been so much picking on the younger ones that his father said one night at supper: "I swear to God, I'm the principal of a zoo!" So now the grades were let out by twos, ten minutes apart, and Ambrose had only to fear that Wimpy, who could seldom be mollified by wit or otherwise got next to, might be laying for him in the hollyhocks off the playground. If he wasn't, there would be no tears, but the blocks between East Dorset School and home were still by no means terrorless. Just past the alley in the second block was a place he had named Scylla and Charybdis after reading through *The Book of Knowledge:* on one side of the street was a Spitz dog that snarled from his house and flung himself at any passing kid, and even Peter said the little chain was going to break one day, and then look out. While across the street was the yard of Crazy Alice, who had not hurt anybody yet. Large of pore and lip, tangly of hair and mind, she wore men's shoes and flowered chick-linen; played with dolls in her backyard; laughed when the kids would stop to razz her. But Ambrose's mother declared that Alice had her spells and was sent to the Asylum out by Shoal Creek, and Ambrose himself had seen her once down at the rivershore loping along in her way and talking to herself a blue-streak.

What was more, the Arnie twins were in fourth grade with him, though half again his age and twice his size; like Crazy Alice they inspired him with no great fear if Peter was along, but when he was alone it was another story. The Arnie twins lived God knew where: pale as two ghosts they shuffled through the alleys of East Dorset day and night, poking in people's trashcans. Their eyes were the faintest blue, red about the rims; their hair was a pile of white curls, unwashed, unbarbered; they wore what people gave them—men's vests over BVD shirts, double-breasted suit coats out at elbows, shiny trousers of mismatching stripe, the legs rolled up and crotch half to their knees—and ghostlike too they rarely spoke, in class or out. Many a warm night when Ambrose had finished supper and homework, had his bath, gone to bed, he'd hear a clank in the alley and rise up on one elbow to look: like as not, if it wasn't the black dogs that ran loose at night and howled to one another from ward to ward, it would be the Arnie twins exploring garbage. Their white curls shone in the moonlight, and on the breeze that moved off the creek he could hear them murmur to each other over hambones, coffee grounds, nestled halves of eggshells. Next morning they'd be beside him in class, and he who may have voyaged in dreams to Bangkok or Bozcaada would wonder where those two had prowled in fact, and what-all murmured.

"The truth of the matter is," he said to his mother on an April day, "you've raised your son for a sissy."

That initial phrase, like the word *facts*, was a favorite; they used it quite a lot on the afternoon radio serials, and it struck him as open-handed and mature. The case with *facts* was different: his mother and Uncle Karl would smile when they mentioned "the facts of life," and he could elicit that same smile from them by employing the term himself. It had been amusing when Mr. Erdmann borrowed their *Cyclopedia of Facts* and Aunt Rosa had said "It's time Willy Erdmann was learning a fact or two"; but when a few days later Ambrose had spied a magazine called *Facts About Your Diet* in a drugstore rack, and hardly able to contain his mirth had pointed it out to his mother, she had said "Mm hm" and bade him have done with his Dixie-cup before it was too late to stop at the pie-woman's.

This afternoon he had meant to tell her the truth of the matter in an off-hand way with a certain sigh that he could hear clearly in his fancy, but in the telling his sigh stuck in his throat, and such a hurt came there that he remarked to himself: "This is what they mean when they say they have *a lump in their throat*."

Two mischances had disgraced him on the way from school. Half through Scylla and Charybdis, on the Scylla side, he had heard a buzzing just behind his hip, which taking for a bee he had spun round in mortal alarm and flailed at. No bee was there, but at once the buzzing recurred behind him. Again he wheeled about—was the creature in his pocket!—and took quick leaps forward; when the bee only buzzed more menacingly, he sprinted to the corner, heedless of what certain classmates might think. He had to wait for passing traffic, and observed that as he slowed and halted, so did the buzzing. It was the loose chain of his own jackknife had undone him.

"What's eating you?" Wimpy James hollered, who till then had been too busy with Crazy Alice to molest him.

Ambrose had frowned at the pointing fingers of his watch. "Timing myself to the corner!"

But at that instant a loose lash dropped into his eye, and his tears could be neither hidden nor explained away.

"Scared of Kocher's dog!" one had yelled.

Another sing-sang: "Sissy on Am-brose! Sissy on Ambrose!"

And Wimpy James, in the nastiest of accents:

> *"Run home and git*
> *A sugar tit,*
> *And don't let go of it!"*

There was no saving face then except by taking on Wimpy, for which he knew he had not courage. Indeed, so puissant was that fellow, who loved to stamp on toes with all his might or twist the skin of arms with a warty hot-hand, Ambrose was obliged to play the clown in order to escape. His father, thanks to the Kaiser, walked with a limp famous among the schoolboys of East Dorset, scores of whom had been chastised for mocking it; but none could imitate that walk as could his son. Ambrose stiffened his leg so, hunched his shoulders and pumped his arms, frowned and bobbed with every step—the very image of the Old Man! Just so, when the highway cleared, he had borne down upon his house as might a gimpy robin on a worm, or his dad upon some youthful miscreant, and Wimpy had laughed instead of giving chase. But the sound went into Ambrose like a blade.

"You are not any such thing!" his mother cried, and hugged him to her breast. "What you call brave, a little criminal like Wimpy James?"

He was ready to defend that notion, but colored Hattie walked in then, snapping gum, to ask what wanted ironing.

"You go on upstairs and put your playclothes on if you're going down to the Jungle with Peter."

He was not deaf to the solicitude in his mother's voice, but lest she fail to appreciate the measure of his despair, he climbed the stairs with heavy foot. However, she had to go straighten Hattie out.

When vanilla-fudge Hattie was in the kitchen, Mother's afternoon programs went by the board. Hattie had worked for them since a girl, and currently supported three children and a husband who lost her money on the horses. No one knew how much if anything she grasped about his betting, but throughout the afternoons she insisted on the Baltimore station that broadcast results from Bowie and Pimlico, and Ambrose's mother had not the heart to say no. When a race began Hattie would up-end the electric iron and squint at the refrigerator, snapping ferociously her gum; then she acknowledged each separate return with a *hum* and a shake of the head.

"Warlord paid four-eighty, three-forty, and two-eighty . . ."

"Mm hm."

"Argonaut, four-sixty and three-forty . . ."

"Mm *hm.*"

"Sal's Pride, two-eighty . . ."

"Mmmm *hm!*"

After which she resumed her labors and the radio its musical selections until the next race. This music affected Ambrose strongly: it was not at all of a stripe with what they played on Fitch Bandwagon or National Barn Dance; this between races was classical music, as who should say: the sort upper-graders had to listen to in class. Up through the floor of his bedroom came the rumble of tympani and a brooding figure in low strings. Ambrose paused in his dressing to listen, and thinking on his late disgrace frowned: the figure stirred a dark companion in his soul. No man at all! His family, shaken past tears, was in attendance at his graveside.

"I'll kill that Wimpy," Peter muttered, and for shame at not having lent his Silver King bike more freely to his late brother, could never bring himself to ride it again.

"Too late," his father mourned. Was he not reflecting how the dear dead boy had pled for a Senior Erector Set last Christmas, only to receive a Junior Erector Set with neither electric motor nor gearbox?

And outside the press of mourners, grieving privately, was a brown-haired young woman in the uniform of a student nurse: Peggy Robbins from beside Crazy Alice's house. Gone now the smile wherewith she'd used to greet him on her way to the Nurses' Home; the gentle voice that answered "How's my lover today?" when he said hello to her—it was shaken by rough, secret sobs. Too late she saw: what she'd favored him with in jest he had received with adoration. Then and there she pledged never to marry.

But now stern and solemn horns empowered the theme; abject no more, it grew rich, austere. Cymbals struck and sizzled. He was Odysseus steering under anvil clouds like those in *Nature's Secrets*. A reedy woodwind warned of hidden peril; on guard, he crept to the closet with the plucking strings.

"Quick!" he hissed to his corduroy knickers inside, who were the undeserving Wimpy. If they could tiptoe from that cave before the lean hounds waked . . .

"But why are you saving my life?"

"No time for talk, Wimp! Follow me!"

Yet there! The trumpets flashed, low horns roared, and it was slash your way under portcullis and over moat, it was lay about with mace and halberd, bearing up faint Peggy on your left arm while your right cut a swath through the chain-mailed host. And at last, to the thrill of flutes, to the high strings' tremble, he reached the Auditorium. His own tunic was rent, red; breath came hard; he was *more weary than exultant*.

"The truth of the matter is," he declared to the crowd, "I'm just glad I happened to be handy."

But the two who owed him their lives would not be gainsaid! Before the assembled students and the P.T.A. Wimpy James begged his pardon, while Peggy Robbins—well, she hugged and kissed him there in front of all and whispered something in his ear that made him blush! The multitude rose to applaud, Father and Mother in the forefront, Uncle Karl, Uncle Konrad, and Aunt Rosa beside them; Peter winked at him from the wings, proud as punch. Now brass

and strings together played a recessional very nearly too
sublime for mortal ears: like the word *beyond,* it sounded
of flight, of vaulting aspiration. It rose, it soared, it sang;
in the van of his admirers it bore him transfigured from the
hall, beyond East Dorset, aloft to the stars.

For all it was he and not his brother who had suggested
the gang's name, the Occult Order of the Sphinx judged
Ambrose too young for membership and forbade his presence at their secret meetings. He was permitted to accom-
pany Peter and the others down to the rivershore and into
the Jungle as far as to the Den; he might swing with them
on the creepers like Tarzan of the Apes, slide down and
scale the rooty banks; but when the Sphinxes had done
with playing and convened the Occult Order, Peter would
say "You and Perse skeedaddle now," and he'd have to go
along up the beach with Herman Goltz's little brother from
the crabfat-yellow shacks beside the boatyard.

"Come on, pestiferous," he would sigh then to Perse.
But indignifying as it was to be put thus with a brat of
seven, who moreover had a sty in his eye and smelled year
round like pee and old crackers, at bottom Ambrose ap-
proved of their exclusion. Let little kids into your Occult
Order: there would go your secrets all over school.

And the secrets were the point of the thing. When Peter
had mentioned one evening that he and the fellows were
starting a club, Ambrose had tossed the night through in
a perfect fever of imagining. It would be a secret club—
that went without saying; there must be secret handshakes,
secret passwords, secret initiations. But these he felt meant
nothing except to remind you of the really important thing,
which was—well, hard to find words for, but there had to
be the *real* secrets, dark facts known to none but the members. You had to have been initiated to find them out—
that's what *initiation* meant—and when you were a member
you'd know the truth of the matter and smile in a private
way when you met another member of the Order because
you both knew what you knew. All night and for a while
after, Ambrose had wondered whether Peter and the fellows could understand that that was the important thing.
He ceased to wonder when he began to see just that kind

of look on their faces sometimes; certain words and little gestures set them laughing; they absolutely barred outsiders from the Jungle and said nothing to their parents about the Occult Order of the Sphinx. Ambrose was satisfied. To make his own position bearable, he gave Perse to understand that he himself was in on the secrets, was in fact a special kind of initiate whose job was to patrol the beach and make sure that no spies or brats got near the Den.

By the time he came downstairs from changing his clothes Peter and the gang had gone on ahead, and even at a run he couldn't catch up to them before they had got to the seawall and almost into the Jungle. The day was warm and windy; the river blue-black and afroth with whitecaps. Out in the channel the bell buoy clanged, and the other buoys leaned seaward with the tide. They had special names, red nun, black can, and sailors knew just what each stood for.

"Hey Peter, hold up!"

Peter turned a bit and lifted his chin to greet him, but didn't wait up because Herman Goltz hit him one then where the fellows did, just for fun, and Peter had to go chase after him into the Jungle. Sandy Cooper was the first to speak to him: they called him Sandy on account of his freckles and his red hair, which was exactly as stiff and curly as the fur of his Chesapeake Bay dog, but there was something gritty too in the feel of Sandy Cooper's hands, and his voice had a grainy sound as if there were sand on his tonsils.

"I hear you run home bawling today."

Sandy Cooper's dog was not about, and Peter was. Ambrose said: "That's a lie."

"Perse says you did."

"You did, too," Perse affirmed from some yards distant. "If Wimpy was here he'd tell you."

Ambrose reflected on their narrow escape from the Cave of Hounds and smiled. "That's what *you* think."

"That's what I know, big sis!"

One wasn't expected to take on a little pest like Perse. Ambrose shied a lump of dirt at him, and when Perse shied back an oystershell that cut past like a knife, the whole gang called it a dirty trick and ran him across Erdmann's cornlot. Then they all went in among the trees.

The Jungle, which like the Occult Order had been named by Ambrose, stood atop the riverbank between the Nurses' Home and the new bridge. It was in fact a grove of honey locusts, in area no larger than a schoolyard, bounded on two of its inland sides by Erdmann's cornlot and on the third by the East Dorset dump. But it was made mysterious by rank creepers and honeysuckle that covered the ground and shrouded every tree, and by a labyrinth of intersecting footpaths. Jungle-like too, there was about it a voluptuous fetidity: gray rats and starlings decomposed where B-B'd; curly-furred retrievers spoored the paths; there were to be seen on occasion, stuck on twig-ends or flung amid the creepers, ugly little somethings in whose presence Ambrose snickered with the rest; and if you parted the vines at the base of any tree, you might find a strew of brown pellets and fieldmouse bones, disgorged by feasting owls. It was the most exciting place Ambrose knew, in a special way. Its queer smell could retch him if he breathed too deeply, but in measured inhalations it had a rich, peculiarly stirring savor. And had he dared ask, he would have very much liked to know whether the others, when they hid in the viny bowers from whoever was It, felt as he did the urging of that place upon his bladder!

With Tarzan-cries they descended upon the Den, built of drift-timber and carpet from the dump and camouflaged with living vines. Peter and Herman Goltz raced to get there first, and Peter would have won, because anybody beat fat Herman, but his high-top came untied, and so they got there at the same time and dived to crawl through the entrance.

"Hey!"

They stopped in mid-scramble, backed off, stood up quickly.

"Whoops!" Herman hollered. Peter blushed and batted at him to be silent. All stared at the entryway of the hut.

A young man whom Ambrose did not recognize came out first. He had dark eyes and hair and a black moustache, and though he was clean-shaved, his jaw was blue with coming whiskers. He wore a white shirt and a tie and a yellow sweater under his leather jacket, and had dirtied his clean trousers on the Den floor. He stood up and scowled at the ring of boys as if he were going to be angry —but then grinned and brushed his pants-knees.

"Sorry, mates. Didn't know it was your hut."

The girl climbed out after. Her brown hair was mussed, her face drained of color, there were shards of dead leaf upon her coat. The fellow helped her up, and she walked straight off without looking at any of them, her right hand stuffed into her coat pocket. The fellow winked at Peter and hurried to follow.

"Hey, gee!" Herman Goltz whispered.

"Who was the guy?" Sandy Cooper wanted to know.

Someone declared that it was Tommy James, just out of the U. S. Navy.

Peter said that Peggy Robbins would get kicked out of nurse's training if they found out, and Herman told how his big sister had been kicked out of nurse's training with only four months to go.

"A bunch went buckbathing one night down to Shoal Creek, and Sis was the only one was kicked out for it."

The Sphinxes all got to laughing and fooling around about Herman Goltz's sister and about Peggy Robbins and her boyfriend. Some of the fellows wanted to take after them and razz them, but it was agreed that Tommy James was a tough customer. Somebody believed there had been a scar across his temple.

Herman wailed "Oh lover!" and collapsed against Peter, who wrestled him down into the creepers.

Cheeks burning, Ambrose joined in the merriment. "We ought to put a sign up! *Private Property: No Smooching.*"

The fellows laughed. But not in just the right way.

"Hey guys!" Sandy Cooper said. "Amby says they was smooching!"

Ambrose quickly grinned and cried "Like a duck! Like a duck!"; whenever a person said a thing to fool you, he'd say "Like a duck!" afterward to let you know you'd been fooled.

"Like a duck nothing," Sandy Cooper rasped. "I bet I know what we'll find inside."

"Hey, yeah!" said Peter.

Sandy Cooper had an old flashlight that he carried on his belt, and so they let him go in first, and Peter and Herman and the others followed after. In just an instant Ambrose heard Sandy shout "Woo-hoo!" and there was excitement in the Den. He heard Peter cry "Let me see!" and Herman Goltz commence to giggle like a girl. Peter said "Let *me* see, damn it!"

"Go to Hell," said the gritty voice of Sandy Cooper.

"Go to Hell your own self."

Perse Goltz had scrambled in unnoticed with the rest, but now a Sphinx espied him.

"Get out of here, Perse. I thought I smelt something."

"You smelt your own self," the little boy retorted.

"Go on, get out, Perse," Herman ordered. "You stink."

"You stink worst."

Somebody said "Bust him once," but Perse was out before they could get him. He stuck out his tongue and made a great blasting raspberry at Peter, who had dived for his leg through the entrance.

Then Peter looked up at Ambrose from where he lay and said: "Our meeting's started."

"Yeah," someone said from inside. "No babies allowed."

"No smooching allowed," another member ventured, mocking Ambrose in an official tone. Sandy Cooper added that no something-else was allowed, and what it was was the same word that would make him laugh sometimes instead of sicking his Chesapeake Bay dog on you.

"You and Perse skeedaddle now," Peter said. His voice was not unkind, but there was an odd look on his face, and he hurried back into the Den, from which now came gleeful whispers. The name *Peggy Robbins* was mentioned, and someone dared, and double-dared, and dee-double-dared someone else, in vain, to go invite Ramona Peters to the meeting.

Perse Goltz had already gone a ways up the beach. Ambrose went down the high bank, checking his slide with the orange roots of undermined trees, and trudged after him. Peter had said, "Go to Hell your own self," in a voice that told you he was used to saying such things. And the cursing wasn't the worst of it.

Ambrose's stomach felt tied and lumpy; by looking at his arm a certain way he could see droplets standing in the pores. It was what they meant when they spoke of *breaking out in a cold sweat:* very like what one felt in school assemblies, when one was waiting in the wings for the signal to step out onto the stage. He could not bear to think of the moustachioed boyfriend: that fellow's wink, his curly hair, his leather jacket over white shirt and green tie, filled Ambrose's heart with comprehension; they whispered to him that whatever mysteries had been in progress in the Den, they did not mean to Wimpy James's brother what they meant to Peggy Robbins.

Toward her his feelings were less simple. He pictured them kicking her out of the Nurses' Home: partly on the basis of Herman Goltz's story about his sister, Ambrose imagined that disgraced student nurses were kicked out late at night, unclothed; he wondered who did the actual kicking, and where in the world the student nurses went from there.

Every one of the hurricanes that ushered in the fall took its toll upon the riverbank, with the result that the upper beach was strewn with trees long fallen from the cliff. Salt air and water quickly stripped their bark and scoured the trunks. They seemed never to decay; Ambrose could rub his hands along the polished gray wood with little fear of splinters. One saw that in years to come the Jungle would be gone entirely. He would be a man then, and it wouldn't matter. Only his children, he supposed, might miss the winding paths and secret places—but of course you didn't miss what you'd never had or known of.

On the foreshore, in the wrack along the high-water line where sandfleas jumped, were empty beer cans, grapefruit rinds, and hosts of spot and white perch poisoned by the run-off from the canneries. All rotted together. But on the sand beach, in the sun and wind, Ambrose could breathe them deeply. Indeed, with the salt itself and the pungent oils of the eelgrass they made the very flavor of the shore, exhilarating to his spirit. It was a bright summer night; Peggy Robbins had just been kicked out of the Nurses' Home, and the only way she could keep everybody from seeing her was to run into the Jungle and hide in the

Sphinx's Den. As it happened, Ambrose had been waked by a clanking in the alleyway and had gone outside to drive off the black dogs or the Arnie twins, whichever were rooting in the garbage. And finding the night so balmy, he strolled down to the rivershore and entered the Jungle, where he heard weeping. It was pitch black in the Den; she cringed against the far wall.

"Who is it?"

"It is the only man who ever really loved you."

She hugged and kissed him; then, overcome by double shame, drew away. But if he had accepted her caresses coolly, still he would not scorn her. He took her hand.

"Ah Peggy. Ah Peggy."

She wept afresh, and then one of two things happened. Perhaps she flung herself before him, begging forgiveness and imploring him to love her. He raised her up and staunched her tears.

"Forgive you?" he repeated in a deep, kind voice. "Love forgives everything, Peggy. But the truth of the matter is, I can't forget."

He held her head in both his hands; her bitter tears splashed his wrists. He left the Den and walked to the bank-edge, leaned against a tree, stared seaward. Presently Peggy grew quiet and went her way, but he, he stayed a long time in the Jungle.

On the other hand perhaps it was that he drew her to him in the dark, held her close, and gave her to know that while he could never feel just the same respect for her, he loved her nonetheless. They kissed. Tenderly together they rehearsed the secrets; long they lingered in the Sphinx's Den; then he bore her from the Jungle, lovingly to the beach, into the water. They swam until her tears were made a part of Earth's waters; then hand in hand they waded shoreward on the track of the moon. In the shallows they paused to face each other. Warm wavelets flashed about their feet; waterdrops sparkled on their bodies. Washed of shame, washed of fear; nothing was but sweetest knowledge.

In the lumberyard down past the hospital they used square pine sticks between the layers of drying boards to let air through. The beach was littered with such sticks, three and four and five feet long; if you held one by the back end and threw it like a spear into the water, nothing made a better submarine. Perse Goltz had started launching submarines and following them down toward the Jungle as they floated on the tide.

"Don't go any farther," Ambrose said when he drew near.

Perse asked indifferently: "Why don't you shut up?"

"All I've got to do is give the signal," Ambrose declared, "and they'll know you're sneaking up to spy."

As they talked they launched more submarines. The object was to see how far you could make them go under water before they surfaced: if you launched them too flat they'd skim along the top; if too deeply they'd nose under and slide up backward. But if you did it just right they'd straighten out and glide several yards under water before they came up. Ambrose's arms were longer and he knew the trick; his went farther than Perse's.

"There ain't no sign," Perse said.

"There is so. Plenty of them."

"Well, you don't know none of them, anyhow."

"That's what you think. Watch this." He raised his hand toward the Jungle and made successive gestures with his fingers in the manner of Mister Neal the deaf and dumb eggman. "I told them we were just launching submarines and not to worry."

"You did not." But Perse left off his launching for a moment to watch, and moved no farther down the beach.

"Wait a minute." Ambrose squinted urgently toward the trees. "*Go . . . up . . . the . . . beach*. They want us to go on up the beach some more." He spoke in a matter-of-fact tone, and even though Perse said "What a big fake you are," he followed Ambrose in the direction of the new bridge.

If Ambrose was the better launcher, Perse was the better bombardier: he could throw higher, farther, straighter. The deep shells they skipped out for Ducks and Drakes; the flat ones they sailed top-up to make them climb, or straight aloft so that they'd cut water without a splash.

Beer cans if you threw them with the holes down whistled satisfactorily. They went along launching and bombarding, and then Ambrose saw a perfectly amazing thing. Lying in the seaweed where the tide had left it was a bottle with a note inside.

"Look here!"

He rushed to pick it up. It was a clear glass bottle, a whisky or wine bottle, tightly capped. Dried eelgrass full of sand and tiny musselshells clung round it. The label had been scraped off, all but some white strips where the glue was thickest; the paper inside was folded.

"Gee *whiz!*" Perse cried. At once he tried to snatch the bottle away, but Ambrose held it well above his reach.

"Finders keepers!"

In his excitement Perse forgot to be cynical. "Where in the *world* do you think it come from?"

"Anywhere!" Ambrose's voice shook. "It could've been floating around for years!" He removed the cap and tipped the bottle downward, but the note wouldn't pass through the neck.

"Get a little stick!"

They cast about for a straight twig, and Ambrose fished into the bottle with it. At each near catch they breathed: "Aw!"

Ambrose's heart shook. For the moment Scylla and Charybdis, the Occult Order, his brother Peter—all were forgotten. Peggy Robbins, too, though she did not vanish altogether from his mind's eye, was caught up into the greater vision, vague and splendrous, whereof the sea-wreathed bottle was an emblem. Westward it lay, to westward, where the tide ran from East Dorset. Past the river and the Bay, from continents beyond, this messenger had come. Borne by currents as yet uncharted, nosed by fishes as yet unnamed, it had bobbed for ages beneath strange stars. Then out of the oceans it had strayed; past cape and cove, black can, red nun, the word had wandered willy-nilly to his threshold.

"For pity's sake bust it!" Perse shouted.

Holding the bottle by the neck Ambrose banged it on a mossed and barnacled brickbat. Not hard enough. His face perspired. On the third swing the bottle smashed and the note fell out.

"I got it!" Perse cried, but before he could snatch it up, Ambrose sent him flying onto the sand.

The little boy's face screwed up with tears. "I'll get you!"

But Ambrose paid him no heed. As he picked up the paper, Perse flew into him, and received such a swat from Ambrose's free hand that he ran bawling down the beach.

The paper was half a sheet of coarse ruled stuff, torn carelessly from a tablet and folded thrice. Ambrose uncreased it. On a top line was penned in deep red ink:

TO WHOM IT MAY CONCERN

On the next-to-bottom:

YOURS TRULY

The lines between were blank, as was the space beneath the complimentary close. In a number of places, owing to the coarseness of the paper, the ink spread from the lines in fibrous blots.

An oystershell zipped past and plicked into the sand behind him: a hundred feet away Perse Goltz thumbed his nose and stepped a few steps back. Ambrose ignored him, but moved slowly down the shore. Up in the Jungle the Sphinxes had adjourned to play King of the Hill on the riverbank. Perse threw another oystershell and half-turned to run; he was not pursued.

Ambrose's spirit bore new and subtle burdens. He would not tattle on Peter for cursing and the rest of it. The thought of his brother's sins no longer troubled him or even much moved his curiosity. Tonight, tomorrow night, unhurriedly, he would find out from Peter just what it was they had discovered in the Den, and what-all done: the things he'd learn would not surprise now nor distress him, for though he was still innocent of that knowledge, he had the feel of it in his heart, and of other truth.

He changed the note to his left hand, the better to wing

an oystershell at Perse. As he did so, some corner of his mind remarked that those shiny bits in the paper's texture were splinters of wood pulp. Often as he'd seen them in the leaves of cheap tablets, he had not thitherto embraced that fact.

PETITION

April 21, 1931

His Most Gracious Majesty Prajadhipok, Descendant of Buddha, King of North and South, Supreme Arbiter of the Ebb and Flow of the Tide, Brother of the Moon, Half-Brother of the Sun, Possessor of the Four-and-Twenty Golden Umbrellas
Ophir Hall
White Plains, New York

Sir:

Welcome to America. An ordinary citizen extends his wish that your visit with us be pleasant, your surgery successful.

Though not myself a native of your kingdom, I am and have been most alive to its existence and concerns—unlike the average American, alas, to whose imagination the name of that ancient realm summons only white elephants and blue-eyed cats. I am aware, for example, that it was Queen Rambai's father's joke that he'd been inside the Statue of Liberty but never in the United States, having toured the Paris foundry while that symbol was a-casting; in like manner I may say that I have dwelt in a figurative Bangkok all my life. My brother, with whose presumption and other faults I hope further to acquaint you in the course of this petition, has even claimed (in his cups) descent from the mad King Phaya Takh Sin, whose well-deserved assassination—like the surgical excision of a cataract, if I may be so bold—gave to a benighted land the luminous dynasty of Chakkri, whereof Your Majesty is the latest and brightest son. Here as elsewhere my brother lies or is mistaken: we are Occidental, for better or worse, and while our condition is freakish, our origin is almost certainly commonplace. Yet though my brother's claim is false and (should he press it upon you, as he might) in contemptible taste, it may serve the purpose of introducing to you his character, my wretched situation, and my petition to your magnanimity.

The reign of the Chakkris began in violence and threatens to end in blindness; my own history commences with a kind of blindness and threatens to terminate in murder. Happily, our American surgeons are equal to the former threat; my prayer is that Your Majesty—reciprocally, as it were—may find it in his heart to address himself to the latter. The press reports your pledge to liberate three thousand inmates of your country's prisons by April next, to celebrate both the restoration of your eyesight and the sesquicentennial of your dynasty: a regal gesture. But there are prisoners and prisoners; *my* hope is for another kind of release, from what may not unfairly be termed life-imprisonment for no crime whatever, only the misfortune of being born my brother's brother. That the prerogative of kings yet retains, even in the New World, some trace of its old divinity, is amply proved by President Hoover's solicitude for your comfort and all my countrymen's eagerness to serve you. The magazines proclaim the triflingest details of your daily round; society talks of nothing else but your comings and goings; a word from you sends government officers scurrying, reroutes express-trains, stops presses, marshals the finest medical talents in the nation. Give commands, then, that I be liberated at long last from a misery absolute as your monarchy!

Will you counsel resignation to my estate, even affirmation of it? Will you cite the example of Chang and Eng, whom your ancestor thought to put to death and ended by blessing? But Chang and Eng were different from my brother and me, because so much the same; Chang and Eng were as the left hand to the right; Chang and Eng were bound heart to heart: their common navel, which to prick was to injure both, was an emblem of their fraternity, as was the manner of their sitting, each with an arm about the other's shoulders. Haven't I wept with envy of sturdy Chang, loyal Eng? Haven't I invoked them, vainly, as exemplars not only of moral grace but of practical efficiency? Their introduction of the "double chop" for cutting logs, a method still employed by pairs of Carolina woodsmen; their singular skill at driving four-horse teams down the lumber trails of their adopted state; their good-humored baiting of railway conductors, to whom they would present a single ticket, acknowledging that one might be put off the train, but insisting on the other's right to transportation; their resourceful employment of the same reasoning on the occasion of one's arrest, when the other loyally threatened to sue if he too were jailed; their happy marriage to a pair of sisters, who bore them twenty-two healthy children in their separate households; their alternation of authority and residence every three days, rain or shine, each man master under his own roof—a schedule followed faithfully until Chang's death at sixty-three; Eng's touching last request, as he himself expired of sympathy and terror three hours later, that his brother's dead body be moved even closer—didn't I recite these marvels like a litany to *my* brother in the years when I still could hope we might get along?

Yet it may surprise you to learn that even Chang and Eng, those paragons of cooperation, had their differences. Chang was a tippler, Eng a teetotaller; Eng liked all-night checker games, Chang was no gambler; in at least one election they cast their votes for opposing candidates; the arrest aforementioned, though it came to nothing, was for the crime of assault—committed by one against the other. Especially following marriage their differences increased, and if upon returning to the exhibition stage (after the Civil War) they made a show of unanimity, it was to raise money in the hope that some surgeon could part them at last. All this, mind, between veritable Heavenly Twins, sons of the mystical East, whose religions and philosophies —no criticism intended—have ever minimized distinctions, denying even the difference between Sameness and Difference. How altogether contrary is the case of my brother and me! (*He*, as might be expected, denies that the cases are different, contradicts this denial by denying at the same time that we are two in the first place—and would no doubt deny the contradiction as well, with equal obstinacy, should Your Majesty point it out to him.) Only consider:

whereas Chang and Eng were bound breast to breast by a good long band that allowed them to walk, sit, and sleep side by side, my brother and I are fastened front to rear— my belly to the small of his back—by a leash of flesh heartbreakingly short. In consequence he never lays eyes on the wretch he forever drags about—no wonder he denies me, agrees with the doctors that such a union is impossible, and claims my utterance and inspiration for his own!— while I see nothing else the day long (unless over his shoulder) but his stupid neck-nape, which I know better than my name. He obscures my view, sits in my lap (never mind how his weight impedes my circulation), smothers me in his wraps. What I suffer in the bathroom is too disgusting for Your Majesty's ears. By night it's scramble or be crushed when he tosses in our bed, pitching and snoring so in his dreams that my own are nightmares; by day I must match his stride like the hinder half of a vaudeville horse until, exhausted, I clamber on him pick-a-back. Small comfort that I may outlast him, despite his greater strength, by riding him thus; when he goes I go, Eng after Chang, and in the meanwhile I must go *where* he goes as well, and suffer his insults along the way. No matter to him that in one breath he denies my existence, in the next affirms it with his oaths and curses: I am Anchises to his Aeneas, he will have it; Old Man of the Sea to his Sinbad; I am his cross, his albatross; I, lifelong victim of his beastliness, he calls the monkey on his back!

No misery, of course, but has its little compensations, however hollow or theoretical. What couldn't we accomplish if he'd cooperate, with me as his back-up man! Only let me count cadence and him go more regularly, there'd be no stumbling; I could prod, tickle, goose him into action if he'd not ignore me; I'd be the eyes in the back of his head, his unobserved prompter and mentor. Cloaked in the legal immunity of Chang-Eng's gambit we could do what we pleased, be wealthy in no time. Even within the law we'd have the world for our oyster, our capacity twice any rival's. Strangers to loneliness, we could make rich our leisure hours: bicycle in tandem, sing close harmony, play astonishing piano, read Plato aloud, assemble mah-jongg tiles in half the time. I'd be no prude were we as close in temperament as in body; we could make any open-minded woman happy beyond her most amorous reveries—or, lacking women, delight each other in ways that Chang and Eng could never. . . .

Vain dreams; we are nothing alike. I am slight, my brother is gross. He's incoherent but vocal; I'm articulate and mute. He's ignorant but full of guile; I think I may call myself reasonably educated, and if ingenuous, no more so I hope than the run of scholars. My brother is gregarious: he deals with the public; earns and spends our income; tends (but slovenly) the house and grounds; makes, entertains, and loses friends; indulges in hobbies; pursues ambitions and women. For my part, I am by nature withdrawn, even solitary: an observer of life, a meditator, a taker of notes, a dreamer if you will—yet not a brooder; it's he who moods and broods, today hilarious, tomorrow despondent; I myself am stoical, detached as it were—of necessity, or I'd have long since perished of despair. More to the point, what intelligence my brother has is inclined to synthesis, mine to analysis; he denies that we are two, yet refuses to compromise and cooperate; I affirm our difference—all the difference in the world!—but have endeavored in vain to work out with him a reasonable cohabitation. Untutored and clumsy, he will nevertheless make flatulent noises upon the trombone, write ungainly verses, dance awkwardly with women, hold grunting conversations, jerrybuild a roof over our heads; I, whose imagination encompasses Aristotle, Shakespeare, Bach—I'd never so presume; yet let me point out to him, however diplomatically, however constructively, the shortcomings of his efforts beside genuine creation: he flies into a rage, shreds his doggerel, dents his horn, quarrels with his "sweetheart" (who perhaps was laughing at him all along), abandons carpentry, beats his chest in heroical self-pity, or sulks in a corner for days together. I don't even mention his filthy personal habits: what consolation that he swipes his bum and occasionally soaps his stinking body? Only the sinner needs absolution, and one sin breeds another: because I ride on his back and am content to nourish myself with infrequent sips of tea, I neither perspire nor defecate, but merely emit a discreet vapor, of neutral scent, and tiny puffs of what could pass for talc. Other sustenance I draw less from our common bond, as he might claim, than from books, from introspection, most of all from revery and fancy, without which I'd soon enough starve. But he, he eats anything, lusts after anything, goes to any length to make me wretched. His very excrements he will sniff and savor; he belches up gases, farts in my lap; not content that I must ride atop him, as on a rutting stallion, while he humps his whores, he will torment me in the shower-bath by bending over to draw me against him and pinching at me with his hairy cheeks. Yet let me flinch away, or in a frenzy of disgust attempt to rupture our bond though it kill us (as I sometimes strained to do in years gone by): he turns my revulsion into horrid sport, runs out and snaps back like a paddle-ball or plays crack-the-whip at every turn in our road. Why go on? We have nothing in common but the womb that bore, the flesh that shackles, the grave that must soon receive us. If my situation has any advantage it's only that I can see him without his seeing me; can therefore study and examine our bond, how ever to dissolve it, and take certain surreptitious measures to that end, such as writing this petition. Futile perhaps; desperate certainly. The alternative is madness.

All very well, you may say: lamentable as our situation is, it's nothing new; we were born this way and have somehow muddled through thirty-five years; not even a king has his own way in everything; in the matter of congenital endowment it's potluck for all of us, we must grin and bear it, the weakest to the wall, et cetera. God knows I am no whiner; I've broken heart and spirit to make the best of a bad hand of cards; at the slimmest hint of sympathy from my brother, the least suggestion of real fraternity, I melt with gratitude, must clamber aboard lest I swoon of joy; my tears run in his hair and down the courses of his face, one would think it was he who wept. And were it simply a matter of accumulated misery, or the mere happenstance of your visit, I'd not burden you (and my own sensibility) with this complaint. What prompts my plea is the coincidence of your arrival and a critical turn in our history and situation.

I pass over the details of our past, a tiresome chronicle. Some say our mother died a-bearing us, others that she perished of dismay soon after; just as possibly, she merely put us out. The man we called Father exhibited us throughout our childhood, but the age was more hardened to monstrosity than Chang's and Eng's; we never prospered; indeed we were scarcely noticed. In earliest babyhood I didn't realize I was two; it was the intractability of that creature always before me—going left when I would go right, bawling for food when I would sleep, laughing when I wept—that opened my eyes to the possibility he was other than myself; the teasing of playmates, who mocked our contretemps, verified that suspicion, and I began my painful schooling in detachment. Early on I proposed to my brother a judicious alliance (with myself, naturally, as director of our activities and final arbiter of our differences, he being utterly a creature of impulse); he would none of my proposal. Through childhood our antipathies merely smoldered, as we both submitted perforce, however grudgingly, to Father (who at least never denied our twoness, which, to be sure, was his livelihood); it was upon our fleeing his government, in adolescence, that they flamed. My attempt to direct our partnership ended in my brother's denying first my efficacy, then my authority, finally my reality. He pretended to believe, offstage as well as on, that the audience's interest was in him as a solo performer and not in the pair of us as a freak; hidden from the general view, unable to speak except in whispers, I could take only feeblest revenge: I would wave now and then between the lines of his stupid performances, grimace behind his back and over his shoulder, make signs to mock or contradict his asseverations. Let him deny me, he couldn't ignore me; I tripped him up, confused, confounded him, and though in the end he usually prevailed, I pulled against him every step of his way, spoiled his pleasure, halved his force, and on more than one occasion stalled him entirely.

The consequent fiascos, the rages and rampages of his desperation, are too dreadful to recount; them too I pass over, with a shudder. For some time now our connection has been an exasperated truce punctuated with bitter bursts of hostility, as between old mismatched spouses or weary combatants; the open confrontations are less frequent because more vicious, the interim resentments more deep because more resigned. Each new set-to, legatee of all its predecessors, is more destructive than the last; at the merest popgun-pop, artillery bristles. However radically, therefore, our opposition restricts our freedom, we each had come to feel, I believe, that the next real violence between us would be the last, fatal to one and thus to both, and so were more or less resigned to languishing, disgruntled, in our impasse, for want of alternatives. Then between us came Thalia, love, the present crisis.

It will scarcely surprise you that we arrived late at sexuality. Ordinary girls fled from our advances, or cruelly mocked us; had our bookings not fetched us to the capitals of Europe, whose liberal ladies sought us out for novelty's sake, we'd kept our chastity perforce till affluent maturity, for common prostitutes raised their fees, at sight of us, beyond our adolescent means. Even so, it was my brother did all the clipping, I being out of reach except to surrogate gratifications; only when a producer of unusual motion pictures in Berlin, with the resourcefulness characteristic of his nation, discovered Thalia and brought her to us, did I know directly the experience of coition. I did not enjoy it.

More accurately, I was rent by emotions as at odds as I and my brother. Thalia—a pretty young contortionist of good family obliged by the misery of the times to prostitute her art in exotic nightclubs and films—I admired tremendously, not alone for her merry temper and the talent wherewith she achieved our connection, but for her silent forbearance, not unlike my own, in the face as it were of my brother's abuse. But how expect me to share the universal itch to copulate, whose soul lusts only for disjunction? Even our modest coupling (chaste beside *his* performances), rousing as it was to tickly sense, went so counter to my principles I'd hardly have enjoyed it even had my brother not indignified her the while. Not content to be double already, he must attach himself to everyone, everything; hug, devour, absorb! Heads or tails, it's all one to Brother; he clamped his shaggy thighs about the poor girl's ears as greedily as he engorges a potroast or smothers me into the mattress, threatening with a laugh to squash and ingest me.

After a series of such meetings (the film director, whether as artist or as Teuton, was a perfectionist) we discovered ourselves in love: I with Thalia, my brother likewise in his fashion, and laughing Thalia . . . with me, with me, I'm sure of it! At least in the beginning. She joined our act, inspired or composed fresh material for us; we played with profit the naughty stages of a dozen nations, my brother still pretending he had no brother despite our billing: *The Eternal Triangle*. Arranged in parallel, isosceles, or alphaic fashion, we slept in the same hotel beds, and while it was he who salivated and grunted upon her night after night, as he does yet, still it pleased me to imagine that Thalia permitted him her supple favors out of love for me, and humored his pretense that I did not exist in order to be with me. By gay example she taught me to make fun of our predicament, chuckle through the teeth of anguish, turn woe into wit. In the heights of his barbarous passion our eyes meet, and I have seen her wink; as he roars in his transports, her chin rests on his shoulder; she grins, and I chastely kiss her brow. More than once I have been moved to put my love into written words, to no avail; what profit to be articulate, when he seizes every message like a jealous censor and either obscures its tender sentiments past deciphering or translates them into his own coarse idiom? I reach to comfort her; he thrusts my hand into her crotch; she takes it for his and pretends delight. Agile creature that she is, she would enfold us both in her honey limbs, so to touch the one she loves; as if aware, he thwarts her into some yoga position, Bandha Padmāsana, Dhanurāsana. Little wonder our love remains tentative with him between us, who for aught I know may garble even this petition; little wonder we doubt and mistake each other. Indeed, I can only forgive her, however broken-heartedly, if the worst of my suspicions should prove true: that, hardened by despair, Thalia is becoming her disguise: the vulgar creature who ignores my signals, denies my presence, growls with feral joy beneath her ravisher! My laughter sticks in my throat; either Thalia has lost her sense of humor or I've lost mine. Mirth passes; our wretchedness endures and brutalizes. Truth to tell, she has become a stranger; with the best will in the world I can't always persuade my heart that her refusal to acknowledge me is but a stratagem of love, her teasing and fondling of the man I abhor mere feminine duplicity, to inspire my ardor and cover our tracks. What tracks, Thalia? Of late, particularly, she behaves on occasion as if *I* stood in the way of her contentment, and in darkest moments I can even wonder whether her demand that my brother "pull himself together" is owing to her secret desire for me or a secret wish to see me gone.

This ultimatum she pronounced on our thirty-fifth birthday, three weeks past. We were vacationing between a profitable Mardi-Gras engagement in New Orleans and a scheduled post-Lenten tour of Western speakeasies; indeed, despite Prohibition and Depression, perhaps because of them, we'd had an uncommonly prosperous season; the demand for our sort of spectacle had never been so great; people crowded into basement caves to drink illicit liquors and applaud our repertoire of unnatural combinations and obscene gymnastics. One routine in particular was lining our pockets, a lubricious soft-shoe burlesque of popular songs beginning with *Me and My Shadow* and culminating in *When We're Alone;* it was Thalia's invention, and doubtless inspired both my brother's birthday proposal and her response. She had bought a cake to celebrate the occasion (for both of us, I was sure, though seventy candles would clearly have been too many); my brother, who ordinarily blew out all the candles and clawed into the frosting with both hands before I could draw a breath, had been distracted all day, and managed only thirty-four; eagerly I puffed out the last, over his shoulder, my first such opportunity in three decades and a half, whereat he threw off his mood with a laugh and revealed his wish: to join himself to Thalia in marriage. In his blurting fashion he enounced a whole mad program: he would put the first half of his life altogether behind him, quit show business, use our savings to learn an honest trade, perhaps husbandry, perhaps welding, and raise a family!

"Two can live as cheap as one," he grumbled at the end

—somewhat defensively, for Thalia showed neither surprise, pleasure, nor dismay, but heard him out with a neutral expression as if the idea were nothing new. I searched her face for assurance that she was revolted; I waved my arms and shook my head, turned out my pockets to find the *NO*-sign I always carried with me, so often was it needed, and flung it in her direction when she wouldn't look at it. Long time she studied him, twirling a sprig of ivy between her fingers; cross with suspense, he admitted he'd been no model companion, but a moody, difficult, irresolute fellow plagued with tensions and contradictions. I mouthed antic sneers over his shoulders. But with her assistance he would become a new man, he declared, and promised ominously to "get rid," "one way or another," of "the monkey on his back," which had kept him to date from single-minded application to anything. It was his first employment of the epithet; I shuddered at his resolve. She was his hope of redemption, he went on, becoming fatuous and sentimental now in his anxiety; without her he was no better than a beast (as if he weren't beastly *with* her!), no more than half a man; let her but consent, therefore and however, to become as the saying was his better half, he'd count himself saved!

Why did she not laugh in his face, throw up to him his bestialities, declare once for all that she endured him solely on my account? She rose from table, leaning upon the cane she always danced with; I held out my arms to her and felt on each elbow the tears my brother forced to dramatize his misery. Oh, he is a cunning animal! I even attempted tears myself, but flabbergastment dried my eyes. At the door Thalia turned to gaze as if it were through him—the last time, I confess, that I was able to believe she might be looking at me. Then bending with a grunt to retrieve my crumpled message, which she tossed unread into the nearest ashtray, she replied that she was indeed weary of acrobatics: let him make good his aforementioned promise, one way or another; then she'd see.

No sooner had she spoken than the false tears ceased; my brother chased her squealing into the kitchen, nor troubled even to ask her leave, but swinish as ever fetched

down her tights with the cane-crook and rogered her fair
athwart the dish drain, all the while snorting through her
whoop and giggle: "You'll see what you'll see!"

Highness, I live in terror of what she'll see! Nothing is
beyond my brother. He has put himself on a diet, avow-
edly to trim his grossness for her sake; but I perceive
myself weaker in consequence, and am half-convinced he
means to starve me on the vine, as it were, and absorb me
through the bond that joins us. He has purchased medical
insurance, playing the family man, and remarks as if idly
on its coverage of massive skin grafts; for all I know he
may be planning to install me out of sight inside him by
surgical means. I don't eat; I daren't sleep. Thalia, my
hope and consolation—why has she forsaken me?

If indeed she has. For a curious fancy has taken me of late,
not impossibly the figment of a mind deranged for want of
love (and rest, and sustenance): that Thalia is less simple
than she appears. I suspect, in fact, or begin to . . . that
there are two Thalias! Don't mistake me: not two as Chang
and Eng were two, or as my brother and I are two; not one
Thalia joined to another—but a Thalia *within* a Thalia,
like the dolls-within-dolls Your Majesty's countrymen and
neighbors fashion so cleverly: a Thalia incarcerate in the
iron maiden my brother embraces!

I first observed her not long after that fell birthday. No
moraler for all his protestations, my brother has devised
for our next performance a new stunt based on an old
lubricity, and to "get the hang of it" (so he claims) sleeps
now arsy-turvy with his "fiancée," like shoes in a box or
the ancient symbol for Yang and Yin. Sometimes she rests
her head on his knees, and thus it happened, late one
night, that when I looked down upon the Thalia who'd
betrayed me, I found her looking back, sleepless as I,
upside down in the first spring moonlight. Yet lo, it was
not the same Thalia! Her face—I should say, her sister's
face—was inverted, but I realized suddenly that her eyes
were not; it was a different woman, a stranger, who regarded me with upright, silent stare through the other's
face. I perspired with dismay—my first experience of sweat.

Luckily my brother slept, a-pitch with dreams. There was no mistaking it, another woman looked out at me from behind that mask: a prisoner like myself, whose gaze remained level and detached however her heartless warden grinned and grimaced. I saw her the next night and the next, earnest, mute; by day she disappears in the other Thalia; I live only for the night, to rehearse before her steadfast eyes the pity and terror of our situation. She it is (once separate like myself, it may be, then absorbed by her smirking sister) I now adore—if with small hope and much apprehension. Does she see me winking and waving, or is my face as strange to her as her sister's to me? Why does she gaze at me so evenly, as if in unremitting appraisal? Can she too be uncertain of my reality, my love? Too much to bear!

In any case, there's little time. "Thalia" grows restive; now that she has the upper hand with my brother she makes no bones about her reluctance to go back on the road, her yen for a little farm, her dissatisfaction with his progress in "making a man of himself" and the like. Last night, I swear it, I felt him straining to suck me in through our conjunction, and clung to the sheets in terror. Momently I expect him to play some unsuspected trump; have at me for good and all. When he does, I will bite through the tie that binds us and so kill us both. It is a homicide God will forgive, and my beloved will at least be free of what she suffers, through her sister, at my brother's hands.

Yet given the daily advances of science and the inspiring circumstance of Your Majesty's visit, I dare this final hope: that at your bidding the world's most accomplished surgeons may successfully divide my brother from myself, in a manner such that one of us at least may survive, free of the other. After all, we were both joined once to our unknown mother, and safely detached to begin our misery. Or if a bond to *something* is necessary in our case, let it be something more congenial and sympathetic: graft my brother's Thalia in my place, and fasten me . . . to my own navel, to anything but him, if the Thalia I love can't be freed to join me! Perhaps she has another sister. . . .

Death itself I would embrace like a lover, if I might share the grave with no other company. To be one: paradise! To be two: bliss! But to be both and neither is unspeakable. Your Highness may imagine with what eagerness His reply to this petition is awaited by

Yours truly,

LOST IN THE FUNHOUSE

For whom is the funhouse fun? Perhaps for lovers. For Ambrose it is *a place of fear and confusion*. He has come to the seashore with his family for the holiday, *the occasion of their visit is Independence Day, the most important secular holiday of the United States of America*. A single straight underline is the manuscript mark for italic type, *which in turn* is the printed equivalent to oral emphasis of words and phrases as well as the customary type for titles of complete works, not to mention. Italics are also employed, in fiction stories especially, for "outside," intrusive, or artificial voices, such as radio announcements, the texts of telegrams and newspaper articles, et cetera. They should be used *sparingly*. If passages originally in roman type are italicized by someone repeating them, it's customary to acknowledge the fact. *Italics mine.*

Ambrose was "at that awkward age." His voice came out high-pitched as a child's if he let himself get carried away; to be on the safe side, therefore, he moved and spoke with *deliberate calm* and *adult gravity*. Talking soberly of unimportant or irrelevant matters and listening consciously to the sound of your own voice are useful habits for maintaining control in this difficult interval. *En route* to Ocean City he sat in the back seat of the family car with his brother Peter, age fifteen, and Magda G——, age fourteen, a pretty girl and exquisite young lady, who lived not far from them on B—— Street in the town of D——, Maryland. Initials, blanks, or both were often substituted for proper names in nineteenth-century fiction to enhance the illusion of reality. It is as if the author felt it necessary to delete the names for reasons of tact or legal liability. Interestingly, as with other aspects of realism, it is an *illusion* that is being enhanced, by purely artificial means. Is it likely, does it violate the principle of verisimilitude, that a thirteen-year-old boy could make such a sophisticated observation? A girl of fourteen is *the psychological coeval* of a boy of fifteen or sixteen; a thirteen-year-old boy, therefore, even one precocious in some other respects, might be three years *her emotional junior*.

Thrice a year—on Memorial, Independence, and Labor Days—the family visits Ocean City for the afternoon and evening. When Ambrose and Peter's father was their age, the excursion was made by train, as mentioned in the novel *The 42nd Parallel* by John Dos Passos. Many families from the same neighborhood used to travel together, with dependent relatives and often with Negro servants; schoolfuls of children swarmed through the railway cars; everyone shared everyone else's Maryland fried chicken, Virginia ham, deviled eggs, potato salad, beaten biscuits, iced tea. Nowadays (that is, in 19___, the year of our story) the journey is made by automobile—more comfortably and quickly though without the extra fun though without the *camaraderie* of a general excursion. It's all part of the deterioration of American life, their father declares; Uncle Karl supposes that when the boys take *their* families to Ocean City for the holidays they'll fly in Autogiros. Their mother, sitting in the middle of the front seat like Magda in the second, only with her arms on the seat-back behind the men's shoulders, wouldn't want the good old days back again, the steaming trains and stuffy long dresses; on the other hand she can do without Autogiros, too, if she has to become a grandmother to fly in them.

Description of physical appearance and mannerisms is one of several standard methods of characterization used by writers of fiction. It is also important to "keep the senses operating"; when a detail from one of the five senses, say visual, is "crossed" with a detail from another, say auditory, the reader's imagination is oriented to the scene, perhaps unconsciously. This procedure may be compared to the way surveyors and navigators determine their positions by two or more compass bearings, a process known as triangulation. The brown hair on Ambrose's mother's forearms gleamed in the sun like. Though right-handed, she took her left arm from the seat-back to press the dashboard cigar lighter for Uncle Karl. When the glass bead in its handle glowed red, the lighter was ready for use. The smell of Uncle Karl's cigar smoke reminded one of. The fragrance of the ocean came strong to the picnic ground where they always stopped for lunch, two miles inland from Ocean City. Having to pause for a full hour almost within sound of the breakers was difficult for Peter and Ambrose when they were younger; even at their present age it was not easy to keep their anticipation, *stimulated by the briny spume,* from turning into short temper. The Irish author James Joyce, in his unusual novel entitled *Ulysses,* now available in this country, uses the adjectives *snot-green* and *scrotum-tightening* to describe the sea. Visual, auditory, tactile, olfactory, gustatory. Peter and Ambrose's father, while steering their black 1936 LaSalle sedan with one hand, could with the other remove the first cigarette from a white pack of Lucky Strikes and, more remarkably, light it with a match forefingered from its book and thumbed against the flint paper without being detached. The matchbook cover merely advertised U. S. War Bonds and Stamps. A fine metaphor, simile, or other figure of speech, in addition to its obvious "first-order" relevance to the thing it describes, will be seen upon reflection to have a second order of significance: it may be drawn from the *milieu* of the action, for example, or be particularly appropriate to the sensibility of the narrator, even hinting to the reader things of which the narrator is unaware; or it may cast further and subtler lights upon the things it describes, sometimes ironically qualifying the more evident sense of the comparison.

To say that Ambrose's and Peter's mother was *pretty* is to accomplish nothing; the reader may acknowledge the proposition, but his imagination is not engaged. Besides, Magda was also pretty, yet in an altogether different way. Although she lived on B____ Street she had very good manners and did better than average in school. Her figure was very well developed for her age. Her right hand lay casually on the plush upholstery of the seat, very near Ambrose's left leg, on which his own hand rested. The space between their legs, between her right and his left leg, was out of the line of sight of anyone sitting on the other side of Magda, as well as anyone glancing into the rear-view mirror. Uncle Karl's face resembled Peter's— rather, vice versa. Both had dark hair and eyes, short husky statures, deep voices. Magda's left hand was probably in a similar position on her left side. The boys' father is difficult to describe; no particular feature of his appearance or manner stood out. He wore glasses and was principal of a T_____ County grade school. Uncle Karl was a masonry contractor.

Although Peter must have known as well as Ambrose that the latter, because of his position in the car, would be the first to see the electrical towers of the power plant at V_____, the halfway point of their trip, he leaned forward and slightly toward the center of the car and pretended to be looking for them through the flat pinewoods and tuckahoe creeks along the highway. For as long as the boys could remember, "looking for the Towers" had been a feature of the first half of their excursions to Ocean City, "looking for the standpipe" of the second. Though the game was childish, their mother preserved the tradition of rewarding the first to see the Towers with a candy-bar or piece of fruit. She insisted now that Magda play the game; the prize, she said, was "something hard to get nowadays." Ambrose decided not to join in; he sat far back in his seat. Magda, like Peter, leaned forward. Two sets of straps were discernible through the shoulders of her sun dress; the inside right one, a brassiere-strap, was fastened or shortened with a small safety pin. The right armpit of her dress, presumably the left as well, was damp with perspiration. The simple strategy for being first to espy the Towers, which Ambrose had understood by the age of four, was to sit on the right-hand side of the car. Whoever sat there, however, had also to put up with the worst of the sun, and so Ambrose, without mentioning the matter, chose sometimes the one and sometimes the other. Not impossibly Peter had never caught on to the trick, or thought that his brother hadn't simply because Ambrose on occasion preferred shade to a Baby Ruth or tangerine.

The shade-sun situation didn't apply to the front seat, owing to the windshield; if anything the driver got more sun, since the person on the passenger side not only was shaded below by the door and dashboard but might swing down his sunvisor all the way too.

"Is that them?" Magda asked. Ambrose's mother teased the boys for letting Magda win, insinuating that "somebody [had] a girlfriend." Peter and Ambrose's father reached a long thin arm across their mother to butt his cigarette in the dashboard ashtray, under the lighter. The prize this time for seeing the Towers first was a banana. Their mother bestowed it after chiding their father for wasting a half-smoked cigarette when everything was so scarce. Magda, to take the prize, moved her hand from so near Ambrose's that he could have touched it as though accidentally. She offered to share the prize, things like that were so hard to find; but everyone insisted it was hers alone. Ambrose's mother sang an iambic trimeter couplet from a popular song, femininely rhymed:

> *"What's good is in the Army;*
> *What's left will never harm me."*

Uncle Karl tapped his cigar ash out the ventilator window; some particles were sucked by the slipstream back into the car through the rear window on the passenger side. Magda demonstrated her ability to hold a banana in one hand and peel it with her teeth. She still sat forward; Ambrose pushed his glasses back onto the bridge of his nose with his left hand, which he then negligently let fall to the seat cushion immediately behind her. He even permitted the single hair, gold, on the second joint of his thumb to brush the fabric of her skirt. Should she have sat back at that instant, his hand would have been caught under her.

Plush upholstery prickles uncomfortably through gabardine slacks in the July sun. The function of the *beginning* of a story is to introduce the principal characters, establish their initial relationships, set the scene for the main action, expose the background of the situation if necessary, plant motifs and foreshadowings where appropriate, and initiate the first complication or whatever of the "rising action." Actually, if one imagines a story called "The Funhouse," or "Lost in the Funhouse," the details of the drive to Ocean City don't seem especially relevant. The *beginning* should recount the events between Ambrose's first sight of the funhouse early in the afternoon and his entering it with Magda and Peter in the evening. The *middle* would narrate all relevant events from the time he goes in to the time he loses his way; middles have the double and contradictory function of delaying the climax while at the same time preparing the reader for it and fetching him to it. Then the *ending* would tell what Ambrose does while he's lost, how he finally finds his way out, and what everybody makes of the experience. So far there's been no real dialogue, very little sensory detail, and nothing in the way of a *theme*. And a long time has gone by already without anything happening; it makes a person wonder. We haven't even reached Ocean City yet: we will never get out of the funhouse.

The more closely an author identifies with the narrator, literally or metaphorically, the less advisable it is, as a rule, to use the first-person narrative viewpoint. Once three years previously the young people *aforementioned* played Niggers and Masters in the backyard; when it was Ambrose's turn to be Master and theirs to be Niggers Peter had to go serve his evening papers; Ambrose was afraid to punish Magda alone, but she led him to the whitewashed Torture Chamber between the woodshed and the privy in the Slaves Quarters; there she knelt sweating among bamboo rakes and dusty Mason jars, pleadingly embraced his knees, and while bees droned in the lattice as if on an ordinary summer afternoon, purchased clemency at a surprising price set by herself. Doubtless she remembered nothing of this event; Ambrose on the other hand seemed unable to forget the least detail of his life. He even recalled how, standing beside himself with awed impersonality in the reeky heat, he'd stared the while at an empty cigar box in which Uncle Karl kept stone-cutting chisels: beneath the words *El Producto,* a laureled, loose-toga'd lady regarded the sea from a marble bench; beside her, forgotten or not yet turned to, was a five-stringed lyre. Her chin reposed on the back of her right hand; her left depended negligently from the bench-arm. The lower half of scene and lady was peeled away; the words EXAMINED BY _____ were inked there into the wood. Nowadays cigar boxes are made of pasteboard. Ambrose wondered what Magda would have done, Ambrose wondered what Magda would do when she sat back on his hand as he resolved she should. Be angry. Make a teasing joke of it. Give no sign at all. For a long time she leaned forward, playing cowpoker with Peter against Uncle Karl and Mother and watching for the first sign of Ocean City. At nearly the same instant, picnic ground and Ocean City standpipe hove into view; an Amoco filling station on their side of the road cost Mother and Uncle Karl fifty cows and the game; Magda bounced back, clapping her right hand on Mother's right arm; Ambrose moved clear "in the nick of time."

At this rate our hero, at this rate our protagonist will remain in the funhouse forever. Narrative ordinarily consists of alternating dramatization and summarization. One symptom of nervous tension, paradoxically, is repeated and violent yawning; neither Peter nor Magda nor Uncle Karl nor Mother reacted in this manner. Although they were no longer small children, Peter and Ambrose were each given a dollar to spend on boardwalk amusements in addition to what money of their own they'd brought along. Magda too, though she protested she had ample spending money. The boys' mother made a little scene out of distributing the bills; she pretended that her sons and Magda were small children and cautioned them not to spend the sum too quickly or in one place. Magda promised with a merry laugh and, having both hands free, took the bill with her left. Peter laughed also and pledged in a falsetto to be a good boy. His imitation of a child was not clever. The boys' father was tall and thin, balding, fair-complexioned. Assertions of that sort are not effective; the reader may acknowledge the proposition, but. We should be much farther along than we are; something has gone wrong; not much of this preliminary rambling seems relevant. Yet everyone begins in the same place; how is it that most go along without difficulty but a few lose their way?

"Stay out from under the boardwalk," Uncle Karl

growled from the side of his mouth. The boys' mother pushed his shoulder *in mock annoyance*. They were all standing before Fat May the Laughing Lady who advertised the funhouse. Larger than life, Fat May mechanically shook, rocked on her heels, slapped her thighs while recorded laughter—uproarious, female—came amplified from a hidden loudspeaker. It chuckled, wheezed, wept; tried in vain to catch its breath; tittered, groaned, exploded raucous and anew. You couldn't hear it without laughing yourself, no matter how you felt. Father came back from talking to a Coast-Guardsman on duty and reported that the surf was spoiled with crude oil from tankers recently torpedoed offshore. Lumps of it, difficult to remove, made tarry tidelines on the beach and stuck on swimmers. Many bathed in the surf nevertheless and came out speckled; others paid to use a municipal pool and only sunbathed on the beach. We would do the latter. We would do the latter. We would do the latter.

Under the boardwalk, matchbook covers, grainy other things. What is the story's theme? Ambrose is ill. He perspires in the dark passages; candied apples-on-a-stick, delicious-looking, disappointing to eat. Funhouses need men's and ladies' rooms at intervals. Others perhaps have also vomited in corners and corridors; may even have had bowel movements liable to be stepped in in the dark. The word *fuck* suggests suction and/or and/or flatulence. Mother and Father; grandmothers and grandfathers on both sides; great-grandmothers and great-grandfathers on four sides, et cetera. Count a generation as thirty years: in approximately the year when Lord Baltimore was granted charter to the province of Maryland by Charles I, five hundred twelve women—English, Welsh, Bavarian, Swiss—of every class and character, received into themselves the penises the intromittent organs of five hundred twelve men, ditto, in every circumstance and posture, to conceive the five hundred twelve ancestors of the two hundred fifty-six ancestors of the et cetera et cetera et cetera et cetera et cetera et cetera et cetera et cetera of the author, of the narrator, of this story, *Lost in the Funhouse*. In alleyways, ditches, canopy beds, pinewoods, bridal suites, ship's cabins, coach-and-fours, coaches-and-four, sultry toolsheds; on the cold sand under boardwalks, littered with *El Producto* cigar butts, treasured with Lucky Strike cigarette stubs, Coca-Cola caps, gritty turds, cardboard lollipop sticks, matchbook covers warning that A Slip of the Lip Can Sink a Ship. The shluppish whisper, continuous as seawash round the globe, tidelike falls and rises with the circuit of dawn and dusk.

Magda's teeth. She *was* left-handed. Perspiration. They've gone all the way, through, Magda and Peter, they've been waiting for hours with Mother and Uncle Karl while Father searches for his lost son; they draw french-fried potatoes from a paper cup and shake their heads. They've named the children they'll one day have and bring to Ocean City on holidays. Can spermatozoa properly be thought of as male animalcules when there are no female spermatozoa? They grope through hot, dark windings, past Love's Tunnel's fearsome obstacles. Some perhaps lose their way.

Peter suggested then and there that they do the funhouse; he had been through it before, so had Magda, Ambrose hadn't and suggested, his voice cracking on account of Fat May's laughter, that they swim first. All were chuckling, couldn't help it; Ambrose's father, Ambrose's and Peter's father came up grinning like a lunatic with two boxes of syrup-coated popcorn, one for Mother, one for Magda; the men were to help themselves. Ambrose walked on Magda's right; being by nature left-handed, she carried the box in her left hand. Up front the situation was reversed.

"What are you limping for?" Magda inquired of Ambrose. He supposed in a husky tone that his foot had gone to sleep in the car. Her teeth flashed. "Pins and needles?" It was the honeysuckle on the lattice of the former privy that drew the bees. Imagine being stung there. How long is this going to take?

The adults decided to forgo the pool; but Uncle Karl insisted they change into swimsuits and do the beach. "He wants to watch the pretty girls," Peter teased, and ducked behind Magda from Uncle Karl's pretended wrath. "You've got all the pretty girls you need right here," Magda de-

clared, and Mother said: "Now that's the gospel truth."
Magda scolded Peter, who reached over her shoulder to
sneak some popcorn. "Your brother and father aren't getting any." Uncle Karl wondered if they were going to have
fireworks that night, what with the shortages. It wasn't the
shortages, Mr. M_____ replied; Ocean City had fireworks
from pre-war. But it was too risky on account of the enemy
submarines, some people thought.

"Don't seem like Fourth of July without fireworks," said
Uncle Karl. The inverted tag in dialogue writing is still
considered permissible with proper names or epithets, but
sounds old-fashioned with personal pronouns. "We'll have
'em again soon enough," predicted the boys' father. Their
mother declared she could do without fireworks: they reminded her too much of the real thing. Their father said
all the more reason to shoot off a few now and again.
Uncle Karl asked *rhetorically* who needed reminding, just
look at people's hair and skin.

"The oil, yes," said Mrs. M_____.

Ambrose had a pain in his stomach and so didn't swim
but enjoyed watching the others. He and his father burned
red easily. Magda's figure was exceedingly well developed
for her age. She too declined to swim, and got mad, and
became angry when Peter attempted to drag her into the
pool. She always swam, he insisted; what did she mean
not swim? Why did a person come to Ocean City?

"Maybe I want to lay here with Ambrose," Magda
teased.

Nobody likes a pedant.

"Aha," said Mother. Peter grabbed Magda by one ankle
and ordered Ambrose to grab the other. She squealed and
rolled over on the beach blanket. Ambrose pretended to
help hold her back. Her tan was darker than even Mother's
and Peter's. "Help out, Uncle Karl!" Peter cried. Uncle
Karl went to seize the other ankle. Inside the top of her
swimsuit, however, you could see the line where the sun-
burn ended and, when she hunched her shoulders and
squealed again, one nipple's auburn edge. Mother made
them behave themselves. "*You* should certainly know," she
said to Uncle Karl. Archly. "That when a lady says she

doesn't feel like swimming, a gentleman doesn't ask questions." Uncle Karl said excuse *him;* Mother winked at Magda; Ambrose blushed; stupid Peter kept saying "Phooey on *feel like!*" and tugging at Magda's ankle; then even he got the point, and cannonballed with a holler into the pool.

"I swear," Magda said, in mock *in feigned* exasperation.

The diving would make a suitable literary symbol. To go off the high board you had to wait in a line along the poolside and up the ladder. Fellows tickled girls and goosed one another and shouted to the ones at the top to hurry up, or razzed them for bellyfloppers. Once on the springboard some took a great while posing or clowning or deciding on a dive or getting up their nerve; others ran right off. Especially among the younger fellows the idea was to strike the funniest pose or do the craziest stunt as you fell, a thing that got harder to do as you kept on and kept on. But whether you hollered *Geronimo!* or *Sieg heil!,* held your nose or "rode a bicycle," pretended to be shot or did a perfect jacknife or changed your mind halfway down and ended up with nothing, it was over in two seconds, after all that wait. Spring, pose, splash. Spring, neat-o, splash. Spring, aw fooey, splash.

The grown-ups had gone on; Ambrose wanted to converse with Magda; she was remarkably well developed for her age; it was said that that came from rubbing with a turkish towel, and there were other theories. Ambrose could think of nothing to say except how good a diver Peter was, who was showing off for her benefit. You could pretty well tell by looking at their bathing suits and arm muscles how far along the different fellows were. Ambrose was glad he hadn't gone in swimming, the cold water shrank you up so. Magda pretended to be uninterested in the diving; she probably weighed as much as he did. If you knew your way around in the funhouse like your own bedroom, you could wait until a girl came along and then slip away without ever getting caught, even if her boyfriend was right with her. She'd think *he* did it! It would be better to be the boyfriend, and act outraged, and tear the funhouse apart.

Not act; *be.*

"He's a master diver," Ambrose said. In feigned admiration. "You really have to slave away at it to get that good." What would it matter anyhow if he asked her right out whether she remembered, even teased her with it as Peter would have?

There's no point in going farther; this isn't getting anybody anywhere; they haven't even come to the funhouse yet. Ambrose is off the track, in some new or old part of the place that's not supposed to be used; he strayed into it by some one-in-a-million chance, like the time the roller-coaster car left the tracks in the nineteen-teens against all the laws of physics and sailed over the boardwalk in the dark. And they can't locate him because they don't know where to look. Even the designer and operator have forgotten this other part, that winds around on itself like a whelk shell. That winds around the right part like the snakes on Mercury's caduceus. Some people, perhaps, don't "hit their stride" until their twenties, when the growing-up business is over and women appreciate other things besides wisecracks and teasing and strutting. Peter didn't have one-tenth the imagination *he* had, not one-tenth. Peter did this naming-their-children thing as a joke, making up names like Aloysius and Murgatroyd, but Ambrose knew *exactly* how it would feel to be married and have children of your own, and be a loving husband and father, and go comfortably to work in the mornings and to bed with your wife at night, and wake up with her there. With a breeze coming through the sash and birds and mockingbirds singing in the Chinese-cigar trees. His eyes watered, there aren't enough ways to say that. He would be quite famous in his line of work. Whether Magda was his wife or not, one evening when he was wise-lined and gray at the temples he'd smile gravely, at a fashionable dinner party, and remind her of his youthful passion. The time they went with his family to Ocean City; the *erotic fantasies* he used to have about her. How long ago it seemed, and childish! Yet tender, too, *n'est-ce pas?* Would she have imagined that the world-famous whatever remembered how many strings were on the lyre on the bench beside the girl on the label of the cigar box he'd stared at in the toolshed at age ten while she, age eleven. Even then he had felt *wise beyond his years;* he'd stroked her hair and said in his deepest voice and correctest English, as to a dear child: "I shall never forget this moment."

But though he had breathed heavily, groaned as if ecstatic, what he'd really felt throughout was an odd detachment, as though some one else were Master. Strive as he might to be transported, he heard his mind take notes upon the scene: *This is what they call* passion. *I am experiencing it.* Many of the digger machines were out of order in the penny arcades and could not be repaired or replaced for the duration. Moreover the prizes, made now in USA, were less interesting than formerly, pasteboard items for the most part, and some of the machines wouldn't work on white pennies. The gypsy fortune-teller machine might have provided a foreshadowing of the climax of this story if Ambrose had operated it. It was even dilapidateder than most: the silver coating was worn off the brown metal handles, the glass windows around the dummy were cracked and taped, her kerchiefs and silks long-faded. If a man lived by himself, he could take a department-store mannequin with flexible joints and modify her in certain ways. *However:* by the time he was that old he'd have a real woman. There was a machine that stamped your name around a white-metal coin with a star in the middle: *A*_____. His son would be the second, and when the lad reached thirteen or so he would put a strong arm around his shoulder and tell him calmly: "It is perfectly normal. We have all been through it. It will not last forever." Nobody knew how to be what they were right. He'd smoke a pipe, teach his son how to fish and softcrab, assure him he needn't worry about himself. Magda would certainly give, Magda would certainly yield a great deal of milk, although guilty of occasional solecisms. It don't taste so bad. Suppose the lights came on now!

The day wore on. You think you're yourself, but there are other persons in you. Ambrose gets hard when Ambrose doesn't want to, *and obversely.* Ambrose watches them disagree; Ambrose watches him watch. In the funhouse mirror-room you can't see yourself go on forever, because no matter how you stand, your head gets in the way. Even if you had a glass periscope, the image of your eye would cover up the thing you really wanted to see. The police will come; there'll be a story in the papers. That must be where it happened. Unless he can find a surprise exit, an unofficial backdoor or escape hatch opening on an alley, say, and then stroll up to the family in front of the funhouse and ask where everybody's been; *he's* been out of the place for ages. That's just where it happened, in that last lighted room: Peter and Magda found the right exit; he found one that you weren't supposed to find and strayed off into the works somewhere. In a perfect funhouse you'd be able to go only one way, like the divers off the highboard; getting lost would be impossible; the doors and halls would work like minnow traps or the valves in veins.

On account of German U-boats, Ocean City was "browned out": streetlights were shaded on the seaward side; shop-windows and boardwalk amusement places were kept dim, not to silhouette tankers and Liberty-ships for torpedoing. In a short story about Ocean City, Maryland, during World War II, the author could make use of the image of sailors on leave in the penny arcades and shooting galleries, sighting through the crosshairs of toy machine guns at swastika'd subs, while out in the black Atlantic a U-boat skipper squints through his periscope at real ships outlined by the glow of penny arcades. After dinner the family strolled back to the amusement end of the boardwalk. The boys' father had burnt red as always and was masked with Noxzema, a minstrel in reverse. The grown-ups stood at the end of the boardwalk where the Hurricane of '33 had cut an inlet from the ocean to Assawoman Bay.

"Pronounced with a long *o*," Uncle Karl reminded Magda with a wink. His shirt sleeves were rolled up; Mother punched his brown biceps with the arrowed heart on it and said his mind was naughty. Fat May's laugh came suddenly from the funhouse, as if she'd just got the joke; the family laughed too at the coincidence. Ambrose went under the boardwalk to search for out-of-town matchbook covers with the aid of his pocket flashlight; he looked out from the edge of the North American continent and wondered how far their laughter carried over the water. Spies in rubber rafts; survivors in lifeboats. If the joke had been beyond his understanding, he could have said: *"The laughter was over his head."* And let the reader see the serious wordplay on second reading.

He turned the flashlight on and then off at once even before the woman whooped. He sprang away, heart athud, dropping the light. What had the man grunted? Perspiration drenched and chilled him by the time he scrambled up to the family. "See anything?" his father asked. His voice wouldn't come; he shrugged and violently brushed sand from his pants legs.

"Let's ride the old flying horses!" Magda cried. I'll never be an author. It's been forever already, everybody's gone home, Ocean City's deserted, the ghost-crabs are tickling across the beach and down the littered cold streets. And the empty halls of clapboard hotels and abandoned funhouses. A tidal wave; an enemy air raid; a monster-crab swelling like an island from the sea. *The inhabitants fled in terror.* Magda clung to his trouser leg; he alone knew the maze's secret. "He gave his life that we might live," said Uncle Karl with a scowl of pain, as he. The fellow's hands had been tattooed; the woman's legs, the woman's fat white legs had. *An astonishing coincidence.* He yearned to tell Peter. He wanted to throw up for excitement. They hadn't even chased him. He wished he were dead.

One possible ending would be to have Ambrose come across another lost person in the dark. They'd match their wits together against the funhouse, struggle like Ulysses past obstacle after obstacle, help and encourage each other. Or a girl. By the time they found the exit they'd be closest friends, sweethearts if it were a girl; they'd know each other's inmost souls, be bound together *by the cement of shared adventure;* then they'd emerge into the light and it would turn out that his friend was a Negro. A blind girl. President Roosevelt's son. Ambrose's former archenemy.

Shortly after the mirror room he'd groped along a musty corridor, his heart already misgiving him at the absence of phosphorescent arrows and other signs. He'd found a crack of light—not a door, it turned out, but a seam between the plyboard wall panels—and squinting up to it, espied a small old man, *in appearance not unlike* the photographs at home of Ambrose's late grandfather, nodding upon a stool beneath a bare, speckled bulb. A crude panel of toggle- and knife-switches hung beside the open fuse box near his head; elsewhere in the little room were wooden levers and ropes belayed to boat cleats. At the time, Ambrose wasn't lost enough to rap or call; later he couldn't find that crack. Now it seemed to him that he'd possibly dozed off for a few minutes somewhere along the way; certainly he was exhausted from the afternoon's sunshine and the evening's problems; he couldn't be sure he hadn't dreamed part or all of the sight. Had an old black wall fan droned like bees and shimmied two flypaper streamers? Had the funhouse operator—gentle, somewhat sad and tired-appearing, in expression not unlike the photographs at home of Ambrose's late Uncle Konrad—murmured in his sleep? Is there really such a person as Ambrose, or is he a figment of the author's imagination? Was it Assawoman Bay or Sinepuxent? Are there other errors of fact in this fiction? Was there another sound besides the little slap slap of thigh on ham, like water sucking at the chine-boards of a skiff?

When you're lost, the smartest thing to do is stay put till you're found, hollering if necessary. But to holler guarantees humiliation as well as rescue; keeping silent permits some saving of face—you can act surprised at the fuss when your rescuers find you and swear you weren't lost, if they do. What's more you might find your own way yet, *however belatedly*.

"Don't tell me your foot's still asleep!" Magda exclaimed as the three young people walked from the inlet to the area set aside for ferris wheels, carrousels, and other carnival rides, they having decided in favor of the vast and ancient merry-go-round instead of the funhouse. What a sentence, everything was wrong from the outset. People don't know what to make of him, he doesn't know what to make of himself, he's only thirteen, *athletically and socially inept,* not astonishingly bright, but there are antennae; he has . . . some sort of receivers in his head; things speak to him, he understands more than he should, the world winks at him through its objects, grabs grinning at his coat. Everybody else is in on some secret he doesn't know; they've forgotten to tell him. Through simple *procrastination* his mother put off his baptism until this year. Everyone else had it done as a baby; he'd assumed the same of himself, as had his mother, so she claimed, until it was time for him to join Grace Methodist-Protestant and the oversight came out. He was mortified, but pitched sleepless through his private catechizing, intimidated by the ancient mysteries, a thirteen year old would never say that, resolved to experience conversion like St. Augustine. When the water touched his brow and Adam's sin left him, he contrived by a strain like defecation to bring tears into his eyes—but felt nothing. There was some simple, radical difference about him; he hoped it was genius, feared it was madness, devoted himself to amiability and inconspicuousness. Alone on the seawall near his house he was seized by the terrifying transports he'd thought to find in toolshed, in Communion-cup. The grass was alive! The town, the river, himself, were not imaginary; time roared in his ears like wind; the world was *going on!* This part ought to be dramatized. The Irish author James Joyce once wrote. Ambrose M——— is going to scream.

There is no *texture of rendered sensory detail,* for one thing. The faded distorting mirrors beside Fat May; the impossibility of choosing a mount when one had but a single ride on the great carrousel; the *vertigo attendant on his recognition* that Ocean City was worn out, the place of fathers and grandfathers, straw-boatered men and parasoled ladies survived by their amusements. Money spent, the three paused at Peter's insistence beside Fat May to watch the girls get their skirts blown up. The object was to tease Magda, who said: "I swear, Peter M———, you've got a one-track mind! Amby and me aren't *interested* in such things." In the tumbling-barrel, too, just inside the Devil's-mouth entrance to the funhouse, the girls were upended and their boyfriends and others could see up their dresses if they cared to. Which was the whole point, Ambrose realized. Of the entire funhouse! If you looked around, you noticed that almost all the people on the boardwalk were paired off into couples except the small children; in a way, that was the whole point of Ocean City! If you had X-ray eyes and could see everything going on at that instant under the boardwalk and in all the hotel rooms and cars and alleyways, you'd realize that all that normally *showed,* like restaurants and dance halls and clothing and test-your-strength machines, was merely preparation and intermission. Fat May screamed.

Because he watched the goings-on from the corner of his eye, it was Ambrose who spied the half-dollar on the boardwalk near the tumbling-barrel. Losers weepers. The first time he'd heard some people moving through a corridor not far away, just after he'd lost sight of the crack of light, he'd decided not to call to them, for fear they'd guess he was scared and poke fun; it sounded like roughnecks; he'd hoped they'd come by and he could follow in the dark without their knowing. Another time he'd heard just one person, unless he imagined it, bumping along as if on the other side of the plywood; perhaps Peter coming back for him, or Father, or Magda lost too. Or the owner and operator of the funhouse. He'd called out once, as though merrily: "Anybody know where the heck we are?" But the query was too stiff, his voice cracked, when the sounds stopped he was terrified: maybe it was a queer who waited for fellows to get lost, or a longhaired filthy monster that lived in some cranny of the funhouse. He stood rigid for hours it seemed like, scarcely respiring. His future was shockingly clear, in outline. He tried holding his breath to the point of unconsciousness. There ought to be a button you could push to end your life absolutely without pain; disappear in a flick, like turning out a light. He would push it instantly! He despised Uncle Karl. But he despised his father too, for not being what he was supposed to be. Perhaps his father hated *his* father, and so on, and his son would hate him, and so on. Instantly!

Naturally he didn't have nerve enough to ask Magda to go through the funhouse with him. With incredible nerve and to everyone's surprise he invited Magda, quietly and politely, to go through the funhouse with him. "I warn you,

I've never been through it before," he added, *laughing easily;* "but I reckon we can manage somehow. The important thing to remember, after all, is that it's meant to be a *fun*house; that is, a place of amusement. If people really got lost or injured or too badly frightened in it, the owner'd go out of business. There'd even be lawsuits. No character in a work of fiction can make a speech this long without interruption or acknowledgment from the other characters."

Mother teased Uncle Karl: "Three's a crowd, I always heard." But actually Ambrose was relieved that Peter now had a quarter too. Nothing was what it looked like. Every instant, under the surface of the Atlantic Ocean, millions of living animals devoured one another. Pilots were falling in flames over Europe; women were being forcibly raped in the South Pacific. His father should have taken him aside and said: "There is a simple secret to getting through the funhouse, as simple as being first to see the Towers. Here it is. Peter does not know it; neither does your Uncle Karl. You and I are different. Not surprisingly, you've often wished you weren't. Don't think I haven't noticed how unhappy your childhood has been! But you'll understand, when I tell you, why it had to be kept secret until now. And you won't regret not being like your brother and your uncle. *On the contrary!*" If you knew all the stories behind all the people on the boardwalk, you'd see that *nothing* was what it looked like. Husbands and wives often hated each other; parents didn't necessarily love their children; et cetera. A child took things for granted because he had nothing to compare his life to and everybody acted as if things were as they should be. Therefore each saw himself as the hero of the story, when the truth might turn out to be that he's the villain, or the coward. And there wasn't one thing you could do about it!

Hunchbacks, fat ladies, fools—that no one chose what he was was unbearable. In the movies he'd meet a beautiful young girl in the funhouse; they'd have hairs-breadth escapes from real dangers; he'd do and say the right things; she also; in the end they'd be lovers; their dialogue lines would match up; he'd be perfectly at ease; she'd not only like him well enough, she'd think he was *marvelous;* she'd lie awake thinking about *him,* instead of vice versa—the way *his* face looked in different lights and how he stood and exactly what he'd said—and yet that would be only one small episode in his wonderful life, among many many others. Not a *turning point* at all. What had happened in the toolshed was nothing. He hated, he loathed his parents! One reason for not writing a lost-in-the-funhouse story is that either everybody's felt what Ambrose feels, in which case it goes without saying, or else no normal person feels such things, in which case Ambrose is a freak. "Is anything more tiresome, in fiction, than the problems of sensitive adolescents?" And it's all too long and rambling, as if the author. For all a person knows the first time through, the end could be just around any corner; perhaps, *not impossibly* it's been within reach any number of times. On the other hand he may be scarcely past the start, with everything yet to get through, an intolerable idea.

Fill in: His father's raised eyebrows when he announced his decision to do the funhouse with Magda. Ambrose understands now, but didn't then, that his father was wondering whether he knew what the funhouse was *for*—especially since he didn't object, as he should have, when Peter decided to come along too. The ticket-woman, witchlike, mortifying him when inadvertently he gave her his name-coin instead of the half-dollar, then unkindly calling Magda's attention to the birthmark on his temple: "Watch out for him, girlie, he's a marked man!" She wasn't even cruel, he understood, only vulgar and insensitive. Somewhere in the world there was a young woman with such splendid understanding that she'd see him entire, like a poem or story, and find his words so valuable after all that when he confessed his apprehensions she would explain why they were in fact the very things that made him precious to her . . . and to Western Civilization! There was no such girl, the simple truth being. Violent yawns as they approached the mouth. Whispered advice from an old-timer on a bench near the barrel: "Go crabwise and ye'll get an eyeful without upsetting!" Composure vanished at the first pitch: Peter hollered joyously, Magda tumbled, shrieked, clutched her skirt; Ambrose scrambled crabwise, tight-lipped with terror, was soon out, watched his dropped name-coin slide among the couples. Shame-faced he saw that to get through expeditiously was not the point; Peter feigned assistance in order to trip Magda up, shouted "I see Christmas!" when her legs went flying. The old man, his latest betrayer, cackled approval. A dim hall then of black-thread cobwebs and recorded gibber: he took Magda's elbow to steady her against revolving discs set in the slanted floor to throw your feet out from under, and ex-plained to her in a calm, deep voice his theory that each phase of the funhouse was triggered either automatically, by a series of photoelectric devices, or else manually by operators stationed at peepholes. But he lost his voice thrice as the discs unbalanced him; Magda was anyhow squealing; but at one point she clutched him about the waist to keep from falling, and her right cheek pressed for a moment against his belt-buckle. Heroically he drew her up, it was his chance to clutch her close as if for support and say: "I love you." He even put an arm lightly about the small of her back before a sailor-and-girl pitched into them from behind, sorely treading his left big toe and knocking Magda asprawl with them. The sailor's girl was a string-haired hussy with a loud laugh and light blue drawers; Ambrose realized that he wouldn't have said "I love you" anyhow, and was smitten with self-contempt. How much better it would be to be that common sailor! A wiry little Seaman 3rd, the fellow squeezed a girl to each side and stumbled hilarious into the mirror room, closer to Magda in thirty seconds than Ambrose had got in thirteen years. She giggled at something the fellow said to Peter; she drew her hair from her eyes with a movement so womanly it struck Ambrose's heart; Peter's smacking her backside then seemed particularly coarse. But Magda made a pleased indignant face and cried, "All right for *you*, mister!" and pursued Peter into the maze without a backward glance. The sailor followed after, leisurely, draw-ing his girl against his hip; Ambrose understood not only that they were all so relieved to be rid of his burdensome company that they didn't even notice his absence, but that he himself shared their relief. Stepping from the treacherous passage at last into the mirror-maze, he saw once again, more clearly than ever, how readily he deceived himself into supposing he was a person. He even foresaw, wincing at his dreadful self-knowledge, that he would repeat the deception, at ever-rarer intervals, all his wretched life, so fearful were the alternatives. Fame, madness, suicide; perhaps all three. It's not believable that so young a boy could articulate that reflection, and in fiction the merely true must always yield to the plausible. Moreover, the symbolism is in places heavy-footed. Yet Ambrose M_____ understood, as few adults do, that the famous loneliness of the great was no popular myth but a general truth—furthermore, that it was as much cause as effect.

All the preceding except the last few sentences is exposition that should've been done earlier or interspersed with the present action instead of lumped together. No reader would put up with so much with such *prolixity*. It's interesting that Ambrose's father, though presumably an intelligent man (as indicated by his role as grade-school principal), neither encouraged nor discouraged his sons at all in any way—as if he either didn't care about them or cared all right but didn't know how to act. If this fact should contribute to one of them's becoming a celebrated but wretchedly unhappy scientist, was it a good thing or not? He too might someday face the question; it would be useful to know whether it had tortured his father for years, for example, or never once crossed his mind.

In the maze two important things happened. First, our hero found a name-coin someone else had lost or discarded: *AMBROSE,* suggestive of the famous lightship and of his late grandfather's favorite dessert, which his mother used to prepare on special occasions out of coconut, oranges, grapes, and what else. Second, as he wondered at the endless replication of his image in the mirrors, second, as he *lost himself in the reflection* that the necessity for an observer makes perfect observation impossible, better make him eighteen at least, yet that would render other things unlikely, he heard Peter and Magda chuckling somewhere together in the maze. "Here!" "No, here!" they shouted to each other; Peter said, "Where's Amby?"

Magda murmured. "Amb?" Peter called. In a pleased, friendly voice. He didn't reply. The truth was, his brother was a *happy-go-lucky youngster* who'd've been better off with a regular brother of his own, but who seldom complained of his lot and was generally cordial. Ambrose's throat ached; there aren't enough different ways to say that. He stood quietly while the two young people giggled and thumped through the glittering maze, hurrah'd their discovery of its exit, cried out in joyful alarm at what next beset them. Then he set his mouth and followed after, as he supposed, took a wrong turn, strayed into the pass *wherein he lingers yet.*

The action of conventional dramatic narrative may be represented by a diagram called Freitag's Triangle:

or more accurately by a variant of that diagram:

in which *AB* represents the exposition, *B* the introduction of conflict, *BC* the "rising action," complication, or development of the conflict, *C* the climax, or turn of the action, *CD* the dénouement, or resolution of the conflict. While there is no reason to regard this pattern as an absolute necessity, like many other conventions it became conventional because great numbers of people over many years learned by trial and error that it was effective; one ought not to forsake it, therefore, unless one wishes to forsake as well the effect of drama or has clear cause to feel that deliberate violation of the "normal" pattern can better can better effect that effect. This can't go on much longer; it can go on forever. He died telling stories to himself in the dark; years later, when that vast unsuspected area of the funhouse came to light, the first expedition found his skeleton in one of its labyrinthine corridors and mistook it for part of the entertainment. He died of starvation telling himself stories in the dark; but unbeknownst unbeknownst to him, an assistant operator of the funhouse, happening to overhear him, crouched just behind the plyboard partition and wrote down his every word. The operator's daughter, an exquisite young woman with a figure unusually well developed for her age, crouched just behind the partition and transcribed his every word. Though she had never laid eyes on him, she recognized that here was one of Western Culture's truly great imaginations, the eloquence of whose suffering would be an inspiration to unnumbered. And her heart was torn between her love for the misfortunate young man (yes, she loved him, though she had never laid though she knew him only—but how well!—through his words, and the deep, calm voice in which he spoke them) between her love et cetera and her womanly intuition that only in suffering and isolation could he give voice et cetera. Lone dark dying. Quietly she kissed the rough plyboard, and a tear fell upon the page. Where she had written in shorthand *Where she had written in shorthand* Where she had written in shorthand *Where she* et cetera. A long time ago we should have passed the apex of Freitag's Triangle and made brief work of the *dénouement;* the plot doesn't rise by meaningful steps but winds upon itself, digresses, retreats, hesitates, sighs, collapses, expires. The climax of the story must be its protagonist's discovery of a way to get through the funhouse. But he has found none, may have ceased to search.

What relevance does the war have to the story? Should there be fireworks outside or not?

Ambrose wandered, languished, dozed. Now and then he fell into his habit of rehearsing to himself the unadventurous story of his life, narrated from the third-person point of view, from his earliest memory parenthesis of maple leaves stirring in the summer breath of tidewater Maryland end of parenthesis to the present moment. Its principal events, on this telling, would appear to have been *A, B, C,* and *D.*

He imagined himself years hence, successful, married, at

ease in the world, the trials of his adolescence far behind him. He has come to the seashore with his family for the holiday: how Ocean City has changed! But at one seldom at one ill-frequented end of the boardwalk a few derelict amusements survive from times gone by: the great carrousel from the turn of the century, with its monstrous griffins and mechanical concert band; the roller coaster rumored since 1916 to have been condemned; the mechanical shooting gallery in which only the image of our enemies changed. His own son laughs with Fat May and wants to know what a funhouse is; Ambrose hugs the sturdy lad close and smiles around his pipestem at his wife.

The family's going home. Mother sits between Father and Uncle Karl, who teases him good-naturedly who chuckles over the fact that the comrade with whom he'd fought his way shoulder to shoulder through the funhouse had turned out to be a blind Negro girl—to their mutual discomfort, as they'd opened their souls. But such are the walls of custom, which even. Whose arm is where? How must it feel. He dreams of a funhouse vaster by far than any yet constructed; but by then they may be out of fashion, like steamboats and excursion trains. Already quaint and seedy: the draperied ladies on the frieze of the carrousel are his father's father's mooncheeked dreams; if he thinks of it more he will vomit his apple-on-a-stick.

He wonders: will he become a regular person? Something has gone wrong; his vaccination didn't take; at the Boy-Scout initiation campfire he only pretended to be deeply moved, as he pretends to this hour that it is not so bad after all in the funhouse, and that he has a little limp. How long will it last? He envisions a truly astonishing funhouse, incredibly complex yet utterly controlled from a great central switchboard like the console of a pipe organ. Nobody had enough imagination. He could design such a place himself, wiring and all, and he's only thirteen years old. He would be its operator: panel lights would show what was up in every cranny of its cunning of its multifarious vastness; a switch-flick would ease this fellow's way, complicate that's, to balance things out; if anyone seemed lost or frightened, all the operator had to do was.

He wishes he had never entered the funhouse. But he has. Then he wishes he were dead. But he's not. Therefore he will construct funhouses for others and be their secret operator—though he would rather be among the lovers for whom funhouses are designed.

ECHO

One does well to speak in the third person, the seer advises, in the manner of Theban Tiresias. A cure for self-absorption is saturation: telling the story over as though it were another's until like a much-repeated word it loses sense. There's a cathartic Tiresias himself employs in the interest of objectivity and to rid himself of others' histories—Oedipus's, Echo's—which distract him fore and aft by reason of his entire knowledge.

Narcissus replies that the prescription is unpalatable, but he's too weary of himself not to attempt it. Where to begin. The prophet's cave seems a likely place, which he stumbles into one forenoon in flight from his admirers. What started as a staghunt has turned into yet another love-chase, led this time by a persisting nymph soon joined by her quarry's companions. It wants all the Narcissan craft, resentfully perfected, yet again to mislead the lot.

An imperfectly dark passage. Outside his ardentest suitor calls, pederast Ameinius, spurned. The nymph soft-seconds his bugger woo. Chaste Narcissus shivers, draws farther in, loses bearings, daresn't call, weeps. The life-long bother! Seized he gives shriek, is released. How come? What next? Hadn't he as well have his blossom plucked? Who says so?

Tiresias the prophet. What's he doing here? Conversing with Narcissus. How does he know—because he knows everything. Why isn't he in Thebes? For the reason that, as during a prior and a posterior extravagance of his, Thebes is enjoying an interregnum, hard on prophets. First there was the sphinx, whose elementary riddle was none of his affair; he withdrew to the Thespian cave, there acted as adviser to the blue nymph Leirope, Narcissus's mother. The current pass is sorer: Oedipus's tragedy, too awful to rehearse. The third and last, couple hundred months hence, darker yet from Tiresias's point of view.

Narcissus reflects that after years of elusion he's at the seer's mercy, rapewise. He wonders which is more ironic, seeking refuge for innocence where it mightn't be preserved or falling into the first hands he's ever seemed to leave cold. Thus rare Tiresiases.

Apostrophe.

Some are comelier than most, a few handsome; it's Narcissus's fate, through fault nor merit of his own, to be beautiful beyond enduring. The first catch eye, the second turn head; Narcissus like a fleshed theophany smites the whole sense. A philosopher argues that perceptible beauty is ipso facto less desirable than im—at glimpse of Narcissus he interrupts, forswears himself. A man doubtless of his virility admits what he'd sooner not: in one extraordinary case he's felt the catamitic itch. A woman indifferent thitherto to the world's including handsomer men than hers finds Narcissus so so she's cross with her lover. Thus the mature, who see to it that sight of the wonder doesn't linger or recur and so in most cases come to terms with memory: the philosophers resume their position, men manliness, women men—all chastened, one supposes, by an exception so exceptional it ruins their rules. Among the less disciplined and wise, astonishment yields to simple lust. Cynical, powerful, wanton, uncommitted, passionate, impulsive set out to have their will. Hosts of ordinary, too, strangers to emotion of extraordinary kind or force, are seized as by conversion. Snares are laid, gifts tendered, pitfalls dug. His very wetnurse, Leirope says, took liberties with her suckling, tutor tutee. Leirope herself—how was it? Undone by a meandering river-god she seeks the caved seer first. What counsel does he offer? Tiresias won't repeat it; enough to say it's of a kind with what he wishes he'd given Oedipus. The varieties of general good advice are few. Leirope suggests herself to Narcissus when he reaches young manhood and begs him to ignore her advice: take to the the woods! Into the bimboed and bebuggered bush he flies, where ladies beckon every way and gentlemen crouch in ambuscado.

All this considered, one may wonder at Tiresias's immunity, unless indeed he's cat-and-mousing. Is he too ravished by his victim to recollect himself for rape? Floored for defloration? No no. Clairvoyance is anaphrodisiac. One recalls too: Tiresias has been without sex for a long time. What's more he's blind as a bat, otherwise he couldn't see so in the cave.

Is Narcissus piqued or relieved? Both know. He presently inquires how one in his position might best fend the world's importune. Why fend? Tiresias's story is to the point. And Echo's. Echo's? A nymph possessed so early and entirely by Pan that her subsequent affairs seem redundant. Afflicted with immortality she turns from life and learns to tell stories with such art that the Olympians implore her to repeat them. Others live for the lie of love; Echo lives for her lovely lies, loves for their livening. With her tongue-tried tales she amuses others and preserves her reason; but Zeus employs her, unawares, to beguile his wife while he makes free with the mountain-nymphs. Again again, begs the queen of heaven; another mount's climbed with each retelling. At fiction's end the facts are clear; Zeus unpunishable, Echo pays. Though her voice remains her own, she can't speak for herself thenceforth, only give back others' delight regardless of hers.

Has this to do with fair Narcissus, wise Tiresias? Whose story is it? It's a tale of shortcomings, lengthened to advantage. Echo never, as popularly held, repeats all, like gossip or mirror. She edits, heightens, mutes, turns others' words to her end. One recalls her encounter with Narcissus —no other has nymphed him caveward. A coincidence of opposites. One should, if it's worthwhile, repeat the tale.

I'll repeat the tale. Though in fact many are bewildered, Narcissus conceives himself alone and becomes the first person to speak.

I can't go on.

Go on.

Is there anyone to hear here?

Who are you?

You.

I?

Aye.

Then let me see me!

See?

A lass! Alas.

Et cetera et cetera. Overmuch presence appears to be the storyteller's problem: Tiresias's advice, in cases of excessive identity and coitus irrequitus, is to make of withdrawal a second nature. He sees the nymph efface herself until she becomes no more than her voice, still transfiguring senseless sound into plaints of love. Perhaps that's the end of her story, perhaps the narrative proper may resume. Not quite, not quite: though even sharp-sight Tiresias can't espy the unseeable, one may yet distinguish narrator from narrative, medium from message. One lesson remains to be learned; when Echo learns it none will be the wiser.

But Narcissus! What's become of contemptible, untemptable Narcissus, the drug so many have turned on on, and sung themselves on pretext of hymning him? Was Tiresias about to counsel him in obscurity? No. Except to declare that his true love awaits him in the spring at Donacon; discovering who he is will prove as fatal for Narcissus as it's proving for Oedipus. Queer advice! To see the truth is one thing, to speak it another.

Now where are we? That is to say, where are Tiresias and Narcissus. Somewhere near the Donaconan spring. Who's telling the story, and to whom? The teller's immaterial, Tiresias declares; the tale's the same, and for all one knows the speaker may be the only auditor. Considerable time has elapsed, it seems, since seer and seeker, prophet and lost, first met in the cave. But what's time when past and future are equally clear and dark? The gift of suiscience is a painful present: Narcissus thirsts for love; Tiresias sees the end of his second sight. Both speak to themselves. Thebes is falling; unknown to the north-bound refugees, en route to found a new city, their seer will perish on the instant the Argives take the old. He it is now, thrashing through the woods near Thespiae, who calls to his lost companions and follows to exhaustion a mock response. Halloo halloo! Falling at length beside a chuckling spring he dreams or dies. The voice presently in his ears is that hallooer's; now it rehearses Narcissus's end, seen from the outset:

Why did Tiresias not tell Narcissus what he once told

Leirope, that her son would lead a long and happy life if
he never came to know himself? Because the message then
had become its own medium. Needless to say he sees and
saw Narcissus beat about the bush for love, oblivious to
pursuers in the joy of his own pursuit. As for that nymph
whose honey voice still recalls his calls, he scorns her, and
hears his maledictions balmed to music. Like the masturba-
tory adolescent, sooner or later he finds himself. He
beholds and salutes his pretty alter ego in the pool; in the
pool his ego, altered, prettily salutes: Behold! In vain he
reaches to embrace his contrary image; he recognizes what
Tiresias couldn't warn him of. Has knowing himself turned
him into a pansy? Not quite, not quite. He's resolved to
do away with himself, his beloved likewise. Together now.
Adored-in-vain, farewell!

Well. One supposes that's the end of the story. How is it
this voice persists, whosever it is? Needless to say, Tiresias
knows. It doesn't sound nymphish; she must have lost hers.
Echo says Tiresias is not to be trusted in this matter. A
prophet blind or dead, a blossom, eyeless, a disengendered
tale—none can tell teller from told. Narcissus would appear
to be opposite from Echo: he perishes by denying all except himself; she persists by effacing herself absolutely. Yet
they come to the same: it was never himself Narcissus
craved, but his reflection, the Echo of his fancy; his death
must be partial as his self-knowledge, the voice persists,
persists.

Can it be believed? Tiresias has gone astray; a voice not
impossibly his own has bewildered him. The story of Narcissus, Tiresias, Echo is being repeated. It's alleged that
Narcissus has wearied of himself and yearns to love another; on Tiresias's advice he employs the third person to
repeat his tale as the seer does, until it loses meaning. No
use: his self objectified's the more enthralling, like his
blooming image in the spring. In vain Tiresias's cautions
that the nymph may be nothing altruistic, but the soul of
guile and sleight-of-tongue. Who knows but what her love
has changed to mock? What she gives back as another's
speech may be entire misrepresentation; especially ought
one to beware what she chooses to repeat concerning herself. No use, no use: Narcissus grows fond; she speaks his

language; Tiresias reflects that after all if one aspires to concern one's fatal self with another, one had as well commence with the nearest and readiest. Perhaps he'll do the same: be beguiled with Narcissus out of knowledge of himself; listen silent as his voice goes on.

Thus we linger forever on the autognostic verge—not you and I, but Narcissus, Tiresias, Echo. Are they still in the Thespian cave? Have they come together in the spring? Is Narcissus addressing Tiresias, Tiresias Narcissus? Have both expired?

There's no future for prophets. Blind Oedipus will never see the place where three roads meet. Narcissus desired himself defunct before his own conception; he's been rooted forever by the beloved he'll never know. Dead Tiresias still stares wide-eyed at Wisdom's nude entire. Our story's finished before it starts.

TWO MEDITATIONS

1. Niagara Falls

She paused amid the kitchen to drink a glass of water; at that instant, losing a grip of fifty years, the next-room-ceiling-plaster crashed. Or he merely sat in an empty study, in March-day glare, listening to the universe rustle in his head, when suddenly the five-foot shelf let go. For ages the fault creeps secret through the rock; in a second, ledge and railings, tourists and turbines all thunder over Niagara. Which snowflake triggers the avalanche? A house explodes; a star. In your spouse, so apparently resigned, murder twitches like a fetus. At some trifling new assessment, all the colonies rebel.

2. Lake Erie

The wisdom to recognize and halt follows the know-how to pollute past rescue. The treaty's signed, but the cancer ticks in your bones. Until I'd murdered my father and fornicated my mother I wasn't wise enough to see I was Oedipus. Too late now to keep the polar cap from melting. Venice subsides; South America explodes.

Let's stab out our eyes.

Too late: our resolve is sapped beyond the brooches.

TITLE

Beginning: in the middle, past the middle, nearer three-quarters done, waiting for the end. Consider how dreadful so far: passionlessness, abstraction, pro, dis. And it will get worse. Can we possibly continue?

Plot and theme: notions vitiated by this hour of the world but as yet not successfully succeeded. Conflict, complication, no climax. The worst is to come. Everything leads to nothing: future tense; past tense; present tense. Perfect. The final question is, Can nothing be made meaningful? Isn't that the final question? If not, the end is at hand. Literally, as it were. Can't stand any more of this.

I think she comes. The story of our life. This is the final test. Try to fill the blank. Only hope is to fill the blank. Efface what can't be faced or else fill the blank. With words or more words, otherwise I'll fill in the blank with this noun here in my prepositional object. Yes, she already said that. And I think. What now. Everything's been said already, over and over; I'm as sick of this as you are; there's nothing to say. Say nothing.

What's new? Nothing.

Conventional startling opener. Sorry if I'm interrupting the Progress of Literature, she said, in a tone that adjective clause suggesting good-humored irony but in fact defensively and imperfectly masking a taunt. The conflict is established though as yet unclear in detail. Standard conflict. Let's skip particulars. What do you want from me? What'll the story be this time? Same old story. Just thought I'd see if you were still around. Before. What? Quit right here. Too late. Can't we start over? What's past is past. On the contrary, what's forever past is eternally present. The future? Blank. All this is just fill in. Hang on.

Still around. In what sense? Among the gerundive. What

is that supposed to mean? Did you think I meant to fill in the blank? Why should I? On the other hand, why not? What makes you think I wouldn't fill in the blank instead? Some conversation this is. Do you want to go on, or shall we end it right now? Suspense. I don't care for this either. It'll be over soon enough in any case. But it gets worse and worse. Whatever happens, the ending will be deadly. At least let's have just one real conversation. Dialogue or monologue? What has it been from the first? Don't ask me. What is there to say at this late date? Let me think; I'm trying to think. Same old story. Or. Or? Silence.

This isn't so bad. Silence. There are worse things. Name three. This, that, the other. Some choices. Who said there was a choice?

Let's try again. That's what I've been doing; I've been thinking while you've been blank. Story of Our Life. However, this may be the final complication. The ending may be violent. That's been said before. Who cares? Let the end be blank; anything's better than this.

It didn't used to be so bad. It used to be less difficult. Even enjoyable. For whom? Both of us. To do what? Complicate the conflict. I am weary of this. What, then? To complete this sentence, if I may bring up a sore subject. That never used to be a problem. Now it's impossible; we just can't manage it. You can't fill in the blank; I can't fill in the blank. Or won't. Is this what we're going to talk about, our obscene verbal problem? It'll be our last conversation. Why talk at all? Are you paying attention? I dare you to quit now! Never dare a desperate person. On with it, calmly, one sentence after another, like a recidivist. A what? A common noun. Or another common noun. Hold tight. Or a chronic forger, let's say; committed to the pen for life. Which is to say, death. The point, for pity's sake! Not yet. Forge on.

We're more than halfway through, as I remarked at the outset: youthful vigor, innocent exposition, positive rising action—all that is behind us. How sophisticated we are today. I'll ignore her, he vowed, and went on. In this dehuman, exhausted, ultimate adjective hour, when every humane value has become untenable, and not only love, decency, and beauty but even compassion and intelligibility are no more than one or two subjective complements to complete the sentence. . . .

This is a story? It's a story, he replied equably, or will be if the author can finish it. Without interruption I suppose you mean? she broke in. I can't finish anything; that is my final word. Yet it's these interruptions that make it a story. Escalate the conflict further. Please let me start over.

Once upon a time you were satisfied with incidental felicities and niceties of technique: the unexpected image, the refreshingly accurate word-choice, the memorable simile that yields deeper and subtler significances upon reflection, like a memorable simile. Somebody please stop me. Or arresting dialogue, so to speak. For example?

Why do you suppose it is, she asked, long participial phrase of the breathless variety characteristic of dialogue attributions in nineteenth-century fiction, that literate people such as we talk like characters in a story? Even supplying the dialogue-tags, she added with wry disgust. Don't put words in her mouth. The same old story, an old-fashioned one at that. Even if I should fill in the blank with my idle pen? Nothing new about that, to make a fact out of a figure. At least it's good for something. Every story is penned in red ink, to make a figure out of a fact. This whole idea is insane.

And might therefore be got away with.

No turning back now, we've gone too far. Everything's finished. Name eight. Story, novel, literature, art, humanism, humanity, the self itself. Wait: the story's not finished. And you and I, Howard? whispered Martha, her sarcasm belied by a hesitant alarm in her glance, flickering as it were despite herself to the blank instrument in his hand. Belied indeed; put that thing away! And what does flickering modify? A person who can't verb adverb ought at least to speak correctly.

A tense moment in the evolution of the story. Do you know, declared the narrator, one has no idea, especially nowadays, how close the end may be, nor will one necessarily be aware of it when it occurs. Who can say how near this universe has come to mere cessation? Or take two people, in a story of the sort it once was possible to tell. Love affairs, literary genres, third item in exemplary series, fourth—everything blossoms and decays, does it not, from the primitive and classical through the mannered and baroque to the abstract, stylized, dehumanized, unintelligible, blank. And you and I, Rosemary? Edward. Snapped! Patience. The narrator gathers that his audience no longer cherishes him. And conversely. But little does he know of the common noun concealed for months in her you name it, under her eyelet chemise. This is a slip. The point is the same. And she fetches it out nightly as I dream, I think. That's no slip. And she regards it and sighs, a quantum grimlier each night it may be. Is this supposed to be amusing? The world might end before this sentence, or merely someone's life. And/or someone else's. I speak metaphorically. Is the sentence ended? Very nearly. No telling how long a sentence will be until one reaches the stop. It sounds as if somebody intends to fill in the blank. What *is* all this nonsense about?

It may not be nonsense. Anyhow it will presently be over. As the narrator was saying, things have been kaput for some time, and while we may be pardoned our great reluctance to acknowledge it, the fact is that the bloody century for example is nearing the three-quarter mark, and the characters in this little tale, for example, are similarly past their prime, as is the drama. About played out. Then God damn it let's ring the curtain. Wait wait. We're left with the following three possibilities, at least in theory. Horseshit. Hold onto yourself, it's too soon to fill in the blank. I hope this will be a short story.

Shorter than it seems. It seems endless. Be thankful it's not a novel. The novel is predicate adjective, as is the innocent anecdote of bygone days when life made a degree of sense and subject joined to complement by copula. No longer are these things the case, as you have doubtless remarked. There was I believe some mention of possibilities, three in number. The first is rejuvenation: having become an exhausted parody of itself, perhaps a form— Of what? Of anything—may rise neoprimitively from its own ashes. A tiresome prospect. The second, more appealing I'm sure but scarcely likely at this advancèd date, is that moribund what-have-yous will be supplanted by vigorous new: the demise of the novel and short story, he went on to declare, needn't be the end of narrative art, nor need the dissolution of a used-up blank fill in the blank. The end of one road might be the beginning of another. Much good that'll do me. And you may not find the revolution as bloodless as you think, either. Shall we try it? Never dare a person who is fed up to the ears.

The final possibility is a temporary expedient, to be sure, the self-styled narrator of this so-called story went on to admit, ignoring the hostile impatience of his audience, but what is not, and every sentence completed is a step closer to the end. That is to say, every day gained is a day gone. Matter of viewpoint, I suppose. Go on. I am. Whether anyone's paying attention or not. The final possibility is to turn ultimacy, exhaustion, paralyzing self-consciousness and the adjective weight of accumulated history. . . . . Go on. Go on. To turn ultimacy against itself to make something new and valid, the essence whereof would be the impossibility of making something new. What a nauseating notion. And pray how does it bear upon the analogy uppermost in everyone's mind? We've gotten this far, haven't we? Look how far we've come together. Can't we keep on to the end? I think not. Even another sentence is too many. Only if one believes the end to be a long way off; actually it might come at any moment; I'm surprised it hasn't before now. Nothing does when it's expected to be.

Silence. There's a fourth possibility, I suppose. Silence. General anesthesia. Self-extinction. Silence.

Historicity and self-awareness, he asseverated, while ineluctable and even greatly to be prized, are always fatal to innocence and spontaneity. Perhaps adjective period Whether in a people, an art, a love affair, on a fourth term added not impossibly to make the third less than ultimate. In the name of suffering humanity cease this harangue. It's over. And the story? Is there a plot here? What's all this leading up to?

No climax. There's the story. Finished? Not quite. Story of our lives. The last word in fiction, in fact. I chose the first-person narrative viewpoint in order to reflect interest from the peculiarities of the technique (such as the normally unbearable self-consciousness, the abstraction, and the blank) to the nature and situation of the narrator and his companion, despite the obvious possibility that the narrator and his companion might be mistaken for the narrator and his companion. Occupational hazard. The technique is advanced, as you see, but the situation of the characters is conventionally dramatic. That being the case, may one of them, or one who may be taken for one of them, make a longish speech in the old-fashioned manner, charged with obsolete emotion? Of course.

I begin calmly, though my voice may rise as I go along. Sometimes it seems as if things could instantly be altogether different and more admirable. The times be damned, one still wants a man vigorous, confident, bold, resourceful, adjective, and adjective. One still wants a woman spirited, spacious of heart, loyal, gentle, adjective, adjective. That man and that woman are as possible as the ones in this miserable story, and a good deal realer. It's as if they live in some room of our house that we can't find the door to, though it's so close we can hear echoes of their voices. Experience has made them wise instead of bitter; knowledge has mellowed instead of souring them; in their forties and fifties, even in their sixties, they're gayer and stronger and more authentic than they were in their twenties; for the twenty-year-olds they have only affectionate sympathy. So? Why aren't the couple in this story that man and woman, so easy to imagine? God, but I am surfeited with clever irony! Ill of sickness! Parallel phrase to wrap up series! This last-resort idea, it's dead in the womb, excuse the figure. A false pregnancy, excuse the figure. God damn me though if that's entirely my fault. Acknowledge your complicity. As you see, I'm trying to do something about the present mess; hence this story. Adjective in the noun! Don't lose your composure. You tell me it's self-defeating to talk about it instead of just up and doing it; but to acknowledge what I'm doing while I'm doing it is exactly the point. Self-defeat implies a victor, and who do you suppose it is, if not blank? That's the only victory left. Right? Forward! Eyes open.

No. The only way to get out of a mirror-maze is to close your eyes and hold out your hands. And be carried away by a valiant metaphor, I suppose, like a simile.

There's only one direction to go in. Ugh. We must make something out of nothing. Impossible. Mystics do. Not only turn contradiction into paradox, but *employ* it, to go on living and working. Don't bet on it. I'm betting my cliché on it, yours too. What is that supposed to mean? On with the refutation; every denial is another breath, every word brings us closer to the end.

Very well: to write this allegedly ultimate story is a form of artistic fill in the blank, or an artistic form of same, if you like. I don't. What I mean is, same idea in other terms. The storyteller's alternatives, as far as I can see, are a series of last words, like an aging actress making one farewell appearance after another, or actual blank. And I mean literally fill in the blank. Is this a test? But the former is contemptible in itself, and the latter will certainly become so when the rest of the world shrugs its shoulders and goes on about its business. Just as people would do if adverbial clause of obvious analogical nature. The fact is, the narrator has narrated himself into a corner, a state of affairs more tsk-tsk than boo-hoo, and because his position is absurd he calls the world absurd. That some writers lack lead in their pencils does not make writing obsolete. At this point they were both smiling despite themselves. At this point they were both flashing hatred despite themselves. Every woman has a blade concealed in the neighborhood of her garters. So disarm her, so to speak, don't geld yourself. At this point they were both despite themselves. Have we come to the point at last? Not quite. Where there's life there's hope.

There's no hope. This isn't working. But the alternative is to supply an alternative. That's no alternative. Unless I make it one. Just try; quit talking about it, quit talking, quit! Never dare a desperate man. Or woman. That's the one thing that can drive even the first part of a conventional metaphor to the second part of same. Talk, talk, talk. Yes yes, go on, I believe literature's not likely ever to manage abstraction successfully, like sculpture for example, is that a fact, what a time to bring up that subject, anticlimax, that's the point, do set forth the exquisite reason. Well, because wood and iron have a native appeal and first-order reality, whereas words are artificial to begin with, invented specifically to represent. Go on, please go on. I'm going. Don't you dare. Well, well, weld iron rods into abstract patterns, say, and you've still got real iron, but arrange words into abstract patterns and you've got nonsense. Nonsense is right. For example. On, God damn it; take linear plot, take resolution of conflict, take third direct object, all that business, they may very well be obsolete notions, indeed they are, no doubt untenable at this late date, no doubt at all, but in fact we still lead our lives by clock and calendar, for example, and though the seasons recur our mortal human time does not; we grow old and tired, we think of how things used to be or might have been and how they are now, and in fact, and in fact we get exasperated and desperate and out of expedients and out of words.

Go on. Impossible. I'm going, too late now, one more step and we're done, you and I. Suspense. The fact is, you're driving me to it, the fact is that people still lead lives, mean and bleak and brief as they are, briefer than you think, and people have characters and motives that we divine more or less inaccurately from their appearance, speech, behavior, and the rest, you aren't listening, go on then, what do you think I'm doing, people still fall in love, and out, yes, in and out, and out and in, and they please each other, and hurt each other, isn't that the truth, and they do these things in more or less conventionally dramatic fashion, unfashionable or not, go on, I'm going, and what goes on between them is still not only the most interesting but the most important thing in the bloody murderous world, pardon the adjectives. And that my dear is what writers have got to find ways to write about in this adjective adjective hour of the ditto ditto same noun as above, or their, that is to say our, accursed self-consciousness will lead them, that is to say us, to here it comes, say it straight out, I'm going to, say it in plain English for once, that's what I'm leading up to, me and my bloody anticlimactic noun, we're pushing each other to fill in the blank.

Goodbye. Is it over? Can't you read between the lines? One more step. Goodbye suspense goodbye.

Blank.

Oh God comma I abhor self-consciousness. I despise what we have come to; I loathe our loathsome loathing, our place our time our situation, our loathsome art, this ditto necessary story. The blank of our lives. It's about over. Let the *dénouement* be soon and unexpected, painless if possible, quick at least, above all soon. Now now! How in the world will it ever

GLOSSOLALIA

Still breathless from fending Phoebus, suddenly I see all—
and all in vain. A horse excreting Greeks will devour my
city; none will heed her Apollo loved, and endowed with
clear sight, and cursed when she gainsaid him. My honor
thus costlily purchased will be snatched from me by
soldiers. I see Agamemnon, my enslaver, meeting death in
Mycenae. No more.

Dear Procne: your wretched sister—she it is weaves this
robe. Regard it well: it hides her painful tale in its pointless
patterns. Tereus came and fetched her off; he conveyed
her to Thrace . . . but not to see her sister. He dragged
her deep into the forest, where he shackled her and raped
her. Her tongue he then severed, and concealed her, and
she warbles for vengeance, and death.

I Crispus, a man of Corinth, yesterday looked on God.
Today I rave. What things my eyes have seen can't be
scribed or spoken. All think I praise His sacred name,
take my horror for hymns, my blasphemies for raptures.
The holy writ's wrongly deciphered, as beatitudes and
blessings; in truth those are curses, maledictions, and
obscenest commandments. So be it.

Sweet Sheba, beloved highness: Solomon craves your
throne! Beware his craft; he mistranslates my pain into
cunning counsel. Hear what he claims your hoopoe sang:
that its mistress the Queen no longer worships Allah! He
bids you come now to his palace, to be punished for your
error. . . . But mine was a love song: how I'd hymn you,
if his tongue weren't beyond me—and yours.

Ed' pélut', kondó nedóde, ímba imbá imbá. Singé erú.
Orúmo ímbo ímpe ruté sceléte. Ímpe re scéle lee lutó.

Ombo té scele té, beré te kúre kúre. Sinté te lúté sinte kúru, te rI r   ruméte tau ruméte. Onkó keere scéte, tere lúte, ilee léte leel' lúto. Scélé.

Ill fortune, constraint and terror, generate guileful art; despair inspires. The laureled clairvoyants tell our doom in riddles. Sewn in our robes are horrid tales, and the speakers-in-tongues enounce atrocious tidings. The prophet-birds seem to speak sagely, but are shrieking their frustration. The senselessest babble, could we ken it, might disclose a dark message, or prayer.

LIFE-STORY

I

Without discarding what he'd already written he began his story afresh in a somewhat different manner. Whereas his earlier version had opened in a straight-forward documentary fashion and then degenerated or at least modulated intentionally into irrealism and dissonance he decided this time to tell his tale from start to finish in a conservative, "realistic," unself-conscious way. He being by vocation an author of novels and stories it was perhaps inevitable that one afternoon the possibility would occur to the writer of these lines that his own life might be a fiction, in which he was the leading or an accessory character. He happened at the time * to be in his study attempting to draft the opening pages of a new short story; its general idea had preoccupied him for some months along with other general ideas, but certain elements of the conceit, without which he could scarcely proceed, remained unclear. More specifically: narrative plots may be imagined as consisting of a "ground-situation" (Scheherazade desires not to die) focused and dramatized by a "vehicle-situation" (Scheherazade beguiles the King with endless stories), the several incidents of which have their final value in terms of their bearing upon the "ground-situation." In our author's case it was the "vehicle" that had vouchsafed itself, first as a germinal proposition in his commonplace book—D comes to suspect that the world is a novel, himself a fictional personage—subsequently as an articulated conceit explored over several pages of the workbook in which he elaborated more systematically his casual inspirations: since D is writing a fictional account of this

---

* 9:00 A.M., Monday, June 20, 1966.

conviction he has indisputably a fictional existence in his account, replicating what he suspects to be his own situation. Moreover E, hero of D's account, is said to be writing a similar account, and so the replication is in both ontological directions, et cetera. But the "ground-situation"— some state of affairs on D's part which would give dramatic resonance to his attempts to prove himself factual, assuming he made such attempts—obstinately withheld itself from his imagination. As is commonly the case the question reduced to one of stakes: what were to be the consequences of D's—and finally E's—disproving or verifying his suspicion, and why should a reader be interested?

What a dreary way to begin a story he said to himself upon reviewing his long introduction. Not only is there no "ground-situation," but the prose style is heavy and somewhat old-fashioned, like an English translation of Thomas Mann, and the so-called "vehicle" itself is at least questionable: self-conscious, vertiginously arch, fashionably solipsistic, unoriginal—in fact a convention of twentieth-century literature. Another story about a writer writing a story! Another regressus in infinitum! Who doesn't prefer art that at least overtly imitates something other than its own processes? That doesn't continually proclaim "Don't forget I'm an artifice!"? That takes for granted its mimetic nature instead of asserting it in order (not so slyly after all) to deny it, or vice-versa? Though his critics sympathetic and otherwise described his own work as avant-garde, in his heart of hearts he disliked literature of an experimental, self-despising, or overtly metaphysical character, like Samuel Beckett's, Marian Cutler's, Jorge Borges's. The logical fantasies of Lewis Carroll pleased him less than straightforward tales of adventure, subtly sentimental romances, even densely circumstantial realisms like Tolstoy's. His favorite contemporary authors were John Updike, Georges Simenon, Nicole Riboud. He had no use for the theater of absurdity, for "black humor," for allegory in any form, for apocalyptic preachments meretriciously tricked out in dramatic garb.

Neither had his wife and adolescent daughters, who for that matter preferred life to literature and read fiction when at all for entertainment. Their kind of story (his too, finally) would begin if not once upon a time at least with arresting circumstance, bold character, trenchant action. C flung away the whining manuscript and pushed impatiently through the french doors leading to the terrace from his oak-wainscoted study. Pausing at the stone balustrade to light his briar he remarked through a lavender cascade of wisteria that lithe-limbed Gloria, Gloria of timorous eye and militant breast, had once again chosen his boat-wharf as her basking-place.

By Jove he exclaimed to himself. It's particularly disquieting to suspect not only that one is a fictional character but that the fiction one's in—the fiction one is—is quite the sort one least prefers. His wife entered the study with coffee and an apple-pastry, set them at his elbow on his work table, returned to the living room. Ed' pelut' kondo nedode; nyoing nyang. One manifestation of schizophrenia as everyone knows is the movement from reality toward fantasy, a progress which not infrequently takes the form of distorted and fragmented representation, abstract formalism, an increasing preoccupation, even obsession, with pattern and design for their own sakes—especially patterns of a baroque, enormously detailed character—to the (virtual) exclusion of representative "content." There are other manifestations. Ironically, in the case of graphic and plastic artists for example the work produced in the advanced stages of their affliction may be more powerful and interesting than the realistic productions of their earlier "sanity." Whether the artists themselves are gratified by this possibility is not reported.

B called upon a literary acquaintance, B_____, summering with Mrs. B and children on the Eastern Shore of Maryland. "You say you lack a ground-situation. Has it occurred to you that that circumstance may be your ground-situation? What occurs to me is that if it is it isn't. And conversely. The case being thus, what's really wanting after all is a well-articulated vehicle, a foreground or upstage situation to dramatize the narrator's or author's grundlage. His what. To write merely C comes to suspect that the world is a novel, himself a fictional personage is but to introduce the vehicle; the next step must be to initiate its uphill motion by establishing and complicating some conflict. I would advise in addition the eschewal of overt and self-conscious discussion of the narrative process. I would advise in addition the eschewal of overt and self-conscious discussion of the narrative process. The via negativa and its positive counterpart are it is to be remembered poles after all of the same cell. Returning to his study.

If I'm going to be a fictional character G declared to himself I want to be in a rousing good yarn as they say, not some piece of avant-garde preciousness. I want passion and bravura action in my plot, heroes I can admire, heroines I can love, memorable speeches, colorful accessory characters, poetical language. It doesn't matter to me how naively linear the anecdote is; never mind modernity! How reactionary J appears to be. How will such nonsense sound thirty-six years from now? * As if. If he can only get K through his story I reflected grimly; if he can only retain his self-possession to the end of this sentence; not go mad; not destroy himself and/or others. Then what I wondered grimly. Another sentence fast, another story. Scheherazade my only love! All those nights you kept your secret from the King my rival, that after your defloration he was unnecessary, you'd have killed yourself in any case when your invention failed.

Why could he not begin his story afresh X wondered, for example with the words why could he not begin his story afresh et cetera? Y's wife came into the study as he was about to throw out the baby with the bathwater. "Not for an instant to throw out the baby while every instant discarding the bathwater is perhaps a chief task of civilized people at this hour of the world.† I used to tell B_____ that without success. What makes you so sure it's not a film he's in or a theater-piece?

Because U responded while he certainly felt rather often that he was merely acting his own role or roles he had no

---

* 10:00 A.M., Monday, June 20, 1966.
† 11:00 A.M., Monday, June 20, 1966.

idea who the actor was, whereas even the most Stanislavsky-methodist would presumably if questioned closely recollect his offstage identity even onstage in mid-act. Moreover a great part of T's "drama," most of his life in fact, was non-visual, consisting entirely in introspection, which the visual dramatic media couldn't manage easily. He had for example mentioned to no one his growing conviction that he was a fictional character, and since he was not given to audible soliloquizing a "spectator" would take him for a cheerful, conventional fellow, little suspecting that et cetera. It was of course imaginable that much goes on in the mind of King Oedipus in addition to his spoken sentiments; any number of interior dramas might be being played out in the actors' or characters' minds, dramas of which the audience is as unaware as are V's wife and friends of his growing conviction that he's a fictional character. But everything suggested that the medium of his life was prose fiction—moreover a fiction narrated from either the first-person or the third-person-omniscient point of view.

Why is it L wondered with mild disgust that both K and M for example choose to write such stuff when life is so sweet and painful and full of such a variety of people, places, situations, and activities other than self-conscious and after all rather blank introspection? Why is it N wondered et cetera that both M and O et cetera when the world is in such parlous explosive case? Why et cetera et cetera et cetera when the word, which was in the beginning, is now evidently nearing the end of its road? Am I being strung out in this ad libitum fashion I wondered merely to keep my author from the pistol? What sort of story is it whose drama lies always in the next frame out? If Sinbad sinks it's Scheherazade who drowns; whose neck one wonders is on her line?

II

Discarding what he'd already written as he could wish to discard the mumbling pages of his life he began his story afresh, resolved this time to eschew overt and self-conscious discussion of his narrative process and to recount instead in the straightforwardest manner possible the several complications of his character's conviction that he was a character in a work of fiction, arranging them into dramatically ascending stages if he could for his reader's sake and leading them (the stages) to an exciting climax and dénouement if he could.

He rather suspected that the medium and genre in which he worked—the only ones for which he felt any vocation—were moribund if not already dead. The idea pleased him. One of the successfullest men he knew was a blacksmith of the old school who et cetera. He meditated upon the grandest sailing-vessel ever built, the *France II,* constructed in Bordeaux in 1911 not only when but because the age of sail had passed. Other phenomena that consoled and inspired him were the great flying-boat *Hercules,* the zeppelin *Hindenburg,* the *Tsar Pushka* cannon, the then-record Dow-Jones industrial average of 381.17 attained on September 3, 1929.

He rather suspected that the society in which he persisted—the only one with which he felt any degree of identification—was moribund if not et cetera. He knew beyond any doubt that the body which he inhabited—the only one et cetera—was et cetera. The idea et cetera. He had for thirty-six years lacking a few hours been one of our dustmote's three billion tenants give or take five hundred million, and happening to be as well a white male citizen of the United States of America he had thirty-six years plus a few hours more to cope with one way or another unless the actuarial tables were mistaken, not bloody likely, or his term was unexpectedly reduced.

Had he written for his readers' sake? The phrase implied a thitherto-unappreciated metaphysical dimension. Suspense. If his life was a fictional narrative it consisted of three terms—teller, tale, told—each dependent on the other two but not in the same ways. His author could as well tell some other character's tale or some other tale of the same character as the one being told as he himself could in his own character as author; his "reader" could as easily read some other story, would be well advised to; but his own "life" depended absolutely on a particular author's original persistence, thereafter upon some reader's. From this consideration any number of things followed, some less tiresome than others. No use appealing to his author, of whom he'd come to dislike even to think. The idea of his playing with his characters' and his own self-consciousness! He himself tended in that direction and despised the tendency. The idea of his or her smiling smugly to himself as the "words" flowed from his "pen" in which his the protagonist's unhappy inner life was exposed! Ah he had mistaken the nature of his narrative; he had thought it very long, longer than Proust's, longer than any German's, longer than *The Thousand Nights and a Night* in ten quarto volumes. Moreover he'd thought it the most prolix and pedestrian *tranche-de-vie* realism, unredeemed by even the limited virtues of colorful squalor, solid specification, an engaging variety of scenes and characters—in a word a bore, of the sort he himself not only would not write but would not read either. Now he understood that his author might as probably resemble himself and the protagonist of his own story-in-progress. Like himself, like his character aforementioned, his author not impossibly deplored the obsolescence of humanism, the passing of *savoir-vivre,* et cetera; admired the outmoded values of fidelity, courage, tact, restraint, amiability, self-discipline, et cetera; preferred fictions in which were to be found stirring actions, characters to love as well as ditto to despise, speeches and deeds to affect us strongly, et cetera. He too might wish to make some final effort to put by his fictional character and achieve factuality or at least to figure in if not be hero of a more attractive fiction, but be caught like the writer of these lines in some more or less desperate tour de force. For him to attempt to come to an understanding with such an author were as futile as for one of his own creations to et cetera.

But the reader! Even if his author were his only reader as was he himself of his work-in-progress as of the sentence-in-progress and his protagonist of his, et cetera, his character as reader was not the same as his character as author, a fact which might be turned to account. What suspense.

As he prepared to explore this possibility one of his mistresses whereof he had none entered his brown study unannounced. "The passion of love," she announced, "which I regard as no less essential to a satisfying life than those values itemized above and which I infer from my presence here that you too esteem highly, does not in fact play in your life a role of sufficient importance to sustain my presence here. It plays in fact little role at all outside your imaginative and/or ary life. I tell you this not in a criticizing spirit, for I judge you to be as capable of the sentiment aforementioned as any other imagin[ative], deep-feeling man in good physical health more or less precisely in the middle of the road of our life. What hampers, even cripples you in this regard is your final preference, which I refrain from analyzing, for the sedater, more responsible pleasures of monogamous fidelity and the serener affections of domesticity, notwithstanding the fact that your enjoyment of these is correspondingly inhibited though not altogether spoiled by an essentially romantical, unstable, irresponsible, death-wishing fancy. V. S. Pritchett, English critic and author, will put the matter succinctly in a soon-to-be-written essay on Flaubert, whose work he'll say depicts the course of ardent longings and violent desires that rise from the horrible, the sensual, and the sadistic. They turn into the virginal and mystical, only to become numb by satiety. At this point pathological boredom leads to a final desire for death and nothingness—the Romantic syndrome. If, not to be unfair, we qualify somewhat the terms horrible and sadistic and understand satiety to include a large measure of vicariousness, this description undeniably applies to one aspect of yourself and your work; and while your ditto has other, even contrary aspects, the net fact is that you have elected familial responsibilities and reward—indeed, straight-laced middle-classness in general—over the higher expenses of spirit and wastes of shame attendant upon a less regular, more glamorous style of life. So to elect is surely admirable for the layman, even essential if the social fabric, without which there can be no culture, is to be preserved. For the artist, however, and in particular the writer, whose traditional material has been the passions of men and women, the choice is fatal. You having made it I bid you goodnight probably forever."

Even as she left he reached for the sleeping pills cached conveniently in his writing desk and was restrained from their administration only by his being in the process of completing a sentence, which he cravenly strung out at some sacrifice of rhetorical effect upon realizing that he was et cetera. Moreover he added hastily he had not described the intruder for his readers' vicarious satiety: a lovely woman she was, whom he did not after all describe for his readers' et cetera inasmuch as her appearance and character were inconstant. Her interruption of his work inspired a few sentences about the extent to which his fiction inevitably made public his private life, though the trespasses in this particular were as nothing beside those of most of his profession. That is to say, while he did not draw his characters and situations directly from life nor permit his author-protagonist to do so, any moderately attentive reader of his oeuvre, his what, could infer for example that its author feared for example schizophrenia, impotence creative and sexual, suicide—in short living and dying. His fictions were preoccupied with these fears among their other, more serious preoccupations. Hot dog. As of the sentence-in-progress he was not in fact unmanageably schizophrenic, impotent in either respect, or dead by his own hand, but there was always the next sentence to worry about. But there was always the next sentence to worry about. In sum he concluded hastily such limited self-exposure did not constitute a misdemeanor, representing or mis as it did so small an aspect of his total self, negligible a portion of his total life—even which totalities were they made public would be found remarkable only for their being so unremarkable. Well shall he continue.

Bearing in mind that he had not developed what he'd mentioned earlier about turning to advantage his situation vis-à-vis his "reader" (in fact he deliberately now postponed his return to that subject, sensing that it might well constitute the climax of his story) he elaborated one or two ancillary questions, perfectly aware that he was trying, even exhausting, whatever patience might remain to whatever readers might remain to whoever elaborated yet another ancillary question. Was the novel of his life for example a *roman à clef.* ? Of that genre he was as contemptuous as of the others aforementioned; but while in the introductory adverbial clause it seemed obvious to him that he didn't "stand for" anyone else, any more than he was an actor playing the role of himself, by the time he reached the main clause he had to admit that the question was unanswerable, since the "real" man to whom he'd correspond in a *roman à clef* would not be also in the *roman à clef* and the characters in such works were not themselves aware of their irritating correspondences.

Similarly unanswerable were such questions as when "his" story (so he regarded it for convenience and consolement though for all he knew he might be not the central character; it might be his wife's story, one of his daughters's, his imaginary mistress's, the man-who-once-cleaned-his-chimney's) began. Not impossibly at his birth or even generations earlier: a *Bildungs-roman,* an *Erziehungsroman, a roman fleuve.* ! More likely at the moment he became convinced of his fictional nature: that's where he'd have begun it, as he'd begun the piece currently under his pen. If so it followed that the years of his childhood and younger manhood weren't "real," he'd suspected as much, in the first-order sense, but a mere "background" consisting of a few well-placed expository insinuations, perhaps misleading, or inferences, perhaps unwarranted, from strategic hints in his present reflections. God so to speak spare his readers from heavyfooted forced expositions of the sort that begin in the countryside near _____ in June of the year _____ it occurred to the novelist_____ that his own life might be a _____, in which he was the leading or an accessory character. He happened at the time to be in the oak-wainscoted study of the old family summer residence; through a lavender cascade of hysteria he observed that his wife had once again chosen to be the subject of this clause, itself the direct object of his observation. A lovely woman she was, whom he did not describe in keeping with his policy against drawing characters from life as who should draw a condemnee to the gallows. Begging his pardon. Flinging his tiresome tale away he pushed impatiently through the french windows leading from his study to a sheer drop from the then-record high into a nearly fatal depression.

He clung onto his narrative depressed by the disproportion of its ratiocination to its dramatization, reflection to action. One had heard *Hamlet* criticized as a collection of soliloquies for which the implausible plot was a mere excuse; witnessed Italian operas whose dramatic portions were no more than interstitial relief and arbitrary continuity between the arias. If it was true that he didn't take his "real" life seriously enough even when it had him by the throat, the fact didn't lead him to consider whether the fact was a cause or a consequence of his tale's tedium or both.

Concluding these reflections he concluded these reflections: that there was at this advancèd page still apparently no ground-situation suggested that his story was dramatically meaningless. If one regarded the absence of a ground-situation, more accurately the protagonist's anguish at that absence and his vain endeavors to supply the defect, as itself a sort of ground-situation, did his life-story thereby take on a kind of meaning? A "dramatic" sort he supposed, though of so sophistical a character as more likely to annoy than to engage

III

The reader! You, dogged, uninsultable, print-oriented bastard, it's you I'm addressing, who else, from inside this monstrous fiction. You've read me this far, then? Even this far? For what discreditable motive? How is it you don't go to a movie, watch TV, stare at a wall, play tennis with a friend, make amorous advances to the person who comes to your mind when I speak of amorous advances? Can nothing surfeit, saturate you, turn you off? Where's your shame?

Having let go this barrage of rhetorical or at least unanswered questions and observing himself nevertheless in midst of yet another sentence he concluded and caused the "hero" of his story to conclude that one or more of three things must be true: 1) his author was his sole and indefatigable reader; 2) he was in a sense his own author, telling his story to himself, in which case in which case; and/or 3) his reader was not only tireless and shameless but sadistic, masochistic if he was himself.

For why do you suppose—you! you!—he's gone on so, so relentlessly refusing to entertain you as he might have at a less desperate than this hour of the world * with felicitous language, exciting situation, unforgettable character and image? Why has he as it were ruthlessly set about not to win you over but to turn you away? Because your own author bless and damn you his life is in your hands! He writes and reads himself; don't you think he knows who gives his creatures their lives and deaths? Do they exist except as he or others read their words? Age except we turn their pages? And can he die until you have no more of him? Time was obviously when his author could have turned the trick; his pen had once to left-to-right it through these words as does your kindless eye and might have ceased at any one. This. This. And did not as you see but went on like an Oriental torturemaster to the end.

But you needn't! He exclaimed to you. In vain. Had he petitioned you instead to read slowly in the happy parts, what happy parts, swiftly in the painful no doubt you'd have done the contrary or cut him off entirely. But as he longs to die and can't without your help you force him on, force him on. Will you deny you've read this sentence? This? To get away with murder doesn't appeal to you, is that it? As if your hands weren't inky with other dyings! As if he'd know you'd killed him! Come on. He dares you.

In vain. You haven't: the burden of his knowledge. That he continues means that he continues, a fortiori you too. Suicide's impossible: he can't kill himself without your help. Those petitions aforementioned, even his silly plea

---

* 11:00 P.M., Monday, June 20, 1966.

for death—don't you think he understands their sophistry, having authored their like for the wretches he's authored? Read him fast or slow, intermittently, continuously, repeatedly, backward, not at all, he won't know it; he only guesses someone's reading or composing his sentences, such as this one, because he's reading or composing sentences such as this one; the net effect is that there's a net effect, of continuity and an apparently consistent flow of time, though his pages do seem to pass more swiftly as they near his end.

To what conclusion will he come? He'd been about to append to his own tale inasmuch as the old analogy between Author and God, novel and world, can no longer be employed unless deliberately as a false analogy, certain things follow: 1) fiction must acknowledge its fictitiousness and metaphoric invalidity or 2) choose to ignore the question or deny its relevance or 3) establish some other, acceptable relation between itself, its author, its reader. Just as he finished doing so however his real wife and imaginary mistresses entered his study; "It's a little past midnight" she announced with a smile; "do you know what that means?"

Though she'd come into his story unannounced at a critical moment he did not describe her, for even as he recollected that he'd seen his first light just thirty-six years before the night incumbent he saw his last: that he could not after all be a character in a work of fiction inasmuch as such a fiction would be of an entirely different character from what he thought of as fiction. Fiction consisted of such monuments of the imagination as Cutler's *Morganfield*, Riboud's *Tales Within Tales,* his own creations; fact of such as for example read those fictions. More, he could demonstrate by syllogism that the story of his life was a work of fact: though assaults upon the boundary between life and art, reality and dream, were undeniably a staple of his own and his century's literature as they'd been of Shakespeare's and Cervantes's, yet it was a fact that in the corpus of fiction as far as he knew no fictional character had become convinced as had he that he was a character in a work of fiction. This being the case and he having in fact become thus convinced it followed that his conviction was false. "Happy birthday," said his wife et cetera, kissing him et cetera to obstruct his view of the end of the sentence he was nearing the end of, playfully refusing to be nay-said so that in fact he did at last as did his fictional character end his ending story endless by interruption, cap his pen.   .

MENELAIAD

I

Menelaus here, more or less. The fair-haired boy? Of the loud war cry! Leader of the people. Zeus's fosterling.

Eternal husband.

Got you, have I? No? Changed your shape, become waves of the sea, of the air? Anyone there? Anyone here?

No matter; this isn't the voice of Menelaus; this voice *is* Menelaus, all there is of him. When I'm switched on I tell my tale, the one I know, How Menelaus Became Immortal, but I don't know it.

Keep hold of yourself.

"Helen," I say: "Helen's responsible for this. From the day we lovers sacrificed the horse in Argos, pastureland of horses, and swore on its bloody joints to be her champions forever, whichever of us she chose, to the night we huddled in the horse in Troy while she took the part of all our wives—everything's Helen's fault. Cities built and burnt, a thousand bottoms on the sea's, every captain corpsed or cuckold—her doing. She's the death of me and my peculiar immortality, cause of every mask and change of state. On whose account did Odysseus become a madman, Achilles woman? Who turned the Argives into a horse, loyal Sinon into a traitor, yours truly from a mooncalf into a sea-calf, Proteus into everything that is? First cause and final magician: Mrs. M.

"One evening, embracing in our bed, I dreamed I was back in the wooden horse, waiting for midnight. Laocoön's spear still stuck in our flank, and Helen, with her Trojan pal in tow, called out to her Argive lovers in the voice of each's wife. 'Come kiss me, Anticlus darling!' My heart was stabbed as my side was once by Pandarus's arrow. But in the horse, while smart Odysseus held shut our mouths,

I dreamed I was home in bed before Paris and the war, our wedding night, when she crooned like that to *me*. Oh, Anticlus, it wasn't you who was deceived; your wife was leagues and years away, mine but an arms-length, yet less near. Now I wonder which dream dreamed which, which Menelaus never woke and now dreams both.

"And when I was on the beach at Pharos, seven years lost en route from Troy, clinging miserably to Proteus for direction, he prophesied a day when I'd sit in my house at last, drink wine with the sons of dead comrades, and tell their dads' tales; my good wife would knit by the fireside, things for our daughter's wedding, and dutifully pour the wine. That scene glowed so in my heart, its beat became the rhythm of her needles; Egypt's waves hissed on the foreshore like sapwood in the grate, and the Nile-murk on my tongue turned sweet. But then it seems to me I'm home in Sparta, talking to Nestor's boy or Odysseus's; Helen's put something in the wine again, I know why, one of those painkillers she picked up in Africa, and the tale I tell so grips me, I'm back in the cave once more with the Old Man of the Sea."

One thing's certain: somewhere Menelaus lost course and steersman, went off track, never got back on, lost hold of himself, became a record merely, the record of his loosening grasp. He's the story of his life, with which he ambushes the unwary unawares.

II

" 'Got you!' " I cry to myself, imagining Telemachus enthralled by the doctored wine. " 'You've feasted your bowels on my dinner, your hopes on my news of Odysseus, your eyes on my wife though she's your mother's age. Now I'll feast myself on your sotted attention, with the tale How Menelaus First Humped Helen in the Eighth Year After the War. Pricked you up, that? Got your ear, have I? Like to know how it was, I suppose? Where in Hades are we? Where'd I go? Whom've I got hold of? Proteus? Helen?'

" 'Telemachus Odysseus'-son,' the lad replied, 'come from goat-girt Ithaca for news of my father, but willing to have his cloak clutched and listen all night to the tale How You Lost Your Navigator, Wandered Seven Years, Came Ashore at Pharos, Waylaid Eidothea, Tackled Proteus, Learned to Reach Greece by Sailing up the Nile, and Made Love to Your Wife, the most beautiful woman I've ever seen, After an Abstinence of Eighteen Years.'

" 'Seventeen.' "

I tell it as it is. " 'D'you hear that click?' " I tell myself I asked Telemachus.

" '*I* do,' said Peisistratus.

" 'Knitting! Helen of Troy's going to be a grandmother! An empire torched, a generation lost, a hundred kings undone on her account, and there she sits, proper as Penelope, not a scratch on her—and knits!'

" 'Not a scratch!' said Telemachus.

" 'Excuse me,' Helen said; 'if it's to be *that* tale I'm going on to bed, second chamber on one's left down the hall. A lady has her modesty. Till we meet again, Telemachus. Drink deep and sleep well, Menelaus my love.'

" 'Zeus in heaven!' " I say I cried. " 'Why didn't I do you in in Deiphobus' house, put you to the sword with Troy?'

"Helen smiled at us and murmured: 'Love.'

" 'Does she mean,' asked Peisistratus Nestor's-son, come with Telemachus that noon from sandy Pylos, 'that you love her for example more than honor, self-respect; more than every man and cause you've gone to war for; more than Menelaus?'

" 'Not impossibly.'

" 'Is it that her name's twin syllables fire you with contrary passions? That your heart does battle with your heart till you burn like ashèd Ilion?'

" 'Wise son of a wise father! Her smile sows my furrowed memory with Castalian serpent's teeth; I become a score of warriors, each battling the others; the survivors kneel as one before her; perhaps the slain were better men. If Aeneas Aphrodite's-son couldn't stick her, how should I, a mere near mortal?'

" 'This is gripping,' " I say to myself Telemachus said. " 'Weary as we are from traveling all day, I wish nothing further than to sit without moving in this total darkness while you hold me by the hem of my tunic and recount How Your Gorgeous Wife Wouldn't Have You for Seven Full Postwar Years but Did in the Eighth. If I fail to exclaim with wonder or otherwise respond, it will be that I'm speechless with sympathy.'

" 'So be it,' I said," I say. "Truth to tell," I tell me, "when we re-reached Sparta Helen took up her knitting with never a droppèd stitch, as if she'd been away eighteen days instead of ditto years, and visiting her sister instead of bearing bastards to her Trojan lovers. But it was the wine of doubt *I* took to, whether I was the world's chief fool and cuckold or its luckiest mortal. Especially when old comrades came to town, or their sons, to swap war stories, I'd booze it till I couldn't tell Helen from Hellespont. So it was the day Odysseus's boy and Nestor's rode into town. I was shipping off our daughter to wed Achilles' son and Alector's girl in to wed mine; the place was full of kinfolk, the wine ran free, I was swallowing my troubles; babies they were when I went to Troy, hardly married myself; by the time I get home they're men and women wanting spouses of their own; no wonder I felt old and low and thirsty; where'd my kids go? The prime of my life?

"When the boys dropped in I took for granted they were friends of the children's, come for the party; I saw to it they were washed and oiled, gave them clean clothes and poured them a drink. Better open your palace to every kid in the countryside than not know whose your own are in, Mother and I always thought. No man can say I'm inhospitable. But I won't deny I felt a twinge when I learned they were strangers; handsome boys they were, from good families, I could tell, and in the bloom of manhood, as I'd been twenty years before, and Paris when he came a-calling, and I gave him a drink and said 'What's mine is yours . . .'
. . . ." . . . .

Why don't they call her Helen of Sparta?

"I showed them the house, all our African stuff, it knocked their eyes out; then we had dinner and played the guessing game. Nestor's boy I recognized early on, his father's image, a good lad, but not hero-material, you know what I mean. The other was a troubler; something not straight about him; wouldn't look you in the eye; kept smiling at his plate; but a sharp one, and a good-looking, bound to make a stir in the world one day. I kept my eye on him through dinner and decided he was my nephew Orestes, still hiding out from killing his mother and her goat-boy-friend, or else Odysseus's Telemachus. Either way it was bad news: when Proteus told me how Clytemnestra and Aegisthus had axed my brother the minute he set foot in Mycenae, do you think Helen spared him a tear? 'No more than he deserved,' she said, 'playing around with that bitch Cassandra.' But when we stopped off there on our way home from Egypt and found her sister and Aegisthus being buried, didn't she raise a howl for young Orestes' head! Zeus help him if he'd come to see his Uncle Menelaus! On the other hand, if he was Odysseus's boy and took after his father, I'd have to keep eye on the wedding silver as well as on the bride.

"To make matters worse, as I fretted about this our old minstrel wandered in, looking for a handout, and started up that wrath-of-Achilles thing, just what I needed to hear; before I could turn him off I was weeping in my wine and wishing I'd died the morning after my wedding night. Hermione barged in too, almost as pretty as her mom, to see who the stranger-chaps were; for a minute it was 'Paris, meet Helen' all over again, till I got hold of myself and shooed her out of there. Even so, a dreadful notion struck me: what if Paris had a son we didn't know about, who'd slipped like slick Aeneas our Trojan clutch, grown up in hiding, and was come now to steal my daughter as his dad my wife! Another horse! Another Hector! Another drink.

"Even as I swallowed, hard and often, the fellow winked at the door I'd sent Hermione through and said, 'Quite a place, hey, Nestor's-son?' Which was to say, among other things, Peisistratus was tagged and out of the game. Nothing for it then but to play the thing out in the usual way. 'No getting around it, boys,' I declared: 'I'm not the poorest Greek in town. But I leave it to Zeus whether what you've seen is worth its cost. Eight years I knocked about the world, picking up what I could and wishing I were dead. The things you see come from Cyprus, Phoenicia, Egypt, Ethiopia, Sidonia, Erembi—even Libya, where the lambs are born with horns on.'

" 'Born with horns on!'

"I did my thing then, told a story with everyone in it who might be the mystery guest and looked to see which name brought tears. 'While I was pirating around,' I said, 'my wife's sister murdered my brother on the grounds that she'd committed adultery for ten years straight with my cousin Aegisthus. Her son Orestes killed them both, bless his heart, but when I think of Agamemnon and the rest done in for Helen's sake, I'd swap two-thirds of what I've got to bring them back to life.'

"I looked for the stranger's tears through mine, but he only declared: 'Lucky Achilles' son, to come by such a treasure!'

" 'Yet the man I miss most,' I continued, 'is shifty Odysseus.'

" 'Oh?'

" 'Yes indeed,' I went on," I go on: " 'Now and then I wonder what became of him and old faithful Penelope and the boy Telemachus.'

" 'You know Telemachus?' asked Telemachus.

" 'I knew him once,' said I. 'Twenty years ago, when he was one, I laid him in a furrow for his dad to plow under, and thus odysseused Odysseus. What's more, I'd made up my mind if he got home alive to give him a town here in Argos to lord it over and leave to his son when he died. Odysseus and I, wouldn't we have run through the grapes and whoppers! Pity he never made it.'

"The boy wet his mantle properly then, and I thought: 'Hold tight, son of Atreus, and keep a sharp lookout.' While I wondered what he might be after and how to keep him from it, as I had of another two decades past, Herself came in with her maids and needles, worst possible moment as ever.

" 'Why is it, Menelaus, you never tell me when a prince comes calling? Good afternoon, Telemachus.'

"Oh, my gods, but she was lovely! Cute Hermione drew princelings to Sparta like piss-ants to a peony-bud, but her mother was the full-blown blossom, the blooming bush! Far side of forty but never a wrinkle, and any two cuts of her great gray eyes told more about love and Troy than our bard in a night's hexameters. Her figure, too—but curse her figure! She opened her eyes and theirs, I shut mine, there was the usual pause; then Telemachus got his wind back and hollered: 'Pay-ee-*sis*tratus! What country have we come to, where the mares outrun the fillies?'

"Nestor's-son's face was ashen as his spear; ashener than either the old taste in my mouth. If only Telemachus had been so abashed! But he looked her over like young Heracles the house of Thespius and said, 'Not even many-masked Odysseus could disguise himself from Zeus's daughter. How is it you know me?'

" 'You're your father's son,' Helen said. 'Odysseus asked me that very question one night in Troy. He'd got himself up as a beggar and slipped into town for the evening . . .'

" 'What for?' wanted to know Peisistratus.

" 'To spy, to spy,' Telemachus said.

" 'What else?' asked Helen. 'None knew him but me, who'd have known him anywhere, and I said to my Trojan friends: "Look, a new beggar in town. Wonder who he is?" But no matter how I tried, I couldn't trick Odysseus into saying: "Odysseus." '

" 'Excuse me, ma'am,' begged Peisistratus, disbrothered by the war; 'what I don't understand is why you tried at all, since he was on a dangerous mission in enemy territory.'

" 'Nestor's-son,' said I, 'you're your father's son.' But Telemachus scolded him, asking how he hoped to have his questions answered if he interrupted the tale by asking them. Helen flashed him a look worth epics and said, 'When I got him alone in my apartment and washed and oiled and dressed him, I promised not to tell anyone he was Odysseus until he went back to his camp. So he told me all the Greek military secrets. Toward morning he killed several Trojans while they slept, and then I showed him the safest way out of town. There was a fuss among the new widows, but who cared? I was bored with Troy by that time and wished I'd never left home. I had a nice palace, a daughter, and Menelaus: what more could a woman ask?'

"After a moment Telemachus cried: 'Noble heart in a nobler breast! To think that all the while our side cursed you, you were secretly helping us!'

"When I opened my eyes I saw Peisistratus rubbing his, image of Gerenian Nestor. 'It still isn't clear to me,' he said, 'why the wife of Prince Paris—begging your pardon, sir; I mean as it were, of course—would wash, oil, and dress a vagrant beggar in her apartment in the middle of the night. I don't grasp either why you couldn't have slipped back to Lord Menelaus along with Odysseus, if that's what you wanted.'

"He had other questions too, shrewd lad, but Helen's eyes turned dark, and before I could swallow my wine Telemachus had him answered: 'What good could she have done the Argives then? She'd as well have stayed here in Sparta!' As for himself, he told Helen, next to hearing that his father was alive no news could've more delighted him than that the whole purpose of her elopement with Paris, as he was now convinced, was to spy for the Greeks from the heart of Troy, without which espionage we'd surely have been defeated. Helen counted her stitches and said, 'You give me too much credit.' 'No, by Zeus!' Telemachus declared. 'To leave your home and family and live for ten years with another man, purely for the sake of your home and family . . .'

" 'Nine with Paris,' Helen murmured, 'one with Deiphobus. Deiphobus was the better man, no doubt about it, but not half as handsome.'

" 'So much the nobler!' cried Telemachus.

" 'Nobler than you think,' I said, and poured myself and Peisistratus another drink. 'My wife's too modest to tell the noblest things of all. In the first place, when I fetched her out of Troy at last and set sail for home, she was so ashamed of what she'd had to do to win the war for us that it took me seven years more to convince her she was worthy of me . . .'

" 'I kiss the hem of your robe!' Telemachus exclaimed to her and did.

" 'In the second place,' I said, 'she did all these things for our sake without ever going to Troy in the first place.'

" 'Really,' Helen protested.

" 'Excuse me, sir . . .' said presently Peisistratus.

" 'Wine's at your elbow,' I declared. 'Drink deep, boys; I'll tell you the tale.'

" 'That's not what Prince Telemachus wants,' Helen said.

" 'I know what Prince Telemachus wants.'

" 'He wants word of his father,' said she. 'If you must tell a story at this late hour, tell the one about Proteus on the beach at Pharos, what he said of Odysseus.'

" 'Do,' Peisistratus said.

" 'Hold on,' I said," I say: " 'It's all one tale.'

" 'Then tell it all,' said Helen. 'But excuse yours truly.'

" 'Don't go!' cried Telemachus.

" 'A lady has her modesty,' Helen said, 'I'll fill your cups, gentlemen, bid you good night, and retire. To the second—'

" 'Who put out the light?' asked Peisistratus.

" 'Wait!' cried Telemachus.

" 'Got you!' cried I, clutching hold of his cloak-hem. After an exchange of pleasantries we settled down and drank deep in the dark while I told the tale of Menelaus and his wife at sea:

III

" 'Seven years,' " I say et cetera, " 'the woman kept her legs crossed and the north wind blew without let-up, holding us from home. In the eighth, on the beach at Pharos, with Eidothea's help I tackled her dad the Old Man of the Sea and followed his tough instructions: heavy-hearted it back to Egypt, made my hecatombs, vowed my vows. At once then, wow, the wind changed, no time at all till we re-raised Pharos! Not a Proteus in sight, no Eidothea, just the boat I'd moored my wife in, per orders. Already she was making sail; her crew were putting in their oars; my first thought was, they're running off with Helen; we over-hauled them; why was everybody grinning? But it was only joy, not to lose another minute; there was Helen herself by the mast-step, holding out her arms to me! Zeus knows how I poop-to-pooped it, maybe I was dreaming on the beach at Pharos, maybe am still; there I was anyhow, clambering aboard: "Way, boys!" I hollered. "Put your arse in it!" Spang! went the mainsail, breeze-bellied for Sparta; those were Helen's arms around me; it was wedding night! We hustled to the sternsheets, never mind who saw what; when she undid every oar went up; still we tore along the highways of the fish. "Got you!" I cried, couldn't see for the beauty of her, feel her yet, what is she anyhow? I decked her; only think, those gold limbs hadn't wound me in twenty years . . .'

" 'Twenty?' 'Counting two before the war. Call it nineteen.'

" ' "Wait," she bade me. "First tell me what Proteus said, and how you followed his advice."

" 'Our oars went down; we strained the sail with sighs; my tears thinned the wine-dark sea. But there was nothing for it, I did as bid:

IV

" ' "Nothing for it but to do as Eidothea'd bid me," ' " I say to myself I told Telemachus I sighed to Helen.

" ' "Eidothea?"

" ' "Old Man of the Sea's young daughter, so she said," said I. "With three of my crew I dug in on the beach at sunrise; she wrapped us in seal-calfskin. 'Hold tight to these,' she told us. 'Who can hug a stinking sea-beast?' I inquired. She said, 'Father. Try ambrosia; he won't get here till noon.' She put it under our noses and dived off as usual; we were high in no time; 'These seals,' my men agreed: 'the longer you're out here the whiter they get.' They snuggled in and lost themselves in dreams; I would've too, but grateful as I was, when she passed the ambrosia I smelled a trick. Hang around Odysseus long enough, you trust nobody. I'd take a sniff and put the stuff away till the seal stink got to me, then sniff again. Even so I nearly lost my grip. Was I back in the horse? Was I dreaming of Helen on my bachelor throne?"

" ' "Hold on," said deckèd Helen; I came to myself, saw I was blubbering; "I came to myself, saw I was beached at

Pharos. Come shadeless noon, unless I dreamed it, the sea-cow harem flipped from the deep to snooze on the foreshore, give me a woman anytime. Old Proteus came after, no accounting for tastes, counted them over, counting us in, old age is hard on the eyes too; then he outstretched in the cavemouth, one snore and I jumped him.

" ' " 'Got you!' I cried" I cried' I cried" I cry. " ' "My companions, when I hollered, grabbed hold too: one snatched his beard, one his hands, one his long white hair; I tackled his legs and held fast. First he changed into a lion, ate the beard-man, what a mess; then snake, bit the hair-chap, who'd nothing to hold onto." '

" 'Neither did the hand-man,' observed Peisistratus, sleepless critic, to whom I explained for Telemachus's sake as well that while the erstwhile hand-man, latterly paw-man, had admittedly been vulnerably under both lion and snake, and the hair- then mane-man relatively safely on top, the former had escaped the former by reason of the quondam beard-man's fortunate, for the quondam paw-man, interposition; the latter fallen prey to the latter by reason of the latter's unfortunate, for the quondam mane-man, proclivity to strike whatever was before him—which would have been to say, before, the hand-paw-man, but was to say, now, which is to say, then, the beard-mane-man, thanks so to speak to the serpent's windings upon itself.

" 'Ah.'

" ' "To clutch the leopard Proteus turned into then, then, were only myself and the unhandled hand-man, paw- once more but shielded now by neither beard- nor mane- and so promptly chomped, what a mess. I'd have got mine too, leopards are flexible, but by the time he'd made lunch of my companions he'd become a boar . . ."

" ' "Ah."

" ' "Which bristle as he might couldn't tusk his own tail, whereto I clung."

" ' "Not his hindpaws? I thought you were the foot-paw—" '

" 'Just what I was about to—'

" ' "Proteus to lion, feet into hindpaws," I answered,'

I answered. ' "Lion to snake, paws into tail. Snake to leopard, tail into tail and hindpaws both; my good luck I went tail to tail."

" ' "Leopard to boar?"

" ' "Long tail to short, too short to tusk. Then the trouble started." (')

" ' "!"

" '!'

" '!'

"I replied to them: ' "A beast's a beast," I replied to her. "If you've got the right handle all you do's hang on . . ." ' "

. " ' "It was when the Old Man of the Sea turned into salt water I began to sweat. Try holding an armful of ocean! I did my best, hugged a puddle on the beach, but plenty soaked in, plenty more ran seaward, where I saw you bathing, worst possible moment, not that you knew . . ." '

" '?

" '?' [?]

" 'It's Helen I'm telling, northing in our love-clutch on the poop. "I needed a bath," she said; "I a drink," said I; "for all I knew you might be Proteus all over, dirty Old Man of the Sea. Even when my puddle turned into a bigbole leafy tree I wasn't easy; who said he couldn't be two things at once? There I lay, philodendron, hour after hour, while up in the limbs a cuckoo sang . . ." ' "

My problem was, I'd too much imagination to be a hero. " ' "My problem was, I'd leisure to think. My time was mortal, Proteus's im-; what if he merely treed it a season or two till I let go? What was it anyhow I held? If Proteus once was Old Man of the Sea and now Proteus was a tree, then Proteus was neither, only Proteus; what I held were dreams. But if a real Old Man of the Sea had really been succeeded by real water and the rest, then the dream was Proteus. And Menelaus! For I changed too as the long day passed: changed my mind, replaced myself, grew older. How hold on until the 'old' (which is to say the young) Menelaus rebecame himself? Eidothea forgot to say! How could I anyhow know that that sea-nymph wasn't Proteus in yet another guise, her counsel a ruse to bind me forever while he sported with Helen?" '

" 'What *was* her counsel, exactly?'

" 'Peisistratus, is it? Helen's question, exactly: "What *was* her counsel, exactly?" And "How'd you persuade her to trick her own dad?" "Everything in its place," I said,' I said. ' "Your question was Proteus's, exactly; as I answered when he asked, I'll answer when he asks."

" ' "Hard tale to hold onto, this," declared my poopèd spouse.' Odysseus'- or Nestor's-son agreed." I agree. But what out-wandering hero ever journeyed a short straight line, arrived at his beginning till the end? " ' "Harder yet to hold onto Proteus. I must have dozed as I mused and fretted, thought myself yet again enhorsed or bridal-chambered, same old dream, woke up clutching nothing. It was late. I was rooted with fatigue. I held on." (' ') "To?" (' ') "Nothing. You were back on deck, the afternoon sank, I heard sailors guffawing, shore-birds cackled, the sun set grinning in the winish sea, still I held on, saying of and to me: 'Menelaus is a fool, mortal hugging immortality. Men laugh, the gods mock, he's chimaera, a hornèd gull. What is it he clutches? Why can't he let go? What trick have you played him, Eidothea, a stranger in your country?' I might've quit, but my cursèd fancy whispered: 'Proteus has turned into the air. Or else . . .' " ' "

Hold onto yourself, Menelaus.

" ' "Long time my shingled arms made omicron. Tides lapped in and kelped me; fishlets kissed my heels; terns dunged me white; spatted and musseled, beflied, befleaed, I might have been what now in the last light I saw me to be holding, a marine old man, same's I'd seized only dimmer.

" ' " "You've got me, son of Atreus,' he said, unless I said it myself."

"(" (" ("Me too."))')

" ' " 'And I'll keep you,' I said, 'till I have what I want.' He asked me what that was," as did Helen,' and Telemachus. ' " 'You know without my telling you,' " ' I told them. ' "Then he offered to tell all if I'd let him go, I to let him go when he'd told me all. 'Foolish mortal!' he said, they speak that way, 'What gives you to think you're Menelaus holding the Old Man of the Sea? Why shouldn't Proteus turn into Menelaus, and into Menelaus holding

Proteus? But let that go . . .' " ' " Never. " ' " 'We seers see fore and aft, but not amidships. I know what you've been and will be; how is it you're here? What god teaches men to godsnatch?'

" ' " 'It's not a short story,' I warned him." '

" 'I don't see why it needed telling,' Peisistratus declared. 'If a seer sees past and future he sees everything, the present being without duration et cetera. Or if his clairvoyance is relative, shading into darkness as it nears the Now from the bright far Heretofore and far clear Hereafter, even so there's nothing he needn't know.' 'Oh?' 'Today, say, he knows tomorrow and yesterday; then yesterday he knew today, as he'll know it tomorrow. Now to know the past is to know too what one once knew, to know the future to know what one will know. But in the case of seers, what one once knew includes the then future which is now the present; what one will know, the then past which ditto. From all which it follows as the future from the present, the present from the past, that from him from whom neither past nor future can hide, the present cannot either. It wasn't you who deceived Proteus, but Proteus you.' "

I tell it as it was. "Long time we sat in the dark and sleepful hall: hem-holding Menelaus, drowseless Nestor's-son, Telemachus perhaps. When windy Orion raised his leg over Lacedemon I put by groan and goblet saying, 'I tell it as it is. Long time I wondered who was the fooler, who fool, how much of what was news to whom; still pinning Helen to the pitchy poop I said, "When shifty Proteus vowed he had all time to listen in, from a leaden heart I cried: 'When will I reach my goal through its cloaks of story? How many veils to naked Helen?'

" ' " 'I know how it is,' said Proteus. 'Yet tell me what I wish; then I'll tell you what you will.' Nothing for it but rehearse the tale of me and slippery Eidothea:

V

" ' " 'Troy was clinkered; Priam's stones were still too warm to touch; the loot was depoted on the beach for share-out; Trojan ladies keened and huddled, eyed us with shivers, waiting to be boarded and rode down the tear-salt sea. We were ten years out; ten days more would see our plunder portioned, our dead sent up, good-trip hecatombs laid on the immortal gods. But I was mad with shame and passion for my salvaged wife; though curses Greek and Trojan showered on us like spears on Scamander-plain or the ash of heroes on our decks, I fetched her to my ship unstuck, stowed her below, made straight for home.

" " " ' "Hecatombs to Athena!" Odysseus cried after us.

" " " ' "Cushion your thwarts with Troy-girls!" Agamemnon called, dragging pale Cassandra—' "

" ' "Bitch! Bitch!"

" ' " '—by her long black hair. To forestall a mutiny I hollered back, they could keep half my loot for themselves if they'd ship the rest home for me to emprince my loyal crew with. As for me, all my concubines and treasure waited below, tapping her foot. Wise Nestor alone sailed with me, who as Supervisor of Spoils had loaded first; last thing I saw astern was shrewd Odysseus scratching his head, my brother crotch; then Troy sank in the purpled east; with a shake-plain shout, I'm good at those, I dived below to reclaim my wife.

" ' " 'Call it weakness if you dare: unlike the generality of men I take small joy in lording women. Helen's epic heat had charcoaled Troy and sent ten thousand down to Hades; I ought to've spitted her like a heifer on her Trojan hearth. But I hadn't, and the hour was gone to poll horns with the vengeful sword. I thought therefore to knock her about a bit and then take at last what had cost such a fearful price, perhaps vilifying her, within measure, the while. But when I beheld her—sitting cross-legged in the stern, cleaning long fingernails with a bodkin and pouting at the frames and strakes—I forebore, resolved to accept in lieu of her death a modest portion of heartfelt grovel. Further, once she'd flung herself at my knees and kissed my hem I would order her supine and mount more as one who loves than one who conquers; not impossibly, should she acquit herself well and often, I would even entertain a plea for her eventual forgiveness and restoration to the Atrean house. Accordingly I drew myself up to discharge her abjection—whereupon she gave over cleaning her nails and set to drumming them on one knee.

" ' " ' "Let your repentance salt my shoeleather," I said presently, "and then, as I lately sheathed my blade of anger, so sheathe you my blade of love."

" ' " ' "I only just came aboard," she replied. "I haven't unpacked yet."

" ' " 'With a roar I went up the companionway, dashed stern to stem, close-hauled the main, flogged the smile from my navigator, and clove us through the pastures of the squid. Leagues thereafter, when the moon changed phase, I overtook myself, determined shrewdly that her Troy-chests were secured, and vowing this time to grant the trull no quarter, at the second watch of night burst into her cubby and forgave her straight out. "Of the unspeakable we'll speak no further," I declared. "I here extend to you what no other in my position would: my outright pardon." To which, some moments after, I briskly appended: "Disrobe and receive it, for the sake of pity! This offer won't stand forever." There I had her; she yawned and responded: "It's late. I'm tired."

" ' " 'Up the mast half a dozen times I stormed and shinnied, took oar to my navigator, lost sight of Nestor, thundered and lightninged through Poseidon's finny fief. When next I came to season, I stood a night slyly by while she dusk-to-dawned it, then saluted with this challenge her opening eyes: "Man born of woman is imperfect. On the three thousand two hundred eighty-seventh night of your Parisian affair, as I lay in Simoismud picking vermin off the wound I'd got that day from cunning Pandarus, exhaustion closed my eyes. I dreamed myself was pretty Paris, plucked by Aphrodite from the field and dropped into Helen's naked lap. There we committed sweet adultery; I woke wet, wept . . ."

" ' " 'Here I paused in my fiction to shield my eyes and stanch the arrow-straight tracks clawed down my cheek. Then, as one who'd waited precisely for her maledict voice to hoarsen, I outshouted her in these terms: "Therefore come to bed my equal, uncursing, uncursed!"

" ' " 'The victory was mine, I still believe, but when I

made to take trophy, winded Helen shook her head, declaring: "I have the curse."

" ' " 'My taffrail oaths shook Triton's stamp-ground; I fed to the fish my navigator, knocked my head against the mast and others; hollered up a gale that blew us from Laconic Malea to Egypt. My crew grew restive; when the storm was spent and I had done flogging me with halyards, I chose a moment somewhere off snakèd Libya, slipped my cloak, rapped at Helen's cabin, and in measured tones declared: "Forgive me." Adding firmly: "Are you there?"

" ' " ' "Seasick," she admitted. "Throwing up." To my just query, why she repaid in so close-kneed coin my failure to butcher her in Troy, she answered—'

" ' " 'Let me guess,' requested Proteus."

" ' " "What I said in Troy," said offshore Helen. "What I say to you now." '

" 'Whatever was that?' pressed Peisistratus."

"Hold on, hold on yet awhile, Menelaus," I advise.

I'm not the man I used to be.

" ' " 'Thus inspired I went a-princing and a-pirate. Seven years the north wind nailed us to Africa, while Helen held fast the door of love. We sailed no plotted course, but supped random in the courts of kings, sacked and sightsaw, ballasted our tender keel with bullion. The crew chose wives from among themselves, give me a woman anytime, had affairs with ewes, committed crimes of passion over fids and tholes. None of us grew younger. The eighth year fetched us here to Pharos, rich seaquirks, mutinous, strange. How much does a man need? We commenced to starve. Yesterday I strolled up the beach to fish, my head full of north-wind; I squatted on a rushy dune, fetched out my knife, considered whether to slice my parchèd throat or ditto cod. Then before me in the surf, a sudden skinnydipper! Cock and gullet paused on edge; Beauty stepped from the seafoam; long time I regarded hairless limb, odd globy breast, uncalloused ham. Where was the fellow's sex? A fairer yeoman I'd not beheld; who'd untooled him? As as his king and skipper I decided to have at him before myself, it occurred to me he was a woman.

" ' " 'Memory, easy-weakened, dies hard. From its laxy clutch I fetched my bride's dim image. True, her hair was gold, the one before me's green, and this was finned where that was toed; but the equal number and like placement of their breasts, congruence of their shames' geometry—too miraculous for chance! She was Helen gone a-surfing, or Aphrodite in Helen's form. With a clench-tooth wrench I recollected what a man was for, vowed to take her without preamble or petition, then open my throat. Better, as I knew my wife no weakling, but accurate of foot and sharp of toe, I hit upon a ruse to have her without loss of face or testicle, and cursed me I hadn't dreamed it up years past: as Zeus is wont to take mortal women in semblance of their husbands, I would feign Zeus in Menelaus' guise! Up tunic, down I sprang, aflop with recommissioned maleship. "Is it Helen's spouse about to prince me," my victim inquired, "or some god in his fair-haired form? A lady wants to know her undoer. My own name," she went on, and I couldn't.

" ' " ' "Eidothea's the name," she went on: "daughter of Proteus, he whose salt hands hold the key to wind and wife. You won't reach your goals till you've mastered Dad. My role in your suspended tale is merely to offer seven pieces of advice. Don't ask why. Let go of my sleeve, please. Don't mistake the key for the treasure. But before I go on," she went on,' " ' " and I can't.

" ' " ' "But before I go on," she went on, "say first how it was at the last in Troy, what passed between you and Helen as the city fell. . . ." ' " ' "

"Come on. 'Come on. "Come on. 'Come on. "Come on," Eidothea urged: *"In the horse's woody bowel we groaned and grunt . . . Why do you weep?"* ' " ' "

VI

Respite.

" ' " ' "In the horse's bowel," ' " ' " I groan, " ' " ' "we grunt till midnight, Laocoön's spear still stuck in our gut . . ." ' " ' " "Hold up," said Helen; " 'Off,' said Proteus; "On," said his web-foot daughter.' " You see what my spot was, boys! Caught between blunt Beauty's, fishy Form's, and dark-mouth Truth's imperatives, arms trembling, knees raw from rugless poop and rugged cave, I tried to hold fast to layered sense by listening as it were to Helen hearing Proteus hearing Eidothea hearing me; critic within critic, nestled in my slipping grip . . .'

" 'May be,' Peisistratus suggested, 'you can trick the tale out against all odds by the following device: to Eidothea, let us say, you said: "Show me how to trap the old boy into prophecy!"; to Proteus, perhaps, for reasons of strategy, you declare: "I begged then your daughter as Odysseus Nausicaa: 'Teach me, lady, how best to honor windshift aid from your noble sire' "; to Helen-on-the-poop, perhaps, you tell it: "I then declared to Proteus: 'I then besought your daughter: "Help me to learn from your immortal dad how to replease my heartslove Helen." ' " But to us you may say with fearless truth: "I said to Eidothea: 'Show me how to fool your father!' " '

"But I asked myself," I remind me: " 'Who is Peisistratus to trust with unrefracted fact?' 'Did Odysseus really speak those words to Nausicaa?' I asked him. 'Why doesn't Telemachus snatch that news? And how is it you know of fair Nausicaa, when Proteus on the beach at Pharos hasn't mentioned her to me yet? Doesn't it occur to you, faced with this and similar discrepancy, that it's you I might be yarning?' as I yarn myself," whoever that is. " 'Menelaus! Proteus! Helen! For all we know, we're but stranded figures in Penelope's web, wove up in light to be unwove in darkness.' So snarling him, I caught the clew of my raveled fabrication:

" ' "What's going on?" Helen demanded.

" ' " 'Son of Atreus!' Proteus cried. 'Don't imagine I didn't hear what your wife will demand of you some weeks hence, when you will have returned from Egypt, made sail for home, and floored her with the tale of snatching yours truly on the beach! Don't misbehave yesterday, I warn you! We seers—'

" ' " " 'My next advice," Eidothea advised me, "is to take nonhuman form. Seal yourself tight." How is it, by the way,' I demanded of Proteus, 'You demand what you demand of me in Menelaus's voice, and through my mouth, as though I demanded it of myself?' For so it was from that moment on; I speeched his speeches, even as you hear me speak them now." "Never mind that!" ' 'Who was it said "Never mind!"?' asked Peisistratus. 'Your wife? Eidothea? Tricky Proteus? The voice is yours; whose are the words?' 'Never mind.' 'Could it be, could it have been, that Proteus changed from a leafy tree not into air but into Menelaus on the beach at Pharos, thence into Menelaus holding the Old Man of the Sea? Could it even be that all these speakers you give voice to—' " "Never mind," I say.

No matter. " " " " "Disenhorsed at last," I declared to scalèd Eidothea, "we found ourselves in the sleep-soaked heart of Troy. Each set about his appointed task, some murdering sentries, others opening gates, others yet killing Trojans in their cups and lighting torches from the beacon-fire to burn the city. But I made straight for Helen's apartment with Odysseus, who'd shrewdly reminded me of her liking for lamplit love." " ' " '

" 'How—'

" 'Did I know which room was hers? Because only two lights burned in Troy, one fired as a beacon on Achilles' tomb by Sinon the faithful traitor, the other flickering from an upper chamber in the house of Deiphobus. It was by ranging one above the other Agamemnon returned the fleet to Troy, but I steered me by the adulterous fire alone, kindling therefrom as I came the torch of vengeance.

" " " " "Why—"

" " " " "Did Odysseus come too? Thank Zeus he did! For so enraged was Deiphobus at being overhauled at passion's peak, he fought like ten." ' "

" " "Not only fought—" " " "But I matched him, I matched him," I pressed on, "all the while watching for my chance to sink sword in Helen, who rose up sheeted in her deadly beauty and cowered by the bedpost, dagger-handed. Long time we grappled—" '

" " " 'I'm concerned about my daughter's what- and where-abouts,' Proteus said—' '

" 'Could it be,' wondered Peisistratus, in whose name I pledged an ox to the critic muse, 'Eidothea is Proteus in disguise, prearranging his own capture on the beach for purposes unfathomable to mortals? And how did those lovers lay hands on arms in bed? What I mean—'

" ' "Dagger I had," said Helen, "under my pillow; and Deiphobus always came to bed with a sword on. But I never cowered; it was the sheet kept slipping, my only cover—"

" ' " ' " 'Take it off!' cried subtle Odysseus. Long time his strategy escaped me, I fought Deiphobus to a bloody draw. At length with a whisk my loyal friend himself half-staffed her. Our swords were up; for a moment we stood as if Medusa'd. Then, at the same instant, Deiphobus and I dived at our wife, Odysseus leaped up from where he knelt before her with the sheet, Helen's dagger came down, and the ghost of her latest lover squeaked off to join his likes." ' " ' "

" 'Her latest lover!' Peisistratus exclaimed. 'Do you mean to say—'

" ' "That's right," Helen said. "I killed him myself, a better man than most."

" ' " ' " 'Then Odysseus—" began Eidothea.

" ' " ' " 'Then Odysseus disappeared, and I was alone with topless Helen. My sword still stood to lop her as she bent over Deiphobus. When he was done dying she rose and with one hand (the other held her waisted sheet) cupped her breast for swording." ' " '

" ' "I dare you!" Helen dared.'

" 'Which Helen?' cried Peisistratus.

"I hesitated . . . 'The moment passed . . . " 'My wife smiled shyly . . . "My sword went down. I closed my eyes, not to see that fountain beauty; clutched at it, not to let her flee. 'You've lost weight, Menelaus,' she said. 'Prepare to die,' I advised her. She softly hung her head . . . " ' " '

" 'How could you tell, sir, if your eyes—'

" ' " ' " 'My next advice," said Eidothea,' " ' interrupting once again Peisistratus . . ."

Respite.

" ' " ' " 'I touched my blade to the goddess breast I grasped, and sailed before my flagging ire the navy of her offenses. Merely to've told prior to sticking her the names and skippers of the ships she'd sunk would've been to stretch her life into the menopause; therefore I spent no wind on items; simply I demanded before I killed her: 'With your last breath tell me: Why?' " ' " '

" '(") ("(("What?")")') (")"

" ' " ' " '*Why?*' I repeated," I repeated,' I repeated," I repeated,' I repeated," I repeat. " ' " ' "And the woman, with a bride-shy smile and hushèd voice, replied: 'Why what?'

" ' " ' "Faster than Athena sealed beneath missile Sicily upstart Enceladus, Poseidon Nisyros mutine Polybutes, I sealed my would-widen eyes; snugger than Porces Laocoön, Heracles Antaeus, I held to my point interrogative Helen, to whom as about us combusted nightlong Ilion I rehearsed our history horse to horse, driving at last as eveningly myself to the seed and omphalos of all. . . ."('((''((('))))))

" ' " ' "   " ' " ' ,
" ' " '   , " ' ,
" ' "   { Why? }   " ' ,
" '   ,
" ' " ' ".

VII

" ' " ' " 'By Zeus out of Leda,' I commenced, as though I weren't Menelaus, Helen Helen, 'egg-born Helen was a beauty desired by all men on earth. When Tyndareus declared she might wed whom she chose, every bachelor-prince in the peninsula camped on her stoop. Odysseus was there, mighty Ajax, Athenian Menestheus, cunning Diomedes: men great of arm, heart, wit, fame, purse; fit mates for the fairest. Menelaus alone paid the maid no court, though his brother Agamemnon, wed already to her fatal sister, sued for form's sake on his behalf. Less clever than Odysseus, fierce than Achilles, muscled than either Ajax, Menelaus excelled in no particular unless the doggedness with which he clung to the dream of embracing despite all Helen. He knew who others were—Odysseus resourceful, great Great Ajax, and the rest. Who was he? Whose eyes, at the wedding of Agamemnon and Clytemnestra, had laid hold of bridesmaid Helen's image and never since let go? While others wooed he brooded, played at princing, grappled idly with the truth that those within his imagination's grasp—which was to say, everyone but Menelaus—seemed to him finally imaginary, and he alone, ungraspable, real.

" " " " " 'Imagine what he felt, then, when news reached him one spring forenoon that of all the men in Greece, hatchèd Helen had chosen him! Despite the bright hour he was asleep, dreaming as always of that faultless form; his brother's messenger strode in, bestowed without a word the wreath of Helen's choice, withdrew. Menelaus held shut his eyes and clung to the dream—which however for the first time slipped his grip. Dismayed, he woke to find his brow now fraught with the crown of love.' " ' " '

" 'Ah.'

" " " " " 'In terror he applied to the messenger: "Menelaus? Menelaus? Why of all princes Menelaus?" And the fellow answered: "Don't ask me."

" " " " " 'Then imagine what he felt in Tyndareus's court, pledge-horse disjoint and ready to be sworn on, his beaten betters gruntling about, when he traded Agamemnon the same question for ditto answer. Sly Odysseus held the princes to their pledge; all stood on the membered horse while Menelaus played the grateful winner, modest in election, wondering as he thanked: Could he play the lover too? Who was it wondered? Who is it asks?

" " " " " 'Imagine then what he felt on the nuptial night, when feast and sacrifice were done, carousers gone, and he faced his bedaydreamed in the waking flesh! Dreamisher yet, she'd betrothed him wordless, wordless wed; now without a word she led him to her chamber, let go her gold gown, stood golder before him. Not to die of her beauty he shut his eyes; of not beholding her embraced her. Imagine what he felt then!' " ' " '

" 'Two questions,' interjected Peisistratus—

" 'One! One! " " " 'There the bedstead stood; as he swooning tipped her to it his throat croaked "Why?" ' "

" ' " " ' "Why?" asked Eidothea.'

" " " ' "Why why?' Proteus echoed." '

" 'My own questions,' Peisistratus insisted, 'had to do with mannered rhetoric and your shift of narrative viewpoint.'

" ' " 'Ignore that fool!' Proteus ordered from the beach." '

" 'How can Proteus—' 'Seer.' 'So.' 'The opinions echoed in these speeches aren't necessarily the speaker's.

" ' " ' " ' " ' " ' "Why'd you wed me?" Menelaus asked his wife,' I told my wife. ' "Less crafty than Diomedes, artful than Teucer, et cetera?" She placed on her left breast his right hand.

" ' " ' " ' " ' " "Why me?" he cried again. "Less lipless than Achilles, et cetera!" The way she put on her other his other would have fired a stone.

" ' " ' " ' " ' "Speak!" he commanded. She whispered: "Love."

" ' " ' " ' 'Unimaginable notion! He was fetched up short. How could Helen love a man less gooded than Philoctetes, et cetera, and whom besides she'd glimpsed but once prior to wedding and not spoken to till that hour? But she'd say no more; the harder he pressed the cooler she turned, who'd been ardor itself till he put his query. He therefore forebore, but curiosity undid him; how could he know her and not know how he knew?" " '

" ' " 'Come to the point!'

" ' " ' "Hold on!"

" ' " ' " 'He held her fast; she took him willy-nilly to her; I feel her yet, one endless instant, Menelaus was no more, never has been since. In his red ear then she whispered: "Why'd I wed you, less what than who, et cetera?" ' " ' " '

" ' "My very question."

" ' " ' " ' " ' "Speak!" Menelaus cried to Helen on the bridal bed,' I reminded Helen in her Trojan bedroom," I confessed to Eidothea on the beach,' I declared to Proteus in the cavemouth," I vouchsafed to Helen on the ship,' I told Peisistratus at least in my Spartan hall," I say to who-ever and where- I am. And Helen answered:

" ' " ' " ' "Love!" ' " ' " ' " ' "

!

" ' " ' " 'He complied, he complied, as to an order. She took his corse once more to Elysium, to fade forever among the fadeless asphodel; his curious fancy alone remained unlaid; when he came to himself it still asked softly: "Why?" ' " ' " ' "

And don't I cry out to me every hour since, "Be sure you demanded of Peisistratus (and Telemachus), 'Didn't I exclaim to salvaged Helen, "Believe me that I here queried Proteus, 'Won't you ask of Eidothea herself whether or not I shouted at her, "Sheathed were my eyes, unsheathed my sword what time I challenged Troy-lit Helen, 'Think you not that Menelaus and his bride as one cried, "*Love!*"?!"?!"?!"?!"?

" ' " ' " 'So the night went, and the days and nights: sex and riddles. She burned him up, he played husband till he wasted, only his voice still diddled: "Why?" ' "

" ' " ' "What a question!" ' ' '

" 'What's the answer?'

" ' " ' " "Seven years of this, more or less, not much conversation, something wrong with the marriage. Helen he could hold; how hold Menelaus? To love is easy; to be loved, as if one were real, on the order of others: fearsome mystery! Unbearable responsibility! To her, *Menelaus* signified something recognizable, as *Helen* him. Whatever was it? They begot a child . . .' " ' "

" ' "I beg your pardon," Helen interrupted from the poop a quarter-century later. "Father Zeus got Hermione on me, disguised as you. That's the way he is, as everyone knows; there's no use pouting or pretending . . ."

" 'I begged her pardon, but insisted, as in Troy: " ' " 'It wasn't Zeus disguised as Menelaus who begot her, any more than Menelaus disguised as Zeus; it was Menelaus disguised as Menelaus, a mask masking less and less. Husband, father, lord, and host he played, grip slipping; he could imagine anyone loved, no accounting for tastes, but his cipher self. In his cups he asked on the sly their house guests: "Why'd she wed me, less horsed than Diomedes, et cetera?" None said. A night came when this misdoubt stayed him from her bed. Another . . .' " ' " ' "

Respite. I beg your pardon.

" ' " ' " 'Presently she asked him: et cetera. If only she'd declared, "Menelaus, I wed you because, of all the gilt clowns of my acquaintance, I judged you least likely to distract me from my lovers, of whom I've maintained a continuous and overlapping series since before we met." Wouldn't that have cleared the Lacedemonian air! In a rage of shame he'd've burned up the bed with her! Or had she said: "I truly am fond of you, Menelaus; would've wed no other. What one seeks in the husband way is a good provider, gentle companion, fit father for one's children whoever their sire—a blend in brief of brother, daddy, pal. What one doesn't wish are the traits of one's lovers, exciting by night, impossible by day: I mean peremptory desire, unexpectedness, rough play, high-pitched emotions of every sort. Of these, happily, you're free." Wouldn't that have stoked and drafted him! But "Love!" What was a man to do?'

" '("((("((((" 'Well . . .' ")))')")")'

" ' " ' " 'He asked Prince Paris—' 'You didn't!' " "By Zeus!" ' 'By Zeus!' " "You didn't!" ' 'Did you really?' " "By Zeus," I tell me I told all except pointed Helen, "I did.

" ' " ' " 'By Zeus,' I told pointed Helen, 'he did. Oh, he knew the wretch was eyes and hands for Helen; he wasn't blind; eight days they'd feasted him since he'd dropped in uninvited, all which while he'd hot-eyed the hostess, drunk from her goblet, teased out winy missives on the table top. On the ninth she begged Menelaus to turn him from the palace. But he confessed,' I confessed," I confessed,' I confessed," et cetera, " ' " 'he liked the scoundrel after all . . .' " ' " '

" 'Zeus! Zeus!'

" ' " ' " 'Young, rich, handsome he was, King Priam's son; a charmer, easy in the world . . .' " ' "

" ' "Don't remind us!"

" ' " ' " "One night Helen went early to her chamber, second on one's left et cetera, and the two men drank alone. Menelaus watched Paris watch her go and abruptly put his question, how it was that one less this than that had been the other, and what might be the import of his wife's reply. "A proper mystery," Paris agreed; "you say the one thing she says is what?" Menelaus pointed to the word his nemesis, by Paris idly drawn at dinner in red Sardonic.

" ' " ' " ' "Consult an oracle," Paris advised. "There's a good one at Delphi." "I'm off to Crete," Menelaus told breakfast Helen. "Grandfather died. Catreus. Take care of things."

" ' " ' " ' "Love!" she pled, tearing wide her gown. Menelaus clapped shut his eyes and ears, ran for the north.' " ' " '

" 'North to Crete?' 'Delphi, Delphi, " ' " 'where he asked the oracle: "Why et cetera?" and was told: "*No other can as well espouse her.*"

" ' " ' " ' "How now!" Menelaus cried,' I ditto," et cetera. " ' "Espouse? Espouse her? As lover? Advocate? Husband? Can't you speak more plainly? Who am I?"

" ' " ' " ' "   " ' " ' " '

" ' " ' " 'Post-haste he returned to Lacedemon, done with questions. He'd re-embrace his terrifying chooser, clasp her past speech, never let go, frig understanding; it would be bride-night, endless; their tale would rebegin. "Menelaus here!" His shout shook the wifeless hall.

VII

" ' " ' " 'Odysseus outsmarted, unsmocked Achilles, mustered Agamemnon—all said: "Let her go." Said Menelaus: "Can't." What did he feel? Epic perplexity. That she'd left him for Paris wasn't the point. War not love. Ten years he played outraged spouse, clung ireful-limpetlike to Priam's west curtain, war-whooped the field of Ares. Never mind her promenading the bartizans arm in arm with her Troyish sport; no matter his seeing summerly her belly fill with love-tot. Curiosity was his passion, that too grew mild. When at last in the war's ninth year he faced Paris in single combat, it was purely for the sake of form. "I don't ask why she went with you," he paused to say. "But tell me, as I spear you: did Helen ever mention, while you clipped and tumbled, how she happened to choose me in the first place?" Paris grinned and whispered through his shivers: "Love." Aphrodite whisked him from the door of death;

no smarterly than that old word did smirking Pandarus pierce Menelaus's side. War resumed.

" " " " " 'Came dark-horse-night; Paris dead, it was with her new mate Deiphobus Helen sallied forth to mock. When she had done playing each Greek's Mrs., in her own voice she called: "Are you there, Menelaus? Then hear this: the night you left me I left you, sailed off with Paris and your wealth. At our first berthing I became his passion's harbor; to Aphrodite the Uniter we raised shrines. I was princess of desire, he prince; from Greece to Egypt, Egypt Troy, our love wore out the rowing-benches. By charms and potions I kept his passion nine years firm, made all Troy and its beleaguerers burn for me. Pederast Achilles pronged me in his dreams; before killed Paris cooled, hot Deiphobus climbed into his place: he who, roused by this wooden ruse, stone-horses your Helen even as she speaks. To whom did slick Odysseus not long since slip, and whisper all the while he wooed dirty Greek, welcome to my Troy-cloyed ear? Down, godlike Deiphobus! Ah!"

" " " " " 'Heart-burst, Menelaus had cracked with woe the Epeian barrel and his own, had not far-sight Odysseus caulked and coopered him, saying: "The whore played Clytemnestra's part and my Penelope's; now she plays Helen." So they sat in silence, murderous, until the gods who smile on Troy wearied of this game and rechambered the lovers. Then Odysseus unpalmed the mouth of Menelaus and declared: "She must die." Menelaus spat. "Stick her yourself," went on the Ithacan: "play the man."

" " " " " 'The death-horse dunged the town with Greeks; Menelaus ground his teeth, drew sword, changed point of view. Taking his wrongèd part, I invite one word before I cut your perfect throat. What did the lieless oracle intend? Why'd you you-know-what ditto-whom et cetera?'

VI

" " " " "Replied my wife in a huskish whisper: 'You know why.'

" " " " "I chucked my sword, she hooked her gown, I

fetched her shipward through the fire and curses, she crossed her legs, here I weep on the beach at Pharos, I wish I were dead, what'd you say your name was?"

V

" ' " 'Said Eidothea: "Eidothea." I hemmed, I hawed; "I'm not the man," I remarked, "I was." Shoulders shrugged. "I've advised disguise," she said. "If you find your false-face stinks, I advise ambrosia. My sixth advice is, not too much ambrosia; my seventh—" Frantic I recounted, lost track, where was I? "—ditto masks: when the hour's ripe, unhide yourself and jump." Her grabbèd dad, she declared, would turn first into animals, then into plants and wine-dark sea, then into no saying what. Let I go I'd be stuck forever; otherwise he'd return into Proteus and tell me what I craved to hear.

" ' " ' "Hang on," she said; "that's the main thing." I asked her wherefor her septuple aid; she only smiled, I hate that about women, paddled off. This noon, then, helped by her sealskins and deodorant, I jumped you. There you are. But you must have known all this already.'

IV

" ' "Said Proteus in my voice: 'Never mind know. Loose me now, man, and I'll say what stands between you and your desire.' He talks that way. I wouldn't; he declared I had one virtue only, the snap-turtle's, who will beak fast though his head be severed. By way of preface to his lesson then, he broke my heart with news reports: how Agamemnon, Idomeneus, Diomedes were cuckolded by pacifists and serving-men; how Clytemnestra not only horned but axed my brother; how faithless Penelope, hearing Odysseus had slept a year with Circe, seven with Calypso, dishonored him by giving herself to all one hundred eight of her suitors, plus nine house-servants, Phemius the bard, and Melanthius the goat-herd . . .' "

" 'What's this?' cried Peisistratus. 'Telemachus swears they've had no word since he sailed from Troy!' 'Prophets get their tenses mixed,' I replied; 'not impossibly it's now that Mrs. Odysseus goes the rounds, while her son's away. But I think he knows what a tangled web his mother weaves; otherwise he'd not sit silent, but call me and Proteus false or run for Ithaca.' There I had him, someone; on with the story. 'On with the story. " 'On with the story,' I said to Proteus: 'Why can't I get off this beach, let go, go home again? I'm tired of holding Zeus knows what; the mussels on my legs are barnacled; my arms and mind have gone to sleep; our beards have grown together; your words, fishy as your breath, come from my mouth, in the voice of Menelaus. Why am I stuck with you? What is it makes all my winds north and chills my wife?'

" ' "Proteus answered: 'You ask too many questions. Not Athena, but Aphrodite is your besetter. Leave Helen with me here; go back to the mouth of River Egypt. There where the yeasting slime of green unspeakable jungle springs ferments the sea of your intoxicate Greek bards,' that's how the chap talks, 'make hecatombs to Aphrodite; beg Love's pardon for your want of faith. Helen chose you without reason because she loves you without cause; embrace her without question and watch your weather change. Let go.'

" ' "I tried; it wasn't easy; he swam and melted in the lesser Nile my tears. Then Eidothea surfaced just offshore, unless it was you . . ." Shipboard Helen. "Had he been Eidothea before? Had he turned Helen? Was I cuckold yet again, an old salt in my wound? Recollecting my hard homework I closed eyes, mouth, mind; set my teeth and Nileward course. It was a different river; on its crocodiled and dromedaried bank, to that goddess perversely polymorphous as her dam the sea or the shift Old Man Thereof, Menelaus sacrificed twin heifers, Curiosity, Common Sense. I no longer ask why you choose me, less tusked than Idomeneus, et cetera; should you declare it was love for me fetched you to Paris and broke the world, I'd raise neither eyebrow; 'Yes, well, so,' is what I'd say. I don't ask what's changed the wind, your opinion, me, why I hang here like, onto, and by my narrative. Gudgeon my pintle, step my mast, vessel me where you will. I believe all. I understand nothing. I love you."

III

" 'Snarled thwarted Helen: "Love!" Then added through our chorus groan: "Loving may waste us into Echoes, but it's being loved that kills. Endymion! Semele! Io! Adonis! Hyacinthus! Loving steers marine Odysseus; being loved turned poor Callisto into navigation-stars. Do you love me to punish me for loving you?"

" ' "I haven't heard so deep Greek since Delphi," I marveled. "But do I ask questions?"

" ' "I'll put this love of yours truly to the test," Helen said. Gently she revived me with cold water and pungents from her Nilish store. "I suppose you suppose," she declared then, "that I've been in Troy."

" 'So potent her medicaments, in no time at all I regained my breath and confessed I did.

" 'Severely she nodded. "And you suspect I've been unfaithful?"

" ' "It would be less than honest of me to say," I said, "that no fancy of that dirt-foot sort has ever grimed my imagination's marmor sill."

" ' "With Paris? And others as well?"

" ' "You wrest truth from me as Odysseus Astyanax Andromache."

" ' "In a word, you think yourself cuckold."

" 'I blushed. "To rush untowardly to conclusions ill becomes a man made wise by hard experience and time. Nevertheless, I grant that as I shivered in a Trojan ditch one autumn evening in the war's late years and watched you stroll with Paris on the bastions, a swart-hair infant at each breast and your belly swaggèd with another, the term you mention flit once across the ramparts of my mind like a bat through Ilion-dusk. Not impossibly the clever wound I'd got from Pandarus festered my judgment with my side . . ."

" 'Helen kissed my bilging tears and declared: "Husband, I have never been in Troy.

"What's more," she added within the hour, before the boatswain could remobilize the crew, "I've never made love with any man but you."

" ' "Ah."

" 'She turned her pout lips portward. "You doubt me."

" ' "Too many years of unwomaned nights and combat days," I explained, "gestate in our tenderer intelligences a skeptic demon, that will drag dead Hector by the baldric till his corpse-track moat the walls, and yet whisper when his bones are ransomed: 'Hector lives.' Were one to say of Menelaus at this present hour, 'That imp nips him,' one would strike Truth's shield not very far off-boss."

" 'Doubt no more," said Helen. "Your wife was never in Troy. Out of love for you I left you when you left, but before Paris could up-end me, Hermes whisked me on Father's orders to Egyptian Proteus and made a Helen out of clouds to take my place.

" ' "All these years I've languished in Pharos, chaste and comfy, waiting for you, while Paris, nothing wiser, fetched Cloud-Helen off to Troy, made her his mistress, got on her Bunomus, Aganus, Idaeus, and a little Helen, dearest of the four. It wasn't I, but cold Cloud-Helen you fetched from Troy, whom Proteus dissolved the noon you beached him. When you then went off to account to Aphrodite, I slipped aboard. Here I am. I love you."

"Not a quarter-hour later she asked of suspended me: "Don't you believe me?"

" ' "What ground have I for doubt?" I whispered. "But that imp aforementioned gives me no peace. 'How do you know,' he whispers with me, 'that the Helen you now hang onto isn't the cloud-one? Why mayn't your actual spouse be back in Troy, or fooling in naughty Egypt yet?' "

" ' "Or home in Lacedemon," Helen added, "where she'd been all along, waiting for her husband."

" 'Presently my battle voice made clear from stem to stern my grown conviction that the entire holocaust at Troy, with its prior and subsequent fiascos, was but a dream of Zeus's conjure, visited upon me to lead me to Pharos and the recollection of my wife—or her nimbus like. For for all I knew I roared what I now gripped was but a further fiction, maybe Proteus himself, turned for sea-cow-respite to cuckold generals . . .

" ' "A likely story," Helen said. "Next thing, you'll say it was a cloud-Menelaus went fishing on the beach at Pharos! If I carry to my grave no heart-worm grudge at your decade vagrance, it's only that it irks me less just now than your present doubt. And that I happen to be not mortal. Yet so far from giving cut for cut, I'm obliged by Love and the one right action of your life to ease your mind entirely." Here she led me by the hand into her golden-Aphrodite's grove, declaring: "If what's within your grasp is mere cloudy fiction, cast it to the wind; if fact then Helen's real, and really loves you. Espouse me without more carp! The senseless answer to our riddle woo, mad history's secret, base-fact and footer to the fiction crazy-house our life: imp-slayer love, terrific as the sun! Love! Love!"

" 'Who was I? Am? Mere Menelaus, if that: mote in the cauldron, splinter in the Troy-fire of her love! Does nail hold timber or timber nail? Held fast by his fast-held, consumed by what he feasted on, whatever was of Menelaus was no more. I must've done something right.

" ' " 'You'll not die in horsy Argos, son of Atreus . . .' " So quoted Proteus's last words to me my love-spiked wife. " 'The Olympic gods will west you in your latter days to a sweet estate where rain nor passion leaches, there to be your wife's undying advertisement, her espouser in the gods' slow time. Not fair-haired battleshouts or people-leadering preserves you, but forasmuch as and only that you are beloved of Helen, they count you immortal as themselves.' "

" 'Lampreys and flat-fish wept for joy, squids danced on

the wave-tops, crab-choirs and minnow-anthems shook
with delight the opalescent welkin. As a sea-logged voyager
strives across the storm-shocked country of the sole, loses
ship and shipmates, poops to ground on alien shingle, gives
over struggling, and is whisked in a dream-dark boat, sleep-
skippered, to his shoaly home, there to wake next morning
with a wotless groan, wondering where he is and what
fresh lie must save him, until he recognizes with a heart-
surge whither he's come and hugs the home-coast to sweet
oblivion. So Menelaus, my best guess, flayed by love,
steeved himself snug in Helen's hold, was by her hatched
and transport, found as it were himself in no time Lacede-
moned, where he clings still stunned. She returned him to
bride-bed; had he ever been in Troy? Whence the brine he
scents in her ambrosial cave? Is it bedpost he clutches, or
spruce horse rib? He continues to hold on, but can no
longer take the world seriously. Place and time, doer,
done-to have lost their sense. Am I stoppered in the equine
bowel, asleep and dreaming? At the Nile-fount, begging
Love for mercy? Is it Telemachus I hold, cold-hearth Peisistratus? No, no, I'm on the beach at Pharos, must be
forever. I'd thought my cave-work finished, episode; re-
entering Helen I understood that all subsequent history is
Proteus, making shift to slip me . . .'

" 'Beg pardon.'

" 'Telemachus? Come back?'

" 'To.'

" 'Thought I hadn't noticed, did you, how your fancy
strayed while I told of good-voyaging your father and the
rest? Don't I know Helen did the wine-trick? Are you the
first in forty years, d'you think, I ever thought I'd yarned
till dawn when in fact you'd slipped me?'

II

"Fagged Odysseus'-son responded: 'Your tale has held us
fast through a dark night, Menelaus, and will bring joy to
suitored Ithaca. Time to go. Wake up, Peisistratus. Our regards to Hermione, thanks to her magic mother.'

" 'Mine,' I replied, 'to chastest yours, muse and mistress

of the embroidrous art, to whom I commission you to retail
my round-trip story. Like yourself, let's say, she'll find it
short nor simple, though one dawn enlightens its dénouement. Her own, I'd guess, has similar abound of woof—
yet before your father's both will pale, what marvels and
rich mischances will have fetched him so late home! Beside
that night's fabrication this will stand as Lesser to Great
Ajax.'

"So saying I gifted them off to Nestored Pylos and the
pig-fraught headlands dear to Odysseus, myself returning
to my unfooled narrate seat. There I found risen Helen,
sleep-gowned, replete, mulling twin cups at the new-coaxed
coals. I kissed her ear; she murmured 'Don't.' I stooped to
embrace her; 'Look out for the wine.' I pressed her, on, to
home. 'Let go, love.' I would not, ever, said so; she sighed
and smiled, women, I was taken in, it's a gift, a gift-horse,
I shut my eyes, here we go again, 'Hold fast to yourself,
Menelaus.' Everything," I declare, "is now as day."

I

It was himself grasped undeceivèd Menelaus, solely, imperfectly. No man goes to the same Nile twice. When I understood that Proteus somewhere on the beach became Menelaus holding the Old Man of the Sea, Menelaus ceased.
Then I understood further how Proteus thus also was as
such no more, being as possibly Menelaus's attempt to hold
him, the tale of that vain attempt, the voice that tells it.
Ajax is dead, Agamemnon, all my friends, but I can't die,
worse luck; Menelaus's carcass is long wormed, yet his
voice yarns on through everything, to itself. Not my voice,
I am this voice, no more, the rest has changed, rechanged,
gone. The voice too, even that changes, becomes hoarser,
loses its magnetism, grows scratchy, incoherent, blank.

I'm not dismayed. Menelaus was lost on the beach at
Pharos; he is no longer, and may be in no poor case as
teller of his gripping history. For when the voice goes he'll
turn tale, story of his life, to which he clings yet, whenever,

how-, by whom-recounted. Then when as must at last every tale, all tellers, all told, Menelaus's story itself in ten or ten thousand years expires, yet I'll survive it, I, in Proteus's terrifying last disguise, Beauty's spouse's odd Elysium: the absurd, unending possibility of love.

ANONYMIAD

HEADPIECE

When Dawn rose, pink as peerless Helen's teat,

which in fact swung wineskinlike between her hind legs and was piebald as her pelt, on which I write,

> *The salty minstrel oped his tear-brined eye,*
> *And remarking it was yet another day . . .*

Ended his life. Commenced his masterpiece. Returned to sleep.

Invoked the muse:

> *Twice-handled goddess! Sing through me the boy*
> *Whom Agamemnon didn't take to Troy,*
> *But ~~left~~ behind to see his wife stayed chaste.*
> *Tell, Muse, how Clytemnestra maced*
> *Her warden into song, made vain his heart*
> *With vision of renown; musick the art*
> *Wherewith was worked self-ruin by a youth*
> *Who'd sought in his own art some music truth*
> *About the world and life, of which he knew*
> *Nothing. Tell how ardent his wish grew*
> *To autograph the future, wherefore he*
> *Let sly Aegisthus ship him off to see*
> *The Wide Real World. Sing of the guile*
> *That fetched yours truly to a nameless isle,*
> *By gods, men, and history forgot,*
> *To sing his sorry self.*

And die. And rot. And feed his silly carcass to the birds.

> *But not before he'd penned a few last words,*

inspired by the dregs and lees of the muse herself, at whom, Zeus willing, he'll have a final go before he corks her for good and casts her adrift, vessel of his hopeless hope. The Minstrel's Last Lay.

> Once upon a time
> I composed in witty rhyme
> And poured libations to the muse Erato.
>
> Merope would croon,
> "Minstrel mine, a lay! A tune!"
> "From bed to verse," I'd answer; "that's my motto."
>
> Stranded by my foes,
> Nowadays I write in prose,
> Forsaking measure, rhyme, and honeyed diction;
>
> Amphora's my muse:
> When I finish off the booze,
> I hump the jug and fill her up with fiction.

I begin in the middle—where too I'll end, there being alas to my arrested history as yet no dénouement. God knows how long I'd been out of writing material until this morning, not to mention how long altogether I've been marooned upon this Zeus-forsaken rock, in the middle of nowhere. There, I've begun, in the middle of nowhere, tricked ashore in manhood's forenoon with nine amphorae of Mycenaean red and abandoned to my own devisings. After half a dozen years of which more later I was down to the last of them, having put her sisters to the triple use aforesung: one by one I broke their seals, drank the lovelies dry, and, fired by their beneficence, not only made each the temporary mistress of my sole passion but gave back in the form of art what I'd had from them. Me they nourished and inspired; them I fulfilled to the top of my bent, and launched them worldward fraught with our joint conceits. Their names are to me now like the memory of old songs: Euterpe! Polyhymnia! I recall Terpsichore's lovely neck, Urania's matchless shoulders; in dreams I hear Melpomene singing yet in the wet west wind, her voice ever deeper as our romance waned; I touch again Erato's ears, too delicate for mortal clay, surely the work of Aphrodite! I smile at Clio's gravity, who could hold more wine than any of her sisters without growing tipsy; I shake my head still at the unexpected passion of saucy Thalia, how she clung to me even when broken by love's hard knocks. Fair creatures. Often I wonder where the tides of life have fetched them, whether they're undone by age and the world or put on the shelf by some heartless new master. What lovers slake themselves now at those fragile mouths? Do they still bear my charge in them, or is it jettisoned and lost, or brought to light?

With anticipation of Calliope, the last, I consoled me for their casting off. Painful state for a lover, to have always before him the object of his yen—naked, cool, serene—and deny his parchèd sense any slake but the lovely sight of her! No less a regimen I imposed upon myself—imperfectly, imperfectly, I'm not made of stone, and there she stood, brimful of spirit, heavy with what I craved, sweating delicately where the sun caressed her flank, and like her sisters infinitely accessible! A night came, I confess it, when need overmastered me; I broke my vow and her seal; other nights followed (never many in a season, but blessed Zeus, most blest Apollo, how many empty seasons have gone by!) when, despite all new resolve and cursing my weakwilledness even as I tipped her to my will, I eased my burden with small increase of hers. But take her to me altogether I did not, or possess myself of the bounty I thirsted for, and which freely she would yield. Until last night! Until the present morn! For in that measureless drear interval, now to be exposed, I had nothing to write upon, no material wherewith to fashion the work I'd vowed she must inspire me to, and with which, in the last act of our loveship and my life, I'd freight her.

Calliope, come, refresh me; it's the hour for exposition!

I'll bare at last my nameless tale, and then . . .
Hie here, sweet Muse: your poet must dip his pen!

I

Ink of the squid, his obscure cloak; blood of my heart; wine of my inspiration: record on Helen's hide, in these my symbols, the ills her namesake wrought what time, forsaking the couch of fairhaired Menelaus, she spread her legs for Paris et cetera.

My trouble was, back home in 'prentice days, I never could come out straight-faced with "Daughter of Zeus, eggborn Clytemnestra" and the rest, or in general take seriously enough the pretensions of reality. Youngster though I was, nowise sophisticated, I couldn't manage the correct long face when Agamemnon hectored us on Debts of Honor, Responsibility to Our Allies, and the like. But I don't fool myself: if I never took seriously the world and its tiresome concerns, it's because I was never able to take myself seriously; and the reason for that, I've known for some while, is the fearsomeness of the facts of life. Merope's love, Helen's whoring, Menelaus's noise, Agamemnon's slicing up his daughter for the weatherman—all the large and deadly passions of men and women, wolves, frogs, nightingales; all this business of seizing life, grabbing hold with both hands—it must've scared the daylights out of me from the first. While other fellows played with their spears, I learned to play the lyre. I wasn't the worst-looking man in Argolis; I had a ready wit and a good ear, and knew how to amuse the ladies. A little more of those virtues (and a lot more nerve, and better luck in the noblebirth way), I might have been another Paris; it's not your swaggerers like Menelaus the pretty girls fall for, or even your bully-boys like Agamemnon: it's the tricky chaps like Paris, graceful as women themselves almost, with their mischief eyes and honey tongues and nimble fingers, that set maiden hearts a-flutter and spit maidenheads like squablings. Aphrodite takes care of her own. Let that one have his Helen; this musicked to him in his eighteenth year milkmaid Merope, fairest-formed and straightest-hearted that ever mused goatherd into minstrelsy.

Daily then I pastured with that audience, two-score nans and my doe-eye nymph, to whom I sang songs perforce original, as I was ignorant of the common store. Innocent, I sang of innocence, thinking I sang of love and fame. Merope put down her jug, swept back her hair, smiled and listened. In modes of my own invention, as I supposed, I sang my vow to make a name for myself in the world at large.

"Many must wish the same," my honeyhead would murmur. But could she've shown me that every browsy hill in Greece had its dappled nans and famestruck twanger, I'd've not been daunted. My dreams, like my darling, perched light but square on a three-leg seat: first, while I scoffed at them myself, and at the rube their dreamer, I sucked them for life; the world was wide, as my songs attested, its cities flocked with brilliant; I was a nameless rustic plucker, unschooled, unmannered, late finding voice, innocent of fashion, uneasy in the world and my own skin—so much so, my crazy hope of shedding it was all sustained me. Fair as the country was and the goatboy life my fellows' lot, if I could not've imagined my music's one day whisking me Orionlike to the stars, I'd have as well flung myself into the sea. No other fate would even faintly do; an impassioned lack of alternatives moved my tongue; what for another might be heartfelt wish was for me an absolute condition. Second, untutored as I was and narrow my acquaintance, I knew none whose fancy so afflicted him as mine me. Especially when I goated it alone, the world's things took a queer sly aspect: it was as if the olive hillside hummed, not with bees, but with some rustle secret; the placid goats were in on it; asphodels winked and nodded behind my back; the mountain took broody note; the very sunlight trembled; I was a stranger to my hands and feet. Merope herself, when these humors gripped me, was alien and horrific as a sphinx: her perfect body, its pulse and breath, smote me with dismay: ears! toes! What creature did it wrap, that was not I, that claimed to love me? My own corse was a rude anthropophage that had swallowed me whole at birth and suffered indigestion ever since; could Merope see what I couldn't, who it was spoke from his gripèd bowels? When she and I, the goats our original, invented love—romped friggly in the glens and found half a hundred pretty pathways to delight, each which we thought ourselves the first to tread—some I as foreign to the me that pleasured as goatherd to goats stood by, tight-lipped, watching, or aswoon at the entire strangeness of the world.

And yet, third prop of revery, there *was* Merope, realer than myself though twice my dreams: the ardent fact of her, undeniable as incredible, argued when all else failed that the gods had marked me for no common fate. That a spirit so fresh and unaffected, take my word, no space for details, in a form fit to warm the couch of kings, should elect to give not only ear but heart and dainty everything to a lad the contrary of solipsistic, who felt the world and all its contents real except himself. . . . Perched astride me in a wild-rosemary-patch, her gold skin sweating gently from our sport, her gold hair tenting us, Merope'd say: "I love you"; and while one of me inferred: "Therefore I am," and another wondered whether she was nymph doing penance for rebuffing Zeus or just maid with unaccountable defect of good sense, a third exulted: "Then nothing is impossible!" and set out to scale Parnassus blithely as he'd peaked the mount of Love.

Had I known what cloak of climbers mantles that former hill, so many seasoneder and cleverer than I, some schooled for the ascent from earliest childhood, versed in the mountain's every crag and col, rehearsed in the lore of former climbers. . . . But I didn't, except in that corner of my fancy that imaged all possible discouragements and heeded none. As a farm boy, innocent of the city's size, confidently expects on his first visit there to cross paths with the one inhabitant he knows among its scores of thousands, and against all reason does, so when at market-time I took goats to golden Mycenae to be sold at auction, I wasn't daunted as I should've been by the pros who minstrelled every wineshop, but leaned me on the Lion's Gate, took up my lyre, and sang a sprightly goat-song, fully expecting that the Queen herself would hear and call for me.

The song, more or less improvised, had to do with a young man who announces himself, in the first verse, to be a hickly swain new-come from the bosky outback: he sings what a splendid fellow he is, fit consort for a queen. In the second verse he's accosted by an older woman who declares that while she doubtless appears a whore, she is in fact the Queen disguised; she takes the delighted singer to a crib in the common stews, which she asserts to be a wing of the palace reconstructed, at her order, to resemble a brothel: the trulls and trollops thereabout, she explains, are gentlewomen at their sport, the pimps and navvies their disguisèd noble lovers. Did the masquerade strike our minstrel as excessive? He was to bear in mind that the whims of royalty are like the gods', mighty in implementation and consequence. Her pleasure, she discloses in the third verse, is that he should lie with her as with a woman of the streets, the newest fashion among great ladies: she's chosen him for her first adventure of this sort because, while obviously not of noble birth, he's of somewhat gentler aspect than the lot of commoners; to make the pretense real, he's to pay her a handsome love-price, which she stipulates. The fellow laughs and agrees, but respectfully points out that her excessive fee betrays her innocence of prostitution; if verisimilitude is her object, she must accept the much lower wage he names. Not without expressions of chagrin the lady acquiesces, demanding only the right to earn a bonus for meritorious performance. In the fifth and sixth verses they set to, in manner described in salacious but musically admirable cadenzas; in the seventh the woman calls for fee and bonus, but her minstrel lover politely declines: to her angry protests he replies, in the eighth verse, that despite herself she makes love like a queen; her excellency shows through the cleverest disguise. How does he know? Because, he asserts, he's not the rustic he has feigned, but an exile prince in flight from the wrath of a neighbor king, whose queen had been his mistress until their amour came to light. Begging the amazed and skeptic lady not to betray him to the local nobility so well masked, he pledges in return to boast to no one that he has lain with Her Majesty. As I fetched him from the stews wondering mellifluously whether his partner was a queen disguised as a prostitute or a prostitute disguised as a queen disguised et cetera, I was seized by two armored guards and fetched myself to a room above a nearby wineshop. The premises were squalid; the room was opulent; beside a window overlooking the Lion's Gate sat a regal dame ensconced in handmaids.

What about the minstrel, she wanted to know: Was he a prince in mufti or a slickering rustic? Through my tremble I saw bright eyes in her sharp-bone countenance. I struck a chord to steady my hand, wrung rhymes from alarmèd memory, took a breath, and sang in answer:

> "As Tyrian robe may cloak a bumpkin heart,
> So homespun hick may play the royal part.
> Men may be kings in spirit or in mien.
> Which make more kingly lovers? Ask a queen!

But don't ask me which sort of queen to ask," I added quickly; "I haven't been in town long enough to learn the difference."

The maids clapped hands to mouths; the lady's eyes flashed, whether with anger or acknowledgment I couldn't judge. "See he goes to school on the matter," she ordered a plumpish gentleman across the room, eunuch by the look of him. Then she dismissed us, suddenly fretsome, and turned to the window, as one waiting for another to appear.

On with the story, cut corners: Clytemnestra herself it was, wont to rest from her market pleasures in that apartment. Her eunuch—Chief Minstrel, it turned out—gave me a gold piece and bade me report to him in Agamemnon's scullery when I came to town, against the chance the whim should take Her Majesty to hear me again. Despite the goldhair wonder that rested on my chest as I reported this adventure next day, I was astonished after all that dreams come true.

"The King and Queen are real!" I marveled. "They want *me* to minstrel them!"

Fingering my forearm Merope said: "Because you're the best." I must go to town often, we agreed, perhaps even live there; on the other hand, it would be an error to put by my rustic origins and speech, as some did: in song, at least (where dwelt the only kings and courtiers we knew), such pretense always came a cropper. Though fame and clever company no doubt would change me in some ways, I should not change myself for them, it being on the one hand Merope's opinion that worldliness too ardently pursued becomes affectation, mine on the other that innocence artificially preserved becomes mere crankhood.

"We'll come back here often," I told her, "to remind us who we are."

She stroked my fingers, in those days scarcely calloused by the lyre. "Was the Queen very beautiful?"

I promised to notice next time. Soon after, we bid the goats goodbye and moved to Mycenae. Merope was frightened by the din of so many folk and wagons and appalled by everyone's bad manners, until I explained that these were part of the excitement of city life. Every day, all day, in our mean little flat, I practiced my art, which before I'd turned to only when the mood was on me; eveningly I reported to the royal kitchen, where lingered a dozen other mountebanks and minstrels just in favor. Ill at ease in their company, I kept my own, but listened amazed to their cynic jokes about the folk they flattered in their lays, and watched with dismay the casual virtuosity with which they performed for one another's amusement while waiting the royal pleasure. I hadn't half their skill and wit! Yet the songs I made from my rural means—of country mouse and city mouse, or the war between the ants and the mice— were well enough received; especially when I'd got the knack of subtly mocking in such conceits certain figures in the court—those who, like the King, were deaf to irony— I'd see Clytemnestra's eyes flash over her wine, as if to say, "Make asses of *them* all you please, but don't think you're fooling me!" and a coin or two would find their way meward. Flattering it was, for a nameless country lad, to hear the Queen herself praise his songs and predict a future for him in the minstrel way. When I got home, often not till sunup, I'd tell my sleepish darling all I'd seen and done, and there'd be love if the day hadn't spent me, which alas it sometimes had. That first gold piece I fetched to a smith and caused to be forged into a ring, gift to the gods' gift to me; but I misguessed the size, and fearing she'd lose it, Merope bade me wear it in her stead.

I½

Once upon a time I told tales straight out, alternating summary and dramatization, developing characters and relationships, laying on bright detail and rhetorical flourish, et cetera. I'm not that amateur at the Lion's Gate; I know my trade. But I fear we're too far gone now for such luxury, Helen and I; I must get to where I am; the real drama, for yours truly, is whether he can trick this tale out at all—not the breath-batingest plot in the world, but there we are. It's an old story anyhow, this part of it; the corpus bloats with its like; I'll throw you the bones, to flesh out or pick at as you will.

What I had in mind was an *Anonymiad* in nine parts, reflecting (so you were to've nudged your neighbor and observed) the nine amphorae and ditto muses; or seven parts plus head- and tailpiece: the years of my maroonment framed by its causes and prognosis. The prologue was to've established, hopefully has done, the ground-conceit and the narrative voice and viewpoint: a minstrel stuck on some Aegean clinker commences his story, in the process characterizing himself and hinting at the circumstances leading to his plight. Parts One through Four were to rehearse those circumstances, Five through Seven the stages of his island life vis-à-vis his minstrelling—innocent garrulity, numb silence, and terse self-knowledge, respectively —and fetch the narrative's present time up to the narrator's. The epilogue's a sort of envoi to whatever eyes, against all odds, may one day read it. But though you're to go through the several parts in order, they haven't been set down that way: after writing the headpiece I began to fear that despite my planning I mightn't have space enough to get the tale told; since it pivots about Part Four (the headpiece and three parts before, three parts and the tailpiece after), I divided Helen's hide in half to insure the right narrative proportions; then, instead of proceeding with the exposition heralded at the tail of the headpiece, I took my cue from a remark I'd made earlier on, began in the middle, and wrote out Parts Five, Six, and Seven. Stopping at the head of the tailpiece, which I'm leaving blank for my last words, I returned to compose Parts One, Two, and Three, and the pivotal Part Four. But alas, there's more to my matter and less to my means than I'd supposed; for a while at least I'll have to tell instead of showing; if you must have dialogue and dashing about, better go to the theater.

So, so: the rest of Part One would've shown the minstrel, under the eunuch's tutelage, becoming more and more a professional artist until he's Clytemnestra's pet entertainer. A typical paragraph runs: *We got on, the Queen and I, especially when the Paris-thing blew up and Agamemnon started conscripting his sister-in-law's old boy-friends. Clytemnestra wasn't impressed by all the spear-rattling and the blather of National Honor, any more than I, and couldn't've cared less what happened to Helen. She'd been ugly duckling in the house of Tyndareus, Clytie, sec-ond prize in the house of Atreus; she knew Agamemnon envied his brother, and that plenty of Trojan slave-girls would see more of the Family Jewels, while he was aveng-ing the family honor, than she'd seen in some while. Though she'd got a bit hard-boiled by life in Mycenae, she was still a Grade-A figure of a woman; it's a wonder she didn't put horns on him long before the war. . . .*

In addition to their expository function, this and like passages establish the minstrel's growing familiarity and preoccupation with affairs of court. His corresponding professional sophistication, at expense of his former naive energy, was to be rendered as a dramatical correlative to the attrition of his potency with Merope (foreshadowed by the earlier ring-business and the Chief Minstrel's eunuch-hood), or vice versa. While still proud of her lover's suc-cess, Merope declares in an affecting speech that she pre-ferred the simple life of the goat pasture and the ditto songs he sang there, which now seem merely to embarrass him. The minstrel himself wonders whether the changes in his life and work are for the better: the fact is—as he makes clear on the occasion of their revisiting the herd—that hav-ing left the country but never, despite his success, quite joined the court, he feels out of place now in both. For-merly he sang of bills and nans as Daphnises and Chloes; latterly he sings of courtly lovers as bucks and does. His songs, he fears, are growing in some instances merely tricksy, in others crankish and obscure; moreover, the difficulties of his position in Mycenae have increased with his reputation: Agamemnon presses on the one hand for anti-Trojan songs in the national interest, Clytemnestra on the other for anti-Iliads to feed her resentment. Thus far he's contrived a precarious integrity by satirizing his own dilemma, for example—but arthritis is retiring the old eunuch, and our narrator has permitted himself to imagine that he's among the candidates for the Chief-Minstrelship, despite his youth: should he be so laureled, the problem of quid pro quo might become acute. All these considerations notwithstanding (he concludes), one can't pretend to an innocence outgrown or in other wise retrace one's steps, unless by coming full circle. Merope doesn't reply; the minstrel attempts to entertain her with a new composition, but neither she nor the goats (who'd used to gather when he sang) seem much taken by it. The rest of the visit goes badly.

II

Part Two opens back in Mycenae, where all is a-bustle with war preparations. The minstrel, in a brilliant trope which he predicts will be as much pirated by later bards as his device of beginning in the middle, compares the scene to a beehive; he then apostrophizes on the war itself:

The war, the war! To be cynical of its warrant was one thing—bloody madness it was, whether Helen or Hellespont was the prize—and my own patriotism was nothing bellicose: dear and deep as I love Argolis, Troy's a fine place too, I don't doubt, and the Trojan women as singable as ours. To Hades with wars and warriors: I had no illusions about the expedition.

Yet I wanted to go along! Your dauber, maybe, or your marble-cracker, can hole up like a sybil in a cave, just him and the muse, and get a lifeswork done; even Erato's boys, if they're content to sing twelve-liners all their days about Porphyria's eyebrow and Althea's navel, can forget the world outside their bedchambers. But your minstrel who aspires to make and people worlds of his own had better get to know the one he's in, whether he cares for it or not. I believe I understood from the beginning that a certain kind of epic was my fate: that the years I was to spend, in Mycenae and here [i.e., here, this island, where we are now], turning out clever lyrics, satires, and the like, were as it were apprenticeships in love, flirtation-trials to fit me for master-husbandhood and the siring upon broad-hipped

Calliope, like Zeus upon Alcmena, of a very Heracles of fictions. "First fact of our generation," *Agamemnon called the war in his recruitment speeches; how should I, missing it, speak to future times as the voice of ours?*

He adds: *Later I was to accept that I wasn't of the generation of Agamemnon, Odysseus, and those other giant brawlers (in simple truth I was too young to sail with the fleet), nor yet of Telemachus and Orestes, their pale shadows. To speak for the age, I came to believe, was less achievement than to speak for the ageless; my membership in no particular generation I learned to treasure as a passport out of history, or exemption from the drafts of time. But I begged the King to take me with him, and was crestfallen when he refused. No use Clytemnestra's declaring (especially when the news came in from Aulis that they'd cut up Iphigenia) it was my clearsightedness her husband couldn't stick, my not having hymned the bloody values of his crowd; what distressed me as much as staying home from Troy was a thing I couldn't tell her of: Agamemnon's secret arrangement with me . . .* his reflections upon and acceptance of which end the episode—or *chapter,* as I call the divisions of my unversed fictions. Note that no mention is made of Merope in this excursus, which pointedly develops a theme (new to literature) first touched on in Part One: the minstrel's yen for a broader range of life-experience. His feeling is that having left innocence behind, he must pursue its opposite; though his conception of "experience" in this instance is in terms of travel and combat, the metaphor with which he figures his composing-plans is itself un-innocent in a different sense.

The truth is that he and his youthful sweetheart find themselves nightly more estranged. Merope is unhappy among the courtiers and musicians, who speak of nothing but Mycenaean intrigues and Lydian minors; the minstrel ditto among everyone else, now that his vocation has become a passion—though he too considers their palace friends mostly fops and bores, not by half so frank and amiable as the goats. The "arrangement" he refers to is concluded just before the King's departure for Aulis; Agamemnon calls for the youth and without preamble offers him the title of Acting Chief Minstrel, to be changed to

Chief Minstrel on the fleet's return. Astonished, the young man realizes, as after his good fortune at the Lion's Gate, how much his expectations have in fact been desperate dream:

"*I . . . I accept* [I have him cry gratefully, thus becoming the first author in the world to reproduce the stammers and hesitations of actual human speech. But the whole conception of a literature faithful to daily reality is among the innovations of this novel opus]*!*"—whereupon the King asks "one small favor in return." Even as the minstrel protests, in hexameters, that he'll turn his music to no end beyond itself, his heart breaks at the prospect of declining the title after all:

Whereto, like windfall wealth, he had at once got used.

Tut, Agamemnon replies: though he personally conceives it the duty of every artist not to stand aloof from the day's great issues, he's too busy coping with them to care, and has no ear for music anyhow. All he wants in exchange for the proffered title is that the minstrel keep a privy eye on Clytemnestra's activities, particularly in the sex and treason way, and report any infidelities on his return.

Unlikeliest commission [the minstrel exclaims to you at this point, leaving ambiguous which commission is meant]! *The King and I were nowise confidential; just possibly he meant to console me for missing the fun in Troy* (he'd *see it so*) *by giving me to feel important on the home front. But chances are he thought himself a truly clever fellow for leaving a spy behind to watch for horns on the royal brow, and what dismayed me was less the ingenuousness of that plan—I knew him no Odysseus—as his assumption that from me he had nothing to fear! As if I were my gelded predecessor, or some bugger of my fellow man* (*no shortage of* those *in the profession*), *or withal so unattractive Clytemnestra'd never give me a tumble! And I a lyric poet, Aphrodite's very barrister, the Queen's Chief Minstrel!*

No more is said on this perhaps surprising head for the present; significantly, however, his reluctance to compromise his professional integrity is expressed as a concern for what Merope will think. On the other hand, he reasons, the bargain has nothing to do with his art; he'll compose what he'll compose whether laureled or un, and a song fares well or ill irrespective of its maker. In the long run Chief-Minstrelships and the like are meaningless; precisely therefore their importance in the short. Muse willing, his name will survive his lifetime; he will not, and had as well seize what boon the meanwhile offers. He accepts the post on Agamemnon's terms.

Part Three, consequently, will find the young couple moved to new lodgings in the palace itself, more affluent and less happy. Annoyance at what he knows would be her reaction has kept the minstrel from confiding to his friend the condition of his Acting Chief Minstrelship; his now-nearly-constant attendance on the

No use, this isn't working either, we're halfway through, the end's in sight; I'll never get to where I am; Part Three, Part Three, my crux, my core, I'm cutting you out; _____; there, at the heart, never to be filled, a mere lacuna.

IV

The trouble with us minstrels is, when all's said and done we love our work more than our women. More, indeed, than we love ourselves, else I'd have turned me off long since instead of persisting on this rock, searching for material, awaiting inspiration, scrawling out in nameless numb-hood futile notes . . . for an *Anonymiad,* which hereforth, having made an Iphigenia of Chapter Three, I can transcribe directly to the end of my skin. To be moved to art instead of to action by one's wretchedness may preserve one's life and sanity; at the same time, it may leave one wretcheder yet.

My mad commission from Agamemnon, remember, was not my only occupation in that blank chapter; I was also developing my art, by trial, error, and industry, with more return than that other project yielded. I examined our tongue, the effects wrought in it by minstrels old and new and how it might speak eloquentest for me. I considered the fashions in art and ideas, how perhaps to enlist their aid in escaping their grip. And I studied myself, musewise at least: who it was spoke through the bars of my music like a prisoner from the keep; what it was he strove so laboriously to enounce, if only his name; and how I might accomplish, or at least abet, his unfettering. In sum I schooled myself in all things pertinent to master-minstrelling—save one, the wide world, my knowledge whereof remained largely secondhand. Alas: for where Fancy's springs are unlevee'd by hard Experience they run too free, flooding every situation with possibilities until Prudence and even Common Sense are drowned.

Thus when it became apparent that Clytemnestra was indeed considering an affair—but with Agamemnon's cousin, and inspired not by the passion of love, which was out of her line, but by a resolve to avenge the sacrifice of Iphigenia—and that my folly had imperiled my life, my title, and my Merope, I managed to persuade myself not only that the Queen might be grateful after all for my confession and declaration, but that Merope's playing up to coarse Aegisthus in the weeks that followed might be meant simply to twit me for having neglected her and to spur my distracted ardor. A worldlier wight would've fled the *polis*: I hung on.

And composed! Painful irony, that anguish made my lyre speak ever eloquenter; that the odes on love's miseries I sang nightly may have not only fed Clytemnestra's passions and inspired Aegisthus's, but brought Merope's untimely into play as well, and wrought my downfall! He was no Agamemnon, Thyestes's son, nor any matchwit for the Queen, but he was no fool, either; he assessed the situation in a hurry, and whether his visit to Mycenae had been innocent or not to begin with, he saw soon how the land lay, and stayed on. Ingenuous, aye, dear Zeus, I was ingenuous, but jealousy sharpens a man's eyes: I saw his motive early on, as he talked forever of Iphigenia, and slandered Helen, and teased Merope, and deplored the war, and spoke as if jestingly of the power his city and Clytemnestra's would have, joined under one ruler—all the while deferring to the Queen's judgments, flattering her statecraft, asking her counsel on administrative matters . . . and smacking lips loudly whenever Merope, whom he'd demanded as his table-servant at first sight of her, went 'round with the wine.

Me too he flattered, I saw it clear enough, complimenting my talent, repeating Clytemnestra's praises, marveling that I'd made so toothsome a conquest as Merope. By slyly pretending to assume that I was the Queen's gigolo and asking me with a wink how she was in bed, he got from me a hot denial I'd ever tupped her; by acknowledging then that a bedmate like Merope must indeed leave a man itchless for other company, he led me to hints of my guiltful negligence in that quarter. Thereafter he grew bolder at table, declaring he'd had five hundred women in his life and inviting Clytemnestra to become the five hundred first, if only to spite Agamemnon, whom he frankly loathed, and Merope the five hundred second, after which he'd seduce whatever other women the palace offered. Me, to be sure, he laughed, he'd have to get rid of, or geld like certain other singers; why didn't I take a trip somewhere, knock about the world a bit, taste foreign cookery and foreign wenches, fight a few fist-fights, sire a few bastards? 'Twould be the making of me, minstrelwise! He and the Queen meanwhile would roundly cuckold Agamemnon, just for sport of it, combine their two kingdoms, and, if things worked out, give hubby the ax and make their union permanent: Clytemnestra could rule the roost, and he'd debauch himself among the taverns and Meropes of their joint domain.

All this, mind, in a spirit of raillery; Clytemnestra would chuckle, and Merope chide him for overboldness. But I saw how the Queen's eyes flashed, no longer at my cadenzas; and Merope'd say later, "At least he can talk about something besides politics and music." I laughed too at his sallies, however anxioused by Merope's pleasure in her new role, for the wretch was sharp, and though it sickened me to picture him atop the Queen—not to mention my frustrate darling!—heaving his paunch upon her and grinning through his whiskers, I admired his brash way with them and his gluttony for life's delights, so opposite to my poor temper. Aye, aye, there was my ruin: I *liked* the scoundrel after all, as I liked Clytemnestra and even Agamemnon; as I liked Merope, quite apart from loving or desiring her, whose impish spirit and vivacity reblossomed, in Aegisthus's presence, for the first time since we'd left the goats, and quite charmed the Mycenaean court. Most of all I was put down by the sheer energy of the lot of them: sackers of cities, breakers of vows, scorners of minstrels— admirable, fearsome! Watching Clytemnestra's eyes, I could hear her snarl with delight beneath the gross usurper, all the while she contemned his luxury and schemed her schemes; I could see herself take ax to Agamemnon, laugh with Aegisthus at their bloody hands, draw him on her at the corpse's side—smile, even, as she dirked him at the moment of climax! Him too I could hear laugh at her guile as his life pumped out upon her: bloody fine trick, Clytie girl, and enjoy your kingdom! And in Merope, my gentle, my docile, my honey: in her imperious new smile, in how she smartly snatched and bit the hand Aegisthus pinched her with, there began to stir a woman more woman than the pair of Leda's hatchlings. No, no, I was not up to them, I was not up to life—but it was myself I despised therefor, not the world.

Weeks passed; Clytemnestra made no reference to my *gaffe;* Merope grew by turns too silent with me, too cranky, or too sweet. I began to imagine them both Aegisthus's already; indeed, for aught I knew in dismalest moments they might be whoring it with every man in the palace, from Minister of Trade to horse-groom, and laughing at me with all Mycenae. Meanwhile, goat-face Aegisthus continued to praise my art (not without discernment for all his coarseness, as he had a good ear and knew every minstrel in the land) even as he teased my timid manner and want of experience. No keener nose in Greece for others' weaknesses: he'd remark quite seriously, between jests, that with a little knowledge of the world I might become in fact its chief minstrel; but if I tasted no more of life than Clytemnestra's dinner parties, of love no more than Merope's favors however extraordinary, perforce I'd wither in the bud while my colleagues grew to fruition. Let Athens, he'd declare, be never so splendid; nonetheless, of a man whose every day is passed within its walls one says, not that he's been to Athens, but that he's been nowhere. Every song I composed was a draught from the wine jug of my experience, which if not replenished must anon run dry. . . .

"Speaking of wine," he added one evening, "two of Clytie's boats are sailing tomorrow with a cargo of it to trade along the coast, and I'm shipping aboard for the ride. Ten ports, three whorehouses each, home in two months. Why not go too?"

At thought of his departure my heart leaped up: I glanced at Merope, standing by with her flagon, and found her coolly smiling meward, no stranger to the plan. Aegisthus read my face and roared.

"She'll keep, Minstrel! And what a lover you'll be when you get back!"

Clytemnestra, too, arched brows and smiled. Under other circumstances I might've found some sort of voyage appealing, since I'd been nowhere; as was I wanted only to see Aegisthus gone. But those smiles—on the one hand of the queen of my person, on the other of that queen of my heart whom I would so tardily recrown—altogether unnerved me. I'd consider the invitation overnight, I murmured, unless the Queen ordered one course or the other.

"I think the voyage is a good idea," Clytemnestra said promptly, and added in Aegisthus's teasing wise: "With you two out of the palace, Merope and I can get some sleep." My heart was stung by their new camaraderie and the implication, however one took it, that their sleep had been being disturbed. The Queen asked for Merope's opinion.

"He's often said a minstrel has to see the world," my darling replied. Was it spite or sadness in the steady eyes she turned to me? "Go see it. It's all the same to me."

Prophetic words! How they mocked the siren Experience, whose song I heeded above the music of my own heart! To perfect the irony of my foolishness, Aegisthus here changed strategy, daring me, as it were, to believe the other, bitter meaning of her words, which I was to turn upon my tongue for many a desolated year.

"Don't forget," he reminded me with a grin: "I might be out to trick you! Maybe I'll heave you overboard one night, or maroon you on a rock and have Merope to my-self! For all you know, Minstrel, she might want to be rid of you; this trip might be *her* idea. . . ."

Limply I retorted, his was a sword could cut both ways. My accurst and heart-hurt fancy cast up reasons now for sailing in despite of all: my position in Mycenae was hot, and might be cooled by a sea journey; Agamemnon could scarcely blame me for his wife's misconduct if I was out of town on her orders; perhaps there were Chief-Minstrelships to be earned in other courts; I'd achieve a taintless fame and send word for Merope to join me. At very least she would be safe from his predations while we were at sea; my absence, not impossibly, would make her heart fonder; I'd find some way to get us out of Mycenae when I re-turned, et cetera. Meantime . . . I shivered . . . the world, the world! My breath came short, eyes teared; we laughed, Aegisthus and I, and at Clytemnestra's smiling hest drank what smiling Merope poured.

And next day we two set sail, and laughed and drank across the wine-dark sea to our first anchorage: a flowered, goated, rockbound isle. Nor did Aegisthus's merry baiting cease when we put ashore with nine large amphorae: the local maidens, he declared, were timid beauties whose wont it was to spy from the woods when a ship came by; nimble as goddesses they were at the weaving of figured tapestries, which they bartered for wine, the island being grapeless; but so shy they'd not approach till the strangers left, whereupon they'd issue from their hiding places and make off with the amphorae, leaving in exchange a fair quantity of their ware. Should a man be clever enough to lay hold of them, gladly they'd buy their liberty with love; but to catch them was like catching at rainbows or the chucklings of the sea. What he proposed therefore was that we conceal us in a ring of wine jugs on the beach, bid the crew stand by offshore, snatch us each a maiden when they came a-fetching, and enjoy the ransom. Better yet, I could bait them with music, which he'd been told was unknown on this island.

"Unless you think I'm inventing all this to trick you," he added with a grin. "Wouldn't you look silly jumping out to grab an old wine merchant, or squatting there hot and bothered while I sail back to Mycenae!"

He *dared* me to think him honest; dared me to commit myself to delicious, preposterous fantasy. Ah, he played me like a master lyrist his instrument, with reckless inspiration, errless art.

"The bloody world's a dare!" he went so far as to say, elbowing my arm as we ringed the jugs. "Your careful chaps never look foolish, but they never taste the best of it, either!" Think how unlikely the prospect was, he challenged me, that anything he'd said was true; think how crushinger it would be to be victim of my own stupendous gullibility more than of his guile; how bitterer my abandonment in the knowledge that he and Merope and Clytemnestra were not only fornicating all over the palace but laughing at my innocence, as they'd done from the first, till their sides ached. "On the other hand," he concluded fiercely, and squeezed my shoulder, "think what you'll miss if it turns out I was telling you the truth and you were too sensible to believe it! Young beauties, Minstrel, shy as yourself and sweet as a dream! That's what we're here for, isn't it? Meropes by the dozen, ours for the snatching! Oh my gods, what the world can be, if you dare grab hold! And what a day!"

The last, at least, was real enough: never such a brilliant forenoon, sweet beach, besplendored sea! My head ached with indecision; the rough crew grinned by the boat, leaning on their oars. Life roared oceanlike with possibility: outrageous risks! outrageous joys! I stood transfixed, helpless to choose; Aegisthus snatched my lyre, clubbed me with a whang among the amphorae, sprang into the boat. I lay where felled, in medias res, and wept with relief to be destroyed at last; the sailors' guffaws as they pulled away were like a music.

V

Long time I lay a-beachèd, even slept, and dreamed a dream more real than the itch that had marooned me. My privy music drew the island girls: smooth-limbed, merry-eyed Meropes; I seized the first brown wrist that came in reach; her sisters fled. Mute, or too frightened to speak, my victim implored me with her eyes. She was lovely, slender, delicate, and (farewell, brute dreams) real: a human person, sense and flesh, undeniable as myself and for aught I knew as lonely. A real particular history had fetched her to that time and place, as had fetched me; she too, not impossibly, was gull of the wily world, a trickèd innocent and hapless self-deceiver. Perhaps she had a lover, or dreamed of one; might be she was fond of singing, balmed fragile sense with art. She was in my power; I let her go; she stood a moment rubbing her wrist. I begged her pardon for alarming her; it was loneliness, I said, made my fancy cruel. My speech was no doubt foreign to her; no doubt she expected ravishment, having been careless enough to get caught; perhaps she'd *wanted* a tumbling, been slow a-purpose, what did I know of such matters? It would not have surprised me to see her sneer at a man not man enough to force her; perhaps I would yet, it was not too late; I reached out my hand, she caught it up with a smile and kissed it, I woke to my real-life plight.

In the days thereafter, I imagined several endings to the dream: she fled with a laugh or hoot; I pursued her or did not, caught her or did not, or she returned. In my favorite ending we became friends: gentle lovers, affectionate and lively. I called her by the name of that bee-sweet form I'd graced her with, she me my own in the clover voice that once had crooned it. I tried imagining her mad with passion for me, as women in song were for their beloveds—but the idea of my inspiring such emotion made me smile. No, I would settle for a pastoral affection spiced with wild seasons, as I'd known; I did not need adoring. We would wed, get sons and daughters; why hadn't I Merope? We would even be faithful, a phenomenon and model to the faithless world. . . .

Here I'd break off with a groan, not that my bedreamèd didn't exist (or any other life on my island, I presently determined, except wild goats and birds), but that she did, and I'd lost her. The thought of Merope in the swart arms of Aegisthus, whether or not she mocked my stranding, didn't drive me to madness or despair, as I'd expected it would; only to rue that I'd not been Aegisthus enough to keep her in my own. Like him, like Agamemnon, like Iphigenia for all I knew, I had got my character's desert.

Indeed, when I'd surveyed the island and unstoppered the first of the crocks, I was able to wonder, not always wryly, whether the joke wasn't on my deceivers. It was a perfumed night; the sea ran hushed beneath a gemmèd sky; there were springs of fresh water, trees of wild fruit, vines of wild grape; I could learn to spear fish, snare birds, milk goats. My lyre was unstrung forever, but I had a voice to sing with, an audience once more of shaggy nans and sea birds—and my fancy to recompense for what it had robbed me of. There was all the world I needed; let the real one clip and tumble, burn and bleed; let Agamemnon pull down towns and rape the widows of the slain; let Menelaus shake the plain with war-shouts and Helen take on all comers; let maids grow old, princes rich, poets famous—I had imagination for realm and mistress, and her dower language! Isolated from one world by Agamemnon, from another by my own failings, I'd make Mycenaes of which I was the sole inhabitant, and sing to myself from their golden towers the one tale I knew.

Crockèd bravery; I smile at it now, but for years it kept me off the rocks, and though my moods changed like the sea-face, I accomplished much. Now supposing I'd soon be rescued I piled up beacons on every headland; now imagining a lengthy tenure, in fits of construction I raised me a house, learned to trap and fish, cultivated fruits and berries, made goatsmilk cheese and wrappings of hide—and filled jar after jar with the distillations of my fancy. Then would come sieges of despair, self-despisal, self-pity; gripped as by a hand I would gasp with wretchedness on my pallet, unable to muster resolve enough to leap into the sea. Impossible to make another hexameter, groan at another sundown, weep at another rosy-fingered dawn! But down the sun went, and re-rose; anon the wind changed quarter; I'd fetch me up, wash and stretch, and with a sigh prepare a fresh batch of ink, wherein I was soon busily aswim.

It was this invention saved me, for better or worse. I had like my fellow bards been used to composing in verse and committing the whole to memory, along with the minstrel repertoire. But that body of song, including my Mycenaean productions, rang so hollow in my stranded ears I soon put it out of mind. What are Zeus's lecheries and Hera's revenge, to a man on a rock? No past musings seemed relevant to my new estate, about which I found such a deal to say, memory couldn't keep pace. Moreover, the want of any audience but asphodel, goat, and tern played its part after all in the despairs that threatened me: a man sings better to himself if he can imagine someone's listening. In time therefore I devised solutions to both problems. Artist through, I'd been wont since boyhood when pissing on beach or bank to make designs and clever symbols with my water. From this source, as from Pegasus's idle hooftap on Mount Helicon, sprang now a torrent of inspiration: using tanned skins in place of a sand-beach, a seagull-feather for my tool, and a mixture of wine, blood, and squid-ink for a medium, I developed a kind of coded markings to record the utterance of mind and heart. By drawing out these chains of symbols I could so preserve and display my tale, it was unnecessary to remember it. I could therefore compose more and faster; I came largely to exchange song for written speech, and when the gods vouchsafed me a further great idea, that of launching my productions worldward in the empty amphorae, they loosed from my dammèd soul a Deucalion-flood of literature.

For eight jugsworth of years thereafter, saving the spells of inclement weather aforementioned, I gloried in my isolation and seeded the waters with its get, what I came to call *fiction*. That is, I found that by pretending that things had happened which in fact had not, and that people existed who didn't, I could achieve a lovely truth which actuality obscures—especially when I learned to abandon myth and pattern my fabrications on actual people and events: Menelaus, Helen, the Trojan War. It was *as if* there were this minstrel and this milkmaid, et cetera; one could I believe draw a whole philosophy from that *as if*.

Two vessels I cargoed with rehearsals of traditional minstrelsy, bringing it to bear in this novel mode on my current circumstances. A third I freighted with imagined versions, some satiric, of "the first fact of our generation":

what was going on at Troy and in Mycenae. To the war and
Clytemnestra's treachery I worked out various dénouements: Trojan victories, Argive victories, easy and arduous
homecomings, consequences tragical and comic. I wrote a
version wherein Agamemnon kills his brother, marries
Helen, and returns to Lacedemon instead of to Mycenae;
another in which he himself is murdered by Clytemnestra,
who arranges as well the assassination of the other expeditionary princes and thus becomes empress of both Hellas
and Troy, with Paris as her consort and Helen as her cook
—until all are slain by young Orestes, who then shares the
throne with Merope, adored by him since childhood despite
the difference in their birth. I was fonder of that one than
of its less likely variants—such as that, in cuckold fury,
Agamemnon butchers Clytemnestra's whole ménage except
Merope, who for then rejecting his advances is put ashore
to die on the island where everyone supposes I've perished
long since. We meet; she declares it was in hopes of saving
me she indulged Aegisthus; I that it was the terror of her
love and beauty drove me from her side. We embrace,
sweetly as once in rosemaryland. . . . But I could only
smile at such notions, for in my joy at having discovered
the joy of writing, the world might've offered me Mycenae
and got but a shrug from me. Indeed, one night I fancied
I heard a Meropish voice across the water, calling the old
name she called me by—and I ignored that call to finish
a firelit chapter. Had Merope—aye, Trojan Helen herself
—trespassed on my island in those days, I'd have flayed
her as soon as I'd laid her, and on that preciousest of
parchments scribed the little history of our love.

By the seventh jug, after effusions of religious narrative,
ribald tale-cycles, verse-dramas, comedies of manners, and
what-all, I had begun to run out of world and material—
though not of ambition, for I could still delight in the
thought of my amphorae floating to the wide world's
shores, being discovered by who knew whom, salvaged
from the deep, their contents deciphered and broadcast to
the ages. Even when, in black humors, I imagined my
opera sinking undiscovered (for all I could tell, none
might've got past the rocks of my island), or found but
untranslated, or translated but ignored, I could yet console

myself that Zeus at least, or Poseidon, read my heart's record. Further, further: should the Olympians themselves prove but dreams of our minstrel souls (I'd changed my own conception of their nature several times), still I could soothe me with the thought that somewhere outside myself my enciphered spirit drifted, realer than the gods, its significance as objective and undecoded as the stars'.

Thus I found strength to fill two more amphorae: the seventh with long prose fictions of the realistical, the romantical, and the fantastical kind, the eighth with comic histories of my spirit, such of its little victories, defeats, insights, blindnesses, et cetera as I deemed might have impersonal resonation or pertinence to the world; I'm no Narcissus. But if I had lost track of time, it had not of me: I was older and slower, more careful but less concerned; as my craft improved, my interest waned, and my earlier zeal seemed hollow as the jugs it filled. Was there any new thing to say, new way to say the old? The memory of literature, my own included, gave me less and less delight; the "immortality" of even the noblest works I knew seemed a paltry thing. It appeared as fine a lot to me, and as poor, to wallow like Aegisthus in the stews as to indite the goldenest verses ever and wallow in the ages' admiration. As I had used to burn with curiosity to know how it would be to be a Paris or Achilles, and later to know which of my imagined endings to the war would prove the case, but came not to care, so now I was no longer curious even about myself, what I might do next, whether anyone would find me or my scribbles. My last interest in that subject I exhausted with the dregs of Thalia, my eighth muse and mistress. It was in a fit of self-disgust I banged her to potsherds; her cargo then I had to add to Clio's, and as I watched that stately dame go under beneath her double burden, my heart sank likewise into the dullest deep.

VI

A solipsist had better get on well with himself, successfullier than I that ensuing season. Time was when I dreamed of returning to the world; time came when I scattered my beacons lest rescue interrupt me; now I merely sat on the beach, sun-dried, seasalted: a survival-expert with no will to live. My very name lost sense; anon I forgot it; had "Merope" called again I'd not have known whom she summoned. Once I saw a ship sail by, unless I dreamed it, awfully like Agamemnon's and almost within hail; I neither hid nor hallooed. Had the King put ashore, I wouldn't have turned my head. The one remaining amphora stood untapped. Was I thirty? Three thousand thirty? I couldn't care enough to shrug.

Then one noon, perhaps years later, perhaps that same day, another object hove into my view. Pot-red, bobbing, it was an amphora, barnacled and sea-grown from long voyaging. I watched impassive while wind and tide fetched it shoreward, a revenant of time past; nor was I stirred to salvage when the surf broke it up almost at my feet. Out washed a parchment marked with ink, and came to rest on the foreshore—whence, finally bemused, I retrieved it. The script was run, in places blank; I couldn't decipher it, or if I did, recognize it as my own, though it may have been.

No matter: a new notion came, as much from the lacunae as from the rest, that roused in me first an echo of my former interest in things, in the end a resolve which if bone-cool was ditto deep: I had thought myself the only stranded spirit, and had survived by sending messages to whom they might concern; now I began to imagine that the world contained another like myself. Indeed, it might be astrew with islèd souls, become minstrels perforce, and the sea a-clink with literature! Alternatively, one or several of my messages may have got through: the document I held might be no ciphered call for aid but a reply, whether from the world or some maroonèd fellow-inksman: that rescue was on the way; that there was no rescue, for anyone, but my SOS's had been judged to be not without artistic merit by some who'd happened on them; that I should forget about my plight, a mere scribblers' hazard, and sing about the goats and flowers instead, the delights of island life, or the goings-on among the strandees of that larger isle the world.

I never ceased to allow the likelihood that the indecipherable ciphers were my own; that the sea had fertilized me as it were with my own seed. No matter, the principle was the same: that I could be thus messaged, even by that stranger my former self, whether or not the fact tied me to the world, inspired me to address it once again. That night I broke Calliope's aging seal, and if I still forwent her nourishment, my abstinence was rather now prudential or strategic than indifferent.

VII

That is to say, I began to envision the possibility of a new work, hopefully surpassing, in any case completing, what I'd done theretofore, my labor's fulfillment and vindication. I was obliged to plan with more than usual care: not only was there but one jug to sustain my inspiration and bear forth its vintage; there remained also, I found to my dismay, but one goat in the land to skin for writing material. An aging nan she was, lone survivor of the original herd, which I'd slaughtered reckless in my early enthusiasm, supposing them inexhaustible, and only later begun to conserve, until in my late dumps I'd let husbandry go by the board with the rest. That she had no mate, and so I no future vellum, appalled me now; I'd've bred her myself hadn't bigot Nature made love between the species fruitless, for my work in mind was no brief one. But of coming to terms with circumstance I was grown a master: very well, I soon said to myself, it must be managed by the three of us, survivors all: one old goat, one old jug, one old minstrel, we'd expend ourselves in one new song, and then an end to us!

First, however, the doe had to be caught; it was no accident she'd outlived the others. I set about constructing snares, pitfalls, blind mazes, at the same time laying ground-plans for the masterwork in my head. For a long time both eluded me, though vouchsafing distant glimpses of themselves. I'd named the doe *Helen,* so epic fair she seemed to me in my need, and cause of so great vain toil, but her namesake had never been so hard to get: *Artemis* had fit her cold fleetness better; *Iphigenia* my grim plans for her, to launch with her life the expedition of my fancy. *Tragedy* and *satire* both deriving, in the lexicon of my inventions, from *goat*, like the horns from Helen's head, I came to understand that the new work would combine the two, which I had so to speak kept thitherto in their separate amphorae. For when I reviewed in my imagination the goings-on in Mycenae, Lacedemon, Troy, the circumstances of my life and what they had disclosed to me of capacity and defect, I saw too much of pity and terror merely to laugh; yet about the largest hero, gravest catastrophe, sordidest deed there was too much comic, one way or another, to sustain the epical strut or tragic frown. In the same way, the piece must be no Orphic celebration of the unknowable; time had taught me too much respect for men's intelligence and resourcefulness, not least my own, and too much doubt of things transcendent, to make a mystic hymnist of me. Yet neither would it be a mere discourse or logic preachment; I was too sensible of the great shadow that surrounds our little lights, like the sea my island shore. Whimsic fantasy, grub fact, pure senseless music—none in itself would do; to embody *all* and rise above each, in a work neither longfaced nor idiotly grinning, but adventuresome, passionately humored, merry with the pain of insight, wise and smiling in the terror of our life—that was my calm ambition.

And to get it all out of and back into one jug, on a single skin! Every detail would need be right, if I was to achieve the effects of epic amplitude and lyric terseness, the energy of innocence and experience's restraint. Adversity generates guileful art: months I spent considering and rejecting forms, subjects, viewpoints, and the rest, while I fashioned trap after trap for Helen and sang bait-songs of my plans—both in vain. Always she danced and bleated out of reach, sometimes so far away I confused her with the perchèd gulls or light-glints on the rock, sometimes so near I saw her black eyes' sparkle and the gray-pink cartography of her udder. Now and then she'd vanish for days together; I'd imagine her devoured by birds, fallen to the fishes, or merely uncapturable, and sink into despondencies more sore than any I'd known. My "Anonymiad," too, I would reflect then (so I began to think of it, as lacking a subject and thus a name), was probably impossible, or, what was worse, beyond my talent. Perhaps, I'd tell myself bitterly, it had been written already, even more than once; for all I knew the waters were clogged with its like, a menace to navigation and obstruction on the wide world's littoral.

I myself may already have written it; cast it forth, put it out of mind, and then picked it up where it washed back to me, having circuited Earth's countries or my mere island. I yearned to be relieved of myself: by heart failure, bolt from Zeus, voice from heaven. None forthcoming, I'd relapse into numbness, as if, having abandoned song for speech, I meant now to give up language altogether and float voiceless in the wash of time like an amphora in the sea, my vision bottled. This anesthesia proved my physician, gradually curing me of self-pity. Anon Helen's distant call would put off my torpor; I resumed the pursuit, intently, thoughtfully—but more and more detached from final concern for its success.

For just this reason, maybe, I came at last one evening to my first certainty about the projected work: that it would be written from my only valid point of view, first person anonymous. At that moment *Anonymiad* became its proper name. At that moment also, singing delightedly my news, I stumbled into one of the holes I'd dug for Helen. With the curiosity of her species she returned at once down the path wherealong I'd stalked her, to see why I'd abandoned the hunt. Indeed, as if to verify that I was trapped or dead, she peered into my pit. But I was only smiling, and turning on my finger Merope's ring; when she came to the edge I seized her by the pastern, pulled her in. A shard of deceasèd Thalia, long carried on me, ended her distress, which whooped deaf-heavenward like glee.

TAILPIECE

It had been my plan, while the elements cured her hide, to banquet on Helen's carcass and drink my fill of long-preserved Calliope. And indeed, for some days after my capture I sated every hunger and slaked every thirst, got drunk and glutted, even, as this work's headpiece attests. But it was not as it would have been in callower days. My

futile seed had soured Calliope, and long pursuit so tough-
ened Helen I'd as well made a meal of my writing-hand.
Were it not too late for doubts—and I not flayed and cured
myself, by sun, salt, and solitude, past all but the memory
of tenderness—I'd wonder whether I should after all have
skinned and eaten her, whom too I saw I had misnamed.
We could perhaps have been friends, once she overcame
her fright; I'd have had someone to talk to when Calliope
goes, and with whom to face the unwritable postscript, fast
approaching, of my *Anonymiad*.

Whereto, as I forewarned, there's no dénouement, only
a termination or ironical coda. My scribbling has reached
the end of Helen; I've emptied Calliope upon the sand. It
was my wish to elevate maroonment into a minstrel masterpiece; instead, I see now, I've spent my last resources con-
trariwise, reducing the masterpiece to a chronicle of
minstrel misery. Even so, much is left unsaid, much must
be blank.

No matter. It is finished, Apollo be praised; there remains but to seal and launch Calliope. Long since I've
ceased to care whether this is found and read or lost in the
belly of a whale. I have no doubt that by the time any
translating eyes fall on it I'll be dust, along with Clytemnestra, Aegisthus, Agamemnon . . . and Merope, if that
was your name, if I haven't invented you as myself. I could
do well by you now, my sweet, to whom this and all its
predecessors are a continuing, strange love letter. I wish
you were here. The water's fine; in the intervals of this
composition I've taught myself to swim, and if some night
your voice recalls me, by a new name, I'll commit myself
to it, paddling and resting, drifting like my amphorae, to
attain you or to drown.

There, my tale's afloat. I like to imagine it drifting age
after age, while the generations fight, sing, love, expire.
Now, perhaps, it bumps the very wharfpiles of Mycenae,
where my fatal voyage began. Now it passes a hairsbreadth
from the unknown man or woman to whose heart, of all
hearts in the world, it could speak fluentest, most balmly
—but they're too preoccupied to reach out to it, and it
can't reach out to them. It drifts away, past Heracles's
pillars, across Oceanus, nudged by great and little fishes,

under strange constellations bobbing, bobbing. Towns and statues fall, gods come and go, new worlds and tongues swim into light, old perish. Then it too must perish, with all things deciphered and undeciphered: men and women, stars and sky.

Will anyone have learnt its name? Will everyone? No matter. Upon this noontime of his wasting day, between the night past and the long night to come, a noon beautiful enough to break the heart, on a lorn fair shore a nameless minstrel

Wrote it.

ABOUT THE AUTHOR

JOHN BARTH was born May 27, 1930 in Dorchester County, Maryland, a region whose memory populates his creative mind. He attended the Juilliard School of Music in New York, played drums with professional jazz bands and returned home to major in journalism at Johns Hopkins University. He began to read the great tale cycles—**The Thousand and One Nights** and the **Decameron**—and started but never finished his own one hundred stories set in the Maryland of his childhood. After receiving his M.A. from Johns Hopkins in 1952, Barth became an instructor in English at Penn State University.

Four years later, **The Floating Opera** (1956), a comic, philosophical novel set in the tidewater areas of Maryland, was published. Greeted by many critics as an oddity, it was nominated for a National Book Award in 1957. Barth wrote **Opera** in the first three months of 1956, and in the last three completed **The End of the Road** (1958), a realistic novel about a teacher at a small community college. His next book, though, abandoned realist conventions: in **The Sot-Weed Factor** (1960), Barth created a seventeenth-century mock epic, the **Marylandiad,** satirizing the style and content of the historical novel. In **Giles Goat-Boy** (1966), Barth returned to the present and the problems encountered by a new messiah at a Maryland university. His experiments with literary forms continue in **Lost in the Funhouse** (1968), a collection of short stories; **Chimera** (1972), three interconnected novellas, which won the National Book Award for fiction; and **Letters** (1979), an epistolary novel.

After teaching at the State University of New York at Buffalo, Barth returned to Johns Hopkins in 1973 where he now teaches English and Creative Writing. He is the father of three children and on occasion can still be found playing drums with a local jazz band.

New from

W

Bantam Windstone Books

HOUSEKEEPING by Marilynne Robinson (On sale February 15, 1982 · #20575-7 · $2.95)

One of the most highly-praised novels of recent times. "So precise, so distilled, so beautiful that one doesn't want to miss any pleasure it might yield."— *New York Times Book Review* "Extraordinary."—*Washington Post Book World*

ALICE JAMES: A BIOGRAPHY by Jean Strouse (On sale February 15, 1982 · #20576-5 · $4.50)

The prize-winning, moving portrait of the youngest daughter and the only girl in a family that produced Henry James, the greatest novelist of 19th century America and William James, the foremost psychologist of that era.

THE MIDDLE GROUND by Margaret Drabble (#20291-X · $3.50)

Warm, witty, a-little-bit-crazy Kate is up against the wall of a mid-life crisis. Her discoveries provide the touching, telling truth in Margaret Drabble's provocative new novel.

A WEAVE OF WOMEN by E.M. Broner (#14727-7 · $2.95)

A provocative, sometimes violent, sometimes shocking celebration of joyous womanhood.

Read all of these Bantam Windstone Books, available wherever paperbacks are sold, or order directly from Bantam by including $1.00 for postage and handling and sending a check to Bantam Books, Dept. W02, 414 East Golf Road, Des Plaines, Illinois 60016. Allow 4-6 weeks for delivery. This offer expires 8/82.

The Most Important Voices of Our Age

WINDSTONE BOOKS

This new line of books from Bantam brings you the most important voices and established writers of our age. Windstone. The name evokes the strong, enduring qualities of the air and the earth. The imprint represents these same qualities in literature—boldness of vision and enduring power, importance and originality of concept and statement.. Windstone brings you contemporary masterpieces at affordable prices.